# TRAPS

A Novel of the FBI

PAUL LINDSAY

SIMON & SCHUSTER
New York   London   Toronto   Sydney   Singapore

SIMON & SCHUSTER
Rockefeller Center
1230 Avenue of the Americas
New York, NY 10020

SIMON & SCHUSTER and colophon are registered
trademarks of Simon & Schuster, Inc.

For information about special discounts for bulk purchases,
please contact Simon & Schuster Special Sales:
1-800-465-6798 or business@simonandschuster.com

Manufactured in the United States of America

10  9  8  7  6  5  4  3  2  1

Library of Congress Cataloging-in-Publication Data
Lindsay, Paul.
    Traps: a novel of the FBI / Paul Lindsay.
        p. cm.
    1. United States. Federal Bureau of Investigation—Fiction.  2. Government investigators—Fiction.  3. Kidnapping—Fiction.  I. Title.

PS3562.I511915 T73 2002
813'.54—dc21                                        2002066915

ISBN 0-7432-1506-0

# Acknowledgments

I wish to express my appreciation to David Rosenthal, my editor and publisher of ten years, for his instruction, his patience, and his humanity. I owe an equal debt of gratitude to my agent, Esther Newberg, whose loyalty and honesty are the standard of the industry. Without her this undertaking would have required a great deal more courage.

Additionally, this book would not have been possible without the tireless efforts of my daughter, Larisa, who had the unenviable task of being the first to discover its flaws and suggest their solution. Also Barbara Yergeau for her unerring eye and flawless ear in making these pages presentable. For the sharp, insightful pencil of my editor, Ruth Fecych, whose safety net of good judgment has allowed me great latitude in finding my way to the end of the maze.

For technical advice, Dr. Werner Spitz and agents past and present: Larry Presley, Stuart Carlisle, and Ron Dibbern. And thank you to my wife, Patti, who has, as always, offered only her encouragement while absorbing all the surrounding distractions.

IN MEMORY OF
DICK VAURIS
A REMARKABLE DETECTIVE, A REMARKABLE FRIEND
KILLED IN THE LINE OF DUTY FEBRUARY 19, 2001

# TRAPS

# 1

OCCASIONALLY, IN THE HOPE OF SLICING THROUGH
the ever-thickening Gordian knot of American justice, FBI
agents have been known to venture across the deeply rutted line
of oath and breach a law or two. While some people might judge
the specifics of such violations to be minor, or even admirable in
their daring, jurists would undoubtedly pronounce these acts
felonies. Earlier in his career, Jack Kincade might have been capable of such dutiful misdirection, but now, as he was about to
commit his fourth bank burglary, justice was the last thing he
wanted to see served.

His only defense, should one become necessary, was that
these were *small* felonies, in dollars and cents, a few thousand, if
that. He had never added them up, he supposed, because he
didn't want to know that he was risking so much for so little. In-
voking a thief's myopia, he told himself that it didn't matter;
there was no way he could be caught. He ran his hand through
his thinning dark brown hair several times, absentmindedly
measuring its density. It had once been thickly baroque, mar-
quee proof of his genetic indestructibility. He picked out two
new casualties from between his fingers and examined them.
The roots were still attached; they weren't going to grow back.
He leaned over the desk and filled the scarred glass in front of
him with vodka.

For the first time since switching brands a month earlier, he noticed a yellow cast to it, like trapped, day-old rainwater. He held the glass up, trying to decide whether the late afternoon light coming through the smeared window of his motel room was the cause, or whether it was simply a consequence of the alcohol's eight-bucks-a-fifth inferiority. He turned the bottle to read its label:

### PISTOL PETE'S VODKA
*Handcrafted for your drinking pleasure*
*in Houston, Texas*

Taking a measured sip, he let it lie on his tongue in a flat ribbon and inhaled across its surface. It had a slippery, carbonous aftertaste, not unlike what he imagined traces of crude oil might leave behind. Apparently Pistol Pete's was best tossed back in large, blanketing doses that bypassed the taste buds of Friday night cowboys, and not sipped by discriminating FBI agents who were about to violate U.S. banking laws.

He gulped a mouthful. The resulting sting temporarily masked the vodka's flaws, but it was too late. A tiny compulsion had barricaded itself in the back of his head, vowing not to be taken alive.

Strangely, that's the way things were now. Through a carefully administered regimen of neglect and apathy, he had learned to disregard the larger things in life almost completely, but the smallest imperfection could wrap its jaws around him with the accelerating panic of a wounded animal.

He tried to rid himself of this latest threat to his euphoric disorder by reciting an all-occasions mantra specifically developed for such emergencies: *Don't give a good goddamn don't give a good goddamn don't give a good goddamn.* He looked at his drink again. The discoloration was just as urgent. Pistol Pete's was going to need fixing.

He looked around the room. Some years earlier, when half of the motel's units were converted to weekly and monthly rentals—a procedure the permanent guests referred to as "going condo"—

tiny kitchenettes were added. The entire modification, while raising the weekly rate thirty dollars, consisted of a waist-high refrigerator recessed under a single three-foot-long shelf. On his counter sat a toaster oven scorched to a spotty black by a succession of frozen-dinner brush fires. Surrounding it were cans of beets, okra, lima beans, and mincemeat, left, maliciously he suspected, by a string of previous tenants. Scattered between them were a few condiments, mostly the kind that came in small packets as part of a carryout meal.

He opened the refrigerator. Except for a single can of Coke, it was empty. He briefly considered the vodka-cola combination, but knew that the soft drink would be considerably more valuable as an antidote the next morning. A search of the envelope-size freezer revealed a single empty ice tray containing only a spiky coating of blue frost.

He fanned out the packets on the shelf and decided against adding the contents of a clear plastic container of earth-brown soy sauce. Then, noticing an almost-full bottle of Tabasco sauce, he took it back to the desk and carefully shook out a single drop into his drink. After swirling it briefly, he could see that the vodka's color hadn't changed enough to affect its taste. Another four drops were added with some precision. Stirring the mixture with his finger, he sipped it cautiously. Then gently, as if one drop too many might cause an explosion, he tapped in a sixth and tasted it again.

It wasn't good, but with as much scrutiny as he allowed himself to examine anything these days, he reasoned that Tabasco would neutralize any undisclosed groundwater ingredients that the great state of Texas had failed to require Pistol Pete to list on its label. He fired back another mouthful. Although it had an old-fashioned medicinal repulsiveness, he decided he liked it. Unlike almost everything else in his increasingly disobedient life, the drink provided its own penance, something an Irish Catholic found illogical, and therefore, perversely reassuring.

That was one of his favorite things about alcohol: its slow, steady warmth never failed to provide a sanctuary from the endless drudgery of logic. At the far end of the room lay his Border collie, its face evenly cleaved, one half black containing a brown eye, the other side white, its eye a frosty blue. The animal's chin rested comfortably between mottled gray paws. Holding up his glass in the direction of the disinterested dog, Kincade let his voice resonate with clear, unarguable authority. "Congratulate me, B.C. Bastardizing something as inferior as Pistol Pete's hand-crafted vodka has qualified me for permanent membership in the ranks of the Great Unwashed." As if seconding his self-denouncement, the ancient black phone on the table next to his bed rang.

If there was an upside to the decaying orbit of his life, it was that he no longer had to concern himself with the consequence of his actions. This, in turn, had a way of reducing all enemies to minor roles. And phone calls, all phone calls, had become ene-mies. Not once since moving into the motel had the device been the bearer of good news. It was the only remaining conduit be-tween him and responsibility, the single, tenuous thread by which he could be tracked down by bill collectors, the friend of the court, the office, or any other group or individual to whom he owed money, time, or feigned passion.

The phone rang a second time. "Friend or foe?" he demanded of the Border collie, which opened its eyes in dutiful response. The ears flagged momentarily until the dog fully recognized the echoing vowels as those of yet another of his master's sputtering soliloquies, which, it had learned, when accompanied by the smell of alcohol, required no actual canine response. Its eyelids slid shut lazily.

Kincade knew to answer the phone was probably a mistake, but anymore that seemed to be less a deterrent to his decisions. In this case, however, experience had taught him that the week-end was normally a sanctuary from the persistence of profes-sional pursuers. Besides, it could be about the card game; maybe it had been called off. He picked up the receiver and spoke with the metallic, arrhythmic voice that people use to record them-selves. "This is Special Agent Jack Kincade. I'm sorry I'm not in right now, but my hundred and eight minutes of paid overtime for the day have expired. You can reach me Monday at eight fifteen A.M. If you wish to leave a message, I'll be sure to ignore it until then."

"Sorry, Jack, Bill Chapman told me to call and give you this." It was Tom Reedy, the Bureau night clerk. He had been with the FBI for five years. During that time, he had used his employment to fund law school and had recently graduated. Although he hadn't taken the bar exam yet, he had already developed—or perhaps, like many lawyers, was born with—an attorney's ability to ignore all unprofitable cries from the wilderness, especially those of agents attempting to keep their off-duty hours uninterrupted.

"How'd you know it wasn't my machine?"

"An answering machine?" Reedy laughed. "Jack, that's a little sophisticated for you, isn't it? You're not even allowed to have a Bureau vehicle."

"Yeah, get caught driving drunk just once and they take away your car. But I figured out a way to make fools out of them."

Reedy didn't want to be in receipt of any complicitous information, at least not until he became a member of the bar when hiding felonies would become not only ethical but billable. However, the rhetorical charge in the agent's voice told Reedy that there would be no escaping Kincade's imminent confession. "How do you do that, Jack?"

"I drive my *own* car drunk."

"Good for you, Jack. That'll show them who the fool is." Kincade laughed, pleased that Reedy had gotten the punch line right. He lit a cigarette and silently took a sip of his iceless drink. "We tried paging you, but you didn't answer."

Kincade looked over at the desk. Next to the black beeper lay its batteries. He had taken them out the day it was issued. "Chapman—he's the fugitive supervisor?" Kincade had been in the Chicago division half a year and still wasn't sure who the supervisors were. For some reason, this lit a small candle of pleasure inside him. He took a long drag on his cigarette, and some ashes fell on his shirtfront. Brushing them off with the flat of his hand, he could feel the paunch that hung over his belt, a sullen emissary of middle age, its inevitability gloating back at him. He grabbed it with a full hand pinch to measure it for new growth. The test, selected specifically for its inaccuracy, convinced him that his waistline was about the same: an inch or so greater in circumference than his trousers. Back in his tennis days, he had hardly had enough of a waist to keep his pants up. But that was three or four lifetimes ago, when the sport had paid his way through Dartmouth.

The days of youth: His only regret was that he had not understood his absolute invulnerability, and hadn't explored more fully the wonder of deeds without consequence. The body or the spirit, no matter how badly abused, then needed only twenty-four hours to recover, to blur all resolutions and readopt Recklessness as its marching order. Aging had been a hypothetical galaxy, an infinite number of light-years away. Unreachable. Unfeared.

"Yes, he is," Reedy said with a patience that seemed more labored as the conversation went on. "We just got a communication in from Portland; one of their fugitives is registered at the Star Crest Motel in De Kalb, room three three one."

"Hold on while I get a pen." Kincade went to the desk and rummaged through its drawers, unable to find a sheet of paper. He picked up an old newspaper and pencil and went back to the phone. "Okay, fire away."

"Subject's name is Daniel Louis O'Keefe," Reedy said.

"What's he wanted for?"

Knowing Kincade was going to see the answer as another reason to object to working on the weekend, Reedy hesitated. "He's wanted for bond jumping."

"What was the original charge?"

"He's a deadbeat dad."

"A deadbeat dad? Come on. This can't wait until Monday?"

"Sorry, Jack, I don't write 'em, I just read 'em."

"There's just something evil about hunting a man with the same misfortunes as oneself."

"I guess it takes one to catch one," Reedy said. "According to Portland, they're not sure he'll be there very long. That's why Chapman wanted me to get ahold of you tonight."

"Portland. It never fails, the smaller the office, the bigger the priority. Okay, give me the rest of it." As the night clerk read the rest of the communication, Kincade absentmindedly took notes along the edge of the newspaper. When Reedy finished reading the communication, Kincade said, "Is that it?"

"That's it, Jack. And thanks for taking the time to fit me in so close to happy hour."

Apparently, Kincade's love of cocktails and other distractions was not as classified as he would have liked. But, as he thought about it, within the achingly pedantic confines of the Bureau, a certain amount of infamy was probably a good thing. He tore the strip containing his notes off the newspaper and stuffed it into his jacket pocket. "That's the problem with today's FBI, Tom: The lowliest employee can be a giant pain in the ass to its most intrepid agents."

"You know what they say: Those of us who can, do; those of us who can't, sodomize."

"Isn't that the motto of the Illinois Bar Association?"

"If you ever need my services, it will be."

# 2

THE RENTED TRUCK PULLED TO A STOP BEHIND THE Cook County Jail and shifted into reverse with an amateurish grinding of gears. Except for the counterfeited logo on the passenger door, the entire vehicle was the customary white of county property. Its cargo consisted of a standard forklift—also rented—and an eight-hundred-pound metal-encased bomb.

The driver was Conrad Ziven, a man thought of as courteous and industrious by his neighbors and coworkers, an electrical engineer who, twenty-five years earlier, had immigrated to the United States with his family to escape the bitter inequities of Eastern Europe. He was born in Croatia, a country where justice was not only complicated but elusive. When the legal system failed there, a man was expected to take matters into his own hands. It had always been a great relief to him that, with the legal protections afforded in his adopted country, he would never have to risk his freedom or safety by reverting to the old ways. Then, three years ago, on a rainy fall afternoon, his sixteen-year-old daughter, Leah, drove off smiling on her way to the orthodontist to have her braces removed. Her car was found later that night at a convenience store, but she was never seen again.

Ziven's face was a strange amalgam of the two cultures in which he had spent his life. The individual features, strongly pronounced, were discernibly those of an Eastern European, but more than two decades of the carbohydrate-rich American diet had left his flesh puffed and jowly. His sad brown eyes were deep-set and tracked the world around him with a relentless curiosity, occasionally pausing for momentary evaluation before continuing on with the permanent bewilderment of an outsider. He was a short man whose dark, unremarkable clothing hung on him crookedly due to a significant weight loss in the last few months.

Dusk was fading into darkness as Ziven backed the truck down the ramp toward the loading dock. His hands, loose on the wheel, guided the truck with some precision. He was surprised how little reluctance he was feeling. He supposed that the old ways did indeed die hard, or maybe insurrection was just in his blood. His father had been a member of the Ustase, a Croatian separatist group that had assassinated King Alexander I in 1934. As soon as they took power, his father inexplicably joined the opposing partisans. Less than a year later, he was killed while fighting his former comrades. Ziven hoped that he, too, wasn't suffering the delusions of the absurdly heroic.

Today was the third anniversary of his daughter's abduction. One thousand and ninety-five days, the last thousand of which the FBI had done little, if anything, to find her. After the first three months, his weekly phone calls, which, with excruciating patience, he waited until each Friday morning to make, went largely unanswered. When he did manage to catch the newest agent assigned to the case, the answers were always given in the lifeless boilerplate that civil servants use to dismiss inquiries. Although he was always assured that the case remained open, there was never anything new to report and after three years, it had become apparent nothing more would be done to find Leah Ziven or her kidnapper.

A thousand days was enough. During that time, his wife, also Croatian, while trying to ease the anger of losing their only child, had become addicted to prescription drugs. Because Ziven thought of those who had survived the purges of Eastern Europe as sturdier emotional stock than most Americans, his wife's surrender to drugs was even more enraging. Two months earlier, she had been arrested for stealing and then forging prescriptions for Valium. As a father, and as a man, he knew he had to do something, no matter the cost. The chances that he would be successful were extremely small, but his only failure now would be not to try.

Croatia was well acquainted with terrorism, and when the tyrannized found the odds impossible, their instinct was to build a bomb. But while his ancestors invariably set out to blow up something or someone, Ziven's device, if all went well, would never be detonated. His purpose was not to destroy property or take life, but rather to bring the FBI to his terms.

Inside the Cook County Jail, the smaller weekend shift of employees had settled in for the night. The rear of the truck eased up to within a few inches of the dock and stopped. Ziven got out and, staying on the driver's side where there was no surveillance camera, walked to the back. With startling ease he threw up the overhead door, causing it to bang into its frame. Although he felt relatively calm, he took this as an indication that his adrenaline was flowing too freely, a condition which could cause a misstep. He took a slow, deep breath and then waited an additional moment before climbing up inside.

The heavy odor of the evening meal—possibly pizza, or maybe ham—was being blown out a heavily barred kitchen vent at the far end of the building. He tried to remember the last time he had eaten and suddenly felt hungry. Inside, the meal hour was a time when most of the guards would be busy keeping order. He started the engine on the forklift. On its blades sat the bomb, a rectangular box about the size of a commercial freezer laid on its side. He raised it a foot above the truck's bed and drove forward.

Once Ziven had devised his plan, he had gone to the jail to scout out any problems he might encounter. The building's architectural configuration suggested where he should plant the device for maximum effect. The loading dock was recessed under the back end of the jail to protect shipments from Chicago's weather. And there were about a dozen feet of space in front of the locked steel overhead doors, enough room to place a good-size pallet load. Ziven knew that, positioned under a portion of the building, the bomb would be considerably more threatening.

But the most important element of his plan was that the building couldn't be evacuated. The jail was notoriously over-crowded. Unbelievably, it housed in excess of fifteen thousand inmates serving not only misdemeanor sentences, but also felons awaiting trial or transfer to the state penitentiaries. That was what had first given him the idea. The news had reported that all the jails and prisons in the state were beyond capacity and civil libertarians were demanding that the federal government inter-vene. To prevent further violations of human rights, they were requesting massive early releases. But, because of public outrage at the thought of Chicago's streets being flooded with crimi-nals—according to the reporter—the authorities didn't seem to be in any hurry to correct the situation.

That was one of the things he couldn't understand about the United States: its coddling of criminals. And not just because his family had become one of their victims. In Croatia, those who vi-olated the law were considered worthy of society's fullest re-venge. But now he was glad that American criminals were treated with such tortured sympathy. Peace between the ac-tivists and prison authorities was hanging by a thread, and Ziven hoped to snap it.

Carefully, he lowered the bomb onto the concrete dock. It was completely encased in sheet metal. Each of the corners had been cleanly welded, leaving flat, smooth seams. On the top were ten toggle switches placed in a line at one end, each marked with a sin-gle hand-numbered digit from zero through nine. There was also a single hole in the middle of the top, about the diameter of a wooden pencil. With a sudden crack of static, a lethargic munici-pal voice came from a speaker that Ziven couldn't see. "Hey, pal, we don't take deliveries after five P.M. on Friday."

Ziven glanced at the surveillance camera and pulled down his large floppy cap. He was wearing sunglasses and a jacket with its collar turned up.

The day of his wife's arrest, he sat up the entire night resisting the need for revenge that steadily began to overwhelm him. By morning, any illusion that justice was simply a matter of patience and given enough time would come to him had been dispatched. With characteristic Croatian resolve, Ziven decided that a man becomes a victim only if he allows it. As much as he wanted to punish the person responsible, he had no idea who had kidnapped his daughter. And at the pace the FBI was working, it didn't look like they were going to find out.

For the last three years, he had been a good citizen and done what he thought was the right thing: let the FBI conduct their investigation and never question their baffling lack of progress. But they were his last hope. There was no higher agency to which an appeal could be begged. The consequences of what he was now doing frightened him greatly, but he knew he no longer had a choice.

For the next two months he became consumed by his plan. As an engineer, and a Croatian at that, he knew, at least in theory, how to build a bomb. But for his plan to work, he had to be sure that the FBI's experts could not disarm or neutralize it. This took some research, first at the library, reading old publications about police cases in which bombs were used, and then the Internet, where virtually anything could be found with enough perseverance.

On the door of the truck which faced the surveillance camera, he had appended a plastic magnetic sign that read: COOK COUNTY FOOD SERVICES. Although it was made for him in a sign shop, he had painted a fairly accurate reproduction of the county logo, at least accurate enough for the video camera. The sign was one of the clues he was leaving so the FBI could find him.

When Ziven didn't answer, the guard's tone became more alert, more indignant. "Did you hear me, pal?" Ziven pulled the forklift back into the truck, cut its engine, and walked calmly over to the device on the loading dock.

"Identify yourself," the voice demanded. That'll be up to the FBI now, Ziven thought. Sufficient clues were being left for them. He wasn't making it easy but hopefully they had someone capable enough to follow the trail, and if they did, that was the person he would demand look for his daughter. Not that he thought she was still alive, that deception had passed a thousand days ago, and then, inexorably, had been reborn countless more times only to wither and die with the unmerciful cycle of all things falsely hoped for. But if she could be found, he wanted her to be properly buried and, more important, properly mourned.

And of course, her kidnapper was still out there, spending the ransom—one hundred thousand dollars, or whatever his extensive stamp collection had been sold for. For this person, Ziven dreamt of Croatian justice: swift, violent, final.

He pulled a thin Phillips-head screwdriver from his hip pocket, inserted it in the single hole in the top of the metal casing, and pushed down carefully until he heard a loud metallic snap. When the FBI reviewed the videotape, they would conclude that the act had armed the device and the only way it could be rendered harmless was by turning off all ten toggle switches in the proper sequence. They would calculate that there were over three million combinations, all of which, except for the single one he had programmed in, would detonate the bomb instantly.

With a device this large, the bomb experts would know enough not to try to move it. Its meticulous construction would cause them to assume that mercury switches were set inside, warning that with the slightest movement out of plumb would complete the circuit and cause it to explode. He had also learned that the most sophisticated, and usually successful, procedure used to neutralize a bomb was to x-ray it, but, as they would soon find out, he had devised a way to defeat that. Keeping his face turned away from the camera, Ziven waved at it to give the guard a few more seconds of confusion.

The warmth of the mid-autumn day had lingered into the evening, and as it did at no other time of the year, lazily melted memories and dreams together. He walked back to the truck's cab and got in. Even with the door closed and the window rolled up, he could hear some of the guard's garbled, crescendoing syllables. He started the engine. From the seat next to him, he picked up his pipe, and, with unpremeditated ceremony, tamped the tobacco-filled bowl several times before touching a match to it. A strange peace settled over him as the smell of just-ripe apples and smoldering briar twined around him like laughing, ribbon-tethered schoolgirls.

As he pulled away, he could see the giant metal box in the rearview mirror. On the front, which was turned away from the camera, eight-inch black letters were neatly stenciled to prevent the appearance of its being a graffitied hoax:

## THIS IS A BOMB
## CALL THE FBI

# 3

"BOYS, HERE'S WHERE WE SEPARATE THE JUNIOR Varsity from those in need of a good twelve-step program . . ." Maurice Wharfman dropped the necessary chips into the pot with an uncharacteristic flair of confidence. ". . . Raise two hundred."

A general groan of surrender swept around the table. The bet was to Manny Tollison. He rolled his half-smoked cigar into the corner of his mouth and bit down on it thoughtfully. Wharfman rarely bluffed, which made it that much more convincing when he did. Tollison shifted his three hundred pounds in the chair as he continued to consider his position. He was holding two pair — a low two pair — and decided the odds were not in his favor. With the slightest flick of his wrist, as if using any more energy than necessary would be an additional victory for Wharfman, he tossed his cards in. The next two players left in the game, Mickey Wallace and Jimmy Diallo, swayed by Tollison's high-percentage instincts, did the same. That left just Jack Kincade.

Each Friday night they came to play poker in the back room of Roxie's Bar and Grill. It was located less than a half mile from the Maywood Racetrack and had a reputation as a gambler's hangout, especially a few hours before or after the races. But the men who came to play cards were mostly regulars, who, for a modest fee, were allowed to continue their game long after the bar was closed. And those who pulled up a chair on Friday night, as implied by Wharfman's taunt, were not likely to leave as long as there was a single dollar left to be won or lost.

The room itself was gloomy, unpainted in years with unsealed wooden floors. A small bar, no longer used, stood at one end. A few small tables and chairs were pushed along the walls, rendering them incidental to the large poker table and the men who now surrounded it. The air, even when no one was smoking, felt thick with the suffocating veneers of nights past. And the distant odor of spilled beer occasionally rose from the floor, reminding them that man's pleasures often leave sour, enduring residues. The walls were filled with dusty photographs, most of which were professional Chicago athletes. All signed to Roxie.

Kincade didn't appear to be in a hurry to call the bet. He was on his third drink, not counting the two he had had in his room. He looked down at the yellow-brown nicotine calluses on the second and third fingers of his right hand. For a moment he studied the cigarette he held there while a ragged pennant of smoke rose and then dissolved into its own weightless updraft. Situations like this were exactly why he gambled, to feel the sting of desperate odds and the occasional surrender of impossibility to recklessness, something he would, in all likelihood, later remember as courage. It seemed such moments were more and more difficult for him to unearth within his muddied psyche. But now, the risk of calling Wharfman's large, dissuasive bet had started throwing those rusting switches. The alcoholic glaze was clearing from his exhausted eyes, and his fingers quickened as they riffed through a stack of chips.

He knew Maurice Wharfman to be a man who, at least metaphorically, never showed his hole card. With cold calculation, he presented himself as simpler than he really was, letting those around him sedate themselves with overconfidence, leaving their flanks unguarded.

"Since my ex-wife's lawyer continues to refer to me as 'the degenerate gambler,' I feel a certain obligation to answer your challenge, Wharf." Kincade dropped two hundred dollars worth of blue plastic disks on top of the pile.

"Continues? I thought your divorce was final," Wharfman said.

"It is, but she's trying to take me back to court. She says she wants more money, but I think she's just mad at me because I've missed a few visits with my son," Kincade said.

Mickey Wallace, who was seventy-three years old, cleared his throat as he always did before he spoke. He was wearing his trademark red-and-white checkered sport coat and snap-brim fedora, which was precariously balanced, as if by some carnival trick, on the top of his small, egg-shaped head. "Maybe they're looking for your hidden assets, Jack." Everyone, including Kincade, laughed.

Jimmy Diallo fingered the gold crucifix around his neck. He was in his mid-thirties and what little of his hair remained was pasted on his scalp in shiny spikes. His cream-colored silk shirt clung luridly to his doughy pecs. It was unbuttoned halfway to his waist, revealing a thick mat of dark chest hair. "When I split with my old lady, it seemed like it took forever. But you know what I found out, she didn't want to lose me."

Everyone looked at one another with half-hidden amusement. Mickey Wallace finally spoke up, "Wharf, I thought you weren't going to allow the institutionally delusional in this game anymore?"

Everyone laughed again and when it died down, Diallo said, "Mickey, don't be so bitter. I'm sure you'll get that part in *Guys and Dolls* next time."

Wallace smiled, putting a hand on Diallo's forearm confidentially, and cleared his throat. "Jimmy, I was asked by the others to tell you that if you're going to wear your shirt like that . . . well . . ."

"Well, what?"

"We'd like you to shave your tits."

Diallo stood up as if to leave. "Where're you going?" Wharfman asked.

"I'm going to see if Roxie has a needle and thread. The old guy just took a giant hunk out of my ass."

Wharfman turned back to the table. "When I got divorced, her lawyers thought I was hiding everything."

"Were you?" Kincade asked.

Wharfman, a bail bondsman, was well acquainted by professional necessity with both the burying and excavating of collateral-size assets. "Of course. But they never found them."

"Well, Wharf, my empire is not quite as far-flung as yours. My wife knew exactly what we had at the time, and was sadly aware that I had prevented the possibility of hidden resources by gambling away almost everything we owned."

"Didn't you get anything?"

"Actually, I did. One previously owned, seventeen-year-old Dodge minivan with 207,000 miles on the odometer. At present, my most valuable possession."

"How long were you two married?" Manny Tollison asked. It was a question, Kincade noticed, that most undivorced gamblers asked, wondering if their own marriage was in some sort of countdown, and if so, how they could handicap its expiration date. Evidently, they feared mistiming the ending and leaving something for their wives, which could just as easily have gone to their bookies.

"Ten years."

Wallace shook his head with a gambler's rare empathy. "Ten years and that's all you got. What did she get?"

"Well, her lawyer thought because of—as he put it—'my ability to enjoy the anarchy of my own life,' she deserved everything else. Not that there was much to argue about. She got the furniture and the small amount of remaining equity in our Pennsylvania home that I had somehow failed to piss away. But by far, the most valuable asset she realized was an extremely healthy cynicism toward the male of the species. And as every one of you degenerates knows, that will take her considerably farther, and with infinitely more safety, than a minivan with *Guinness Book* mileage."

Wharfman laughed. "Are you going to raise or call?"

"I call."

Wharfman flipped over his hole cards to reveal two pair.

Kincade smiled. "Three queens." He turned over the third one and started raking in the pot.

"Just out of curiosity," Wallace said, "does she get half of your winnings, too?"

"Absolutely, and she told me, out of her half she wanted me to buy every one of my dickhead friends a drink."

As everyone toasted his generous ex-wife, Kincade said, "B.C.!" Instantly, the Border collie's black and white head appeared above the table, its eager eyes locked on him. "Cocktails." With no wasted motion, the dog headed for the bar at a determined trot. Using a paw, it pulled the partially open door wide enough to exit.

"You've never told us, Jack, what's 'B.C.' stand for?" Wallace asked.

"Border collie."

"Border collie, that's it? That's a pretty smart dog; don't you think he deserves a real name?"

"Not until he's off probation."

"Probation?"

"He came with my motel room. First day I moved in, he started scratching on the door. The manager said the family who lived there before me must have left him behind. I'm not going to bother naming him until I'm sure he's sticking around."

"So I'm assuming your wife used to call you J.K.," Tollison said.

"No, but she did regularly refer to me as A. Hole."

Five minutes later, Sue, the waitress summoned by the Border collie, came in with their drinks. Kincade tucked two twenties into her apron pocket and found himself distracted as the back of his hand explored the fleshy curve of her stomach. "Don't start anything you can't finish right here, right now, G-man," she said, her voice filled with a veteran waitress's ability never to give quarter to a room filled with men.

Kincade considered his options and then withdrew his hand. "So many vices, so little time," he said. "Keep the change, darlin'."

For the next two hours, Kincade failed to win another hand, and the six hundred dollars he was ahead had steadily dwindled. He let his chips riff through his fingers, discreetly counting and re-counting the remaining two hundred dollars. He glanced at Wharfman and realized that the bondsman had also been counting them.

"Raise a hundred." Wharfman held his chips above the pot with a confident smile. Being an FBI agent did give Kincade one advantage as a poker player. After years of listening to suspects whose believability would result not in simply winning a few dollars but their freedom, he had learned that, invariably, the most accurate judgments about deception were made by observing the smallest of details. Wharfman leaned back and put his hands behind his head. That was the second indication the bondsman had given of his optimism. One could be revealing, but for Maurice Wharfman, normally a man of Byzantine motives, two were extremely confusing. Was he trying to buy the pot again?

His fingers, thick and rough, could have come from generations of stone cutters or cabinetmakers. They moved with quick, surgical certainty. Kincade had always noticed that as the betting moved around the table, even though Wharf's turn was at least three players away, he would anticipate how much to wager, his fingers deftly separating the necessary number of chips far in advance. The other players invariably waited to the last possible moment, using the size and flow of the other bets to help determine their chances of success. Wharfman seemed to have everyone's position charted as soon as each card was turned over. Consequently, he rarely seemed surprised or disappointed, which allowed him to remain stoic, a sizable advantage during the rape-and-pillage exuberance of the Friday night game. But now he *was* sending signals. Everything considered, to wager further would be ill-advised, but once again Kincade felt himself drawn to the paper-thin line between failure and success.

Wharfman noticed Kincade watching his hands and pulled them down into his lap out of sight. But then his elbows bowed out and his forearms rotated up, suggesting he was steepling his fingers. To an interrogator, it was an unmistakable sign of sureness. But Wharfman was certainly smart enough to understand that the FBI agent could read such a sign, even off the table. Kincade checked the cards again. The five overturned cards showing were an ace, a ten, a three, and a pair of jacks. He had a pair of nines in the hole, so with the jacks, he had two pair. But Wharfman was trying to sell the idea that he had an ace in the hole, giving him aces and jacks, which would beat Kincade's hand. Or he could possibly have a third jack.

Kincade knew the odds were not in his favor. But Wharfman knew that, too. If he did have a better hand, why would he be sending out all the uncharacteristic body language? Kincade decided that Wharfman was probably bluffing. Everyone knew he rarely bluffed, so for him to do it twice in a night would be completely unexpected. Besides, for only the second time tonight, Kincade was feeling a jolt of uncertainty. "I'll see your hundred and raise a hundred." He threw in the last of his chips, hoping the doubled bet would warn Wharfman that if he was bluffing, it wasn't going to work this time, either.

When Wharfman reached into his stacks of chips and started counting past a hundred, Kincade realized it wasn't going to be that easy. "I'll raise five hundred," the bondsman said with a chilling lack of emotion.

Kincade took a long pull on his drink and lit another cigarette, stalling. Whether Wharfman was bluffing or not, it no longer mattered; he was broke. If this hand were lost, he would be done for the night, which left only the aching solitude of his room. Illogically searching his pockets for money he knew wasn't there, he pulled out the torn piece of newspaper that he had used to write down the information about the wanted Portland, Oregon, deadbeat dad. "Any out-of-state bond jumpers, if you pick them up, you get ten percent of the bond forfeited, right?"

"It's negotiable, but that's the normal deal."

"This guy bolted on a ten-thousand-dollar bond. He's staying at the Star Crest Motel in De Kalb." Kincade handed the newspaper to Wharfman. "It's worth a grand to you; you can have it for five hundred."

As though it were the possible source of a virus, Wharf held the ragged piece of newsprint with two fingertips. "Is this an official FBI document?"

"Don't worry, it's good."

"Let me go make a call."

Kincade took a full swallow of his drink. The room had become quiet and he felt everyone's eyes on him. Normally, chronic gamblers, due to their own ample imperfections, were reluctant to judge others, especially when it came to which part of their lives they chose to trade away across a poker table. They had seen weaknesses of all shades and accepted them as part of the human landscape in which they chose to live. But here was something they hadn't encountered before, a strain of human behavior they hadn't realized could exist within their ranks. Even though they had gambled with Kincade for months and had witnessed many of their own weaknesses in him, they thought of him ultimately as an FBI agent, someone who, at some point, could rise above the fray and say, *Enough*. It was important for them to believe that a certain incorruptibility existed out there beyond their four walls, even though they would never dare to take the initiative for its maintenance themselves. Someone had to protect their right to be irresponsible.

Tollison took out a small silver lighter and relit his cigar, blowing the smoke toward the ceiling. He continued to watch it long after it disappeared into the light. The others silently sipped their drinks or shuffled their chips or brushed away stubborn, imaginary lint. Mickey Wallace leaned over and massaged B.C.'s black velvety ear.

Kincade understood their indignation because, in a way, he sensed his own betrayal. For an FBI agent, his or her sense of duty should be ultimately incorruptible. At least he had believed that when he joined the Bureau, but the intervening mileage had led him to conclude that such idealism existed only in the hollow tunnels of a young man's imagination.

Wharfman came back into the room. "If I decide to accept this and he's not at the motel, you'll still owe me five hundred."

Kincade knew that after paying his bounty hunters for their services, Wharfman wouldn't make the five hundred dollars profit that the bet was supposed to represent. But he imagined that Wharfman was not able to resist the unusual trophy—an FBI agent actually losing one of his cases to him. "That seems reasonable."

When Wharfman had first met Kincade, he couldn't help but like him. He was an Ivy League–educated FBI agent with a sense of humor who liked to drink and gamble, maybe a little too much at times, and was completely uninhibited. But each week there seemed to be a little less to admire. Presently, he was in need of a haircut. His suits were chronically rumpled, and he always wore the same pair of cheap, casual suedes. As a bondsman, he had seen a thousand lives unravel. With Kincade betting his fugitive case so contemptuously, he was lowering himself from that final rung, becoming someone who no longer held anything sacred. There was no fear left. Gambling had become a necessity, its bite one of the few things left he could feel.

While everyone else in the room decided, in low tones, which hand was going to win, the two men sat in silence.

"Are you calling then?" Wharfman asked.

"I'm a-calling, Bondsman."

Wharfman turned over his hole cards. He had the third jack.

Kincade gave a single snort of laughter as he tossed his hand in. Wharfman had used the agent's ability to read body language against him. The earlier hand that Kincade won from him was a setup for this larger one. Kincade had known the depth of Wharfman's ability and still chose to ignore his own instincts. "Nice double reverse."

Wharfman nodded graciously. "Thank you." Kincade got up, his lips drawn back, slightly embarrassed. B.C. was already standing at his side. "You're not leaving, are you, Jack?"

Kincade leaned over the table and crushed out his cigarette in the overflowing ashtray. "Sorry, Wharf, I'm all out of fugitives."

"Want to borrow a couple of hundred?"

"No. I might actually win some money back and interrupt my plans for a nice quiet suicide."

"You sure? This looks like it's going to run for a while."

"I'll probably be back. I'm going to see about picking up some cash."

"You, an ATM? I thought you told me you didn't have any bank accounts?"

"Fortunately, the FBI has trained me to be resourceful."

# 4

TO ILLUMINATE THE DARKNESS BEHIND THE COOK County Jail at 1:30 in the morning, a wide semicircle of portable, high-intensity lights had been aimed at the bomb. Moving through the blinding sodium-white glare with the broad, labored movements of hard-hat divers were two Chicago Bomb Squad officers covered head to toe in heavily padded black armor.

The overhead doors on the loading dock had been opened so the two men could inspect the device easily from all sides. After walking completely around it, the taller of the two, Lt. Dan Elkins, motioned for his partner to step back. He then carefully pulled off his helmet and set it on the dock. The scorching light turned his blond hair white and gave his fair skin the purple cast of a newborn. The lieutenant's thin, bladed face was too long to be considered handsome, but his clear blue eyes, now fully excited with danger, had gained an appeal all their own. Moving to within inches of the bomb, he lowered himself to his hands and knees. For the next five minutes he crawled around it carefully, stopping every two or three feet to place his face against the ground, using a small flashlight to eliminate secondary shadows so the entire bottom edge of the device could be examined.

Before putting his helmet back on, he said to his partner, "Okay, let's set the X-ray canisters and get out of here." Working with the silent understanding that comes from sharing danger, the two men placed a series of film holders behind the bomb, abutting the ends to one another to ensure full coverage. Then, with as much haste as was possible in the protective suits, they walked back beyond the lights and behind a six-foot-high double wall of sandbags.

Another Chicago Bomb Squad officer sat at a folding table checking the contrast on an oversize laptop computer screen. Behind him, in thin blue nylon jackets with their agency's initials printed across them in large yellow letters, were a dozen or so FBI agents clustered around the acting SAC, Albert Bartoli. His official title was Assistant Special Agent in Charge, but the previous head of the Chicago office had retired prematurely, leaving Bartoli to run the division until FBI headquarters could send someone more seasoned. He was thirty-one, which was considered young to be an ASAC in a field office the size of Chicago. At first glance, his face presented itself as uncomplicated and easy to interpret. Its upper portions, thanks to his pronounced cheekbones, were large and pleasantly shaped. But his lower jaw was relatively underdeveloped and weak, giving his face a vague, unsophisticated quality. This, combined with a practiced tilt of the head, gave the impression that Al Bartoli was somewhat in awe of everything around him, too inexperienced to be a threat, lacking the ambition or cunning to involve himself in the daily hand-to-hand combat of Bureau politics.

He wore a moustache, and like everything else about him, it was neatly trimmed, except for the lower edge, which was left ragged to hang over his upper lip, an attempt to mute the waxy, feminine curve of his mouth. In like manner, as those who had underestimated him in the past could attest to, there was a calculation to everything he did. It had not been an accident that he was now the agent in charge of one of the largest offices in the FBI. He had circuitously arranged a job offer for the previous SAC from a corporation with which he had been responsible for maintaining liaison. The offer was so lucrative that his boss had no choice but to take it immediately, leaving Bartoli to fill the void while distant Washington pondered a replacement. The title, even though qualified by the "acting" that preceded it, undoubtedly looked good in his personnel file, and demonstrated his ability to head a field office in the near future.

He wore a suit and tie with a freshly starched white shirt, and because he did not have on one of the flimsy blue FBI jackets, he was that much more distinguishable in the group of agents. All the men around him were noticeably younger and less experienced. Not one of them seemed to notice that Bartoli had positioned himself so that most of them were between him and the bomb.

Another larger group, consisting of uniformed police officers and sheriff's deputies, stood off in a second cluster. In the darkness, a car stopped quickly. A black man wearing the uniform of a Chicago Police Department deputy chief got out and greeted his men, also shaking hands with several of the sheriff's deputies.

Billy Hatton was in his fifties and had hard brown eyes; his hair, a finely crimped silver, was visible under the edges of his hat. He looked over at the FBI agents. "Who's in charge?"

The agents parted and Bartoli stepped forward extending his hand. "Al Bartoli. I'm the acting SAC."

"Billy Hatton." The deputy chief shook his hand and gave him a quick smile. "Acting? Does that mean it's temporary or you're just pretending?"

Still holding the deputy chief's hand, Bartoli used it to pull him closer and in a mock-confidential whisper said, "Both, I'm afraid."

Hatton released his grip and leaned back slightly. He had learned about the legendary agency as a young detective working stolen autos. Like clockwork on Monday mornings, one or two of the Bureau's agents would show up looking for cars stolen out-of-state that had been recovered over the weekend. A day later, those "stats" were on their way to Washington. The occasional glimpse he had been afforded of the Bureau in recent years had done nothing to reduce his caution when dealing with them. But if there was one thing that set his warning lights flashing, it was an FBI agent who tried to ingratiate himself by the use of self-deprecating humor. He had seen thirty-five years of agents come and go and knew they didn't become bosses because they took themselves lightly. "What happened to, ah . . . ?"

"Jay Johnson," Bartoli finished for him. "He got a quick job offer and took it. Didn't really give the Bureau any notice so they could get a replacement here on time. They have named somebody but he wasn't scheduled to be here for another month. Because of this"—Bartoli waved his hand toward the wall of sandbags—"he'll be here tomorrow morning. His name is Roy K. Thorne."

"Why is that name familiar?"

"He's kind of a legend in the Bureau. Remember when that U.S. representative from California was murdered about eight years ago? Thorne was brought in to solve it. They said he slept on the floor next to his desk for the first three weeks. And that Coast Guard cutter that was blown up down in Miami by the Colombians a couple of years ago, he solved that, too. He was supposed to be coming here as a nice farewell assignment until he retired in a year or two, you know, to find a job. He's originally from here."

"Doesn't sound like he's going to ease into retirement, at least not yet."

"If there's anyone in the Bureau that can figure this out, it's him."

Hatton walked over to the break in the sandbag wall, looked at the stenciled message on the front of the bomb quickly, and then asked, "Any idea who your latest admirer is?"

"Your men were just getting a closer look at it. Our best guess is that it isn't terrorists."

"Who plants bombs besides terrorists?"

"You're right, it is meant to terrorize. But when it comes to traditional terrorist groups, we don't think this belongs to any of the usual suspects. Their method of informing us of the presence of a bomb is usually to explode it, and then provide the rhetoric afterward. This is meant to intimidate, but to what end we don't have a clue."

Hatton called Lt. Elkins over. "Dan, what's it look like?"

"I've never seen anything like it, sir. If it wasn't a bomb, you could sell it as a piece of furniture. Whoever built it was a real craftsman. The exterior is made up of five perfectly fitted pieces of sheet metal. All the seams are neatly welded and then, I'd guess some sort of high-speed grinder was used to smooth them. This guy knew what he was doing."

"I understand they already brought the bomb dog in."

"Yes, sir, he hit on it immediately. It's definitely hot. That's another interesting detail to this device. At each of the four corners, there are two small holes drilled out. At first we couldn't figure what they were for, but those are the exact points where the dog hit. They must have been drilled specifically so the dog could confirm the presence of explosives."

The deputy chief said, "You're not making me warm with optimism."

Elkins smiled respectfully at his boss. "Maybe I'm overestimating this guy. We won't know anything for sure until we get some X rays." Elkins called behind him, "Is Ralph ready?"

"Ready," someone called back from the darkness.

"Okay, send him in." A CPD Bomb Squad officer stepped forward with a remote-control device held forward in both his hands. Beside him was Ralph, a three-foot-tall bomb robot. It whirred past the lights, headed up a ramp at the far end of the loading dock and straight toward the bomb. Elkins looked down at the computer. The robot's television camera was transmitting the area immediately in front of it onto the screen. "Okay, I want to work it left to right in two-foot intervals."

The police officer with the remote stepped over in front of the computer screen and used its image to guide the robot's movement. He made it back up slightly, turn a couple of degrees, and then go forward until it was less than twenty-four inches from the bomb. "That's it, right there," Elkins said. A metallic click from the robot signaled that the X ray had been taken. The officer at the computer hit a couple of keys and, except for a few fuzzy white squiggles on the right-hand side, the screen showed black. Elkins rocked forward to get a closer look. "Did you check the camera?" he asked the officer with the remote.

"It was working fine." He bent down and scrutinized the characters at the right end of the display. "Are those letters?"

Elkins looked again. "Could be." He looked up over the laptop. "Shoot the next section."

Again the robot backed up and was repositioned. "Snapping it now," said the officer.

Another mostly black screen resulted but a few white letters were now plainly visible. "Get the next section," Elkins ordered.

Again the robot was maneuvered into position and the X ray taken. When the entire length of the bomb had been photographed and the images were consolidated, a two-line message was visible on the laptop:

Pb

3M possible

Bartoli said, "Pb?"

Elkins answered, "It's the chemical symbol for lead. He's telling us the entire bomb is encased in lead, which means x-raying it isn't going to do any good. The X rays are blocked and the light can't get through. Everything just appears black, everything but the message. This guy's letting us know he's way ahead of us."

"Is x-raying absolutely necessary to disarm it?" the deputy chief asked.

"A self-contained device like this has to have a power pack, a battery wired to an electrical blasting cap. What we try to do is interrupt that detonation chain. If the device was in something like a briefcase, we might employ a water cannon, which is like a shotgun attachment for the robot. A water slug is fired at the power pack in an attempt to destroy it. When the container is something more impenetrable like this metal shell, a precision explosive charge can be used to sever the chain. That's usually a shape charge, or, if we know where everything is, we can strategically place a det cord, which, when set off properly, can also interrupt the electrical connection. But without X rays, we don't have a clue where anything is and using any of these techniques would in all likelihood just explode the bomb."

"What about moving it?" Bartoli asked.

"As sophisticated as this is, we have to assume there are mercury switches installed, which have only one purpose—immobility. The slightest jostle could set it off."

"So, if we can't disarm it, and we can't move it, what's left?" Hatton asked.

"Either leave it in place or blow it up."

"With the political pressure this thing is already generating, letting it remain is not an option. If you blow it, how much damage are we talking about?"

"I'd estimate there could be as much as a thousand pounds of explosives packed inside. It could take out a major portion of the jail, maybe even all of it."

"Is there any chance it could blow up by itself?"

"With an explosive device, there's always that possibility. But if you're asking if it contains any type of countdown clock, I'd guess, no. His message would have warned us about that. Given us a deadline."

The deputy chief's face filled with consternation. "What does that second line in the message mean, Dan?"

"There are ten switches on the top. I haven't done the math, but if you figure the number of possible combinations, I'm guessing there'll be somewhere around three million. He's telling us that the bomb can be disarmed only by throwing all ten switches in proper sequence. Which means one switch out of turn would trigger it. We have one chance in three million."

"Any idea why he's doing this?" Bartoli asked.

"I'm just a bomb technician. You're the ones with all the profilers. This guy could be anyone from a wacko with a messiah complex to somebody the FBI *framed*. Whoever he is, he's telling us the only way to make this bomb go away is to find out who he is, and get him to do it."

Hatton looked at Bartoli with the same smile he had used when they introduced themselves. "Well, Al, here's your chance to quit *acting*."

"The new SAC will be here in a few hours. He's already contacted me and I've briefed him. We're calling out every agent in the division to find out who did this." The final sentence had an exploratory cadence to it, one of someone testing his credibility as a commander.

Hatton looked at him carefully. "This Thorne, does he know what he's in for?"

Bartoli started to answer but then realized there was something in Hatton's tone that indicated that the old cop might not be talking about the bomb.

# 5

FROM A QUARTER MILE AWAY, KINCADE SCANNED THE deserted parking lot one last time with his binoculars. Earlier, during rush hour, he had placed a trap in the Barrington Community Savings night depository. He knew from experience that it was the optimum time. Even though daylight was quickly fading, not all the homeward-bound drivers had turned on their headlights. It was Friday evening and with that liberation came the tiny, earned pleasure of delaying such minor rules, a time when the summons of family and the first cocktail blurred the world along the way and would hopefully leave Kincade's movements unnoticed. But now, hours later, even though the area was darker and with far less traffic, retrieving the device was filled with even more risk than its installation. Kincade's biggest fear was the device being discovered by a depositor. If someone had, and reported it, the police could be waiting for the thief to retrieve it.

He took a last drag on his cigarette and dropped it out the window. He blew the smoke in a long, controlled stream against the inside of the windshield, momentarily obliterating the world in front of him, and with it, what he was about to do.

Trapping night depositories was a crime rarely committed anymore simply because the old-style unlocked chutes had been upgraded to more sophisticated equipment in all but a relatively small number of banks across the country. The suburban Chicago area, long a holdout against branch banking, still had a few.

Kincade had learned the finer points of the all-but-vanished crime more than a decade earlier from Alfred James Manning, who, before being caught, had been known to the FBI only as "The Trapper." Eluding them for over a year, he had set more than a hundred of his customized devices in the night depositories of banks throughout southeastern Pennsylvania. He was finally identified and sent to prison by Kincade himself, then a Philadelphia bank robbery agent.

While the design of Manning's traps had been refined by sheer repetition, his rules for deploying them changed little. He would always set them on Friday or Saturday, the most lucrative nights because of weekly business receipts. He avoided patterns, such as targeting the same bank twice, or trapping two weekends in a row. Patterns led to stakeouts, and stakeouts, sooner or later, led to arrests. But the one caution Manning failed to postulate, as did most thieves, was *Never get overconfident.* Although the total loot from his traps had topped $200,000 after one particularly unproductive weekend, he incautiously cashed some checks that had been snared. The resulting paper trail led Kincade and most of the bank robbery squad straight to Manning's suburban Philadelphia apartment.

Kincade had been in his car for the better part of an hour. The town's single patrol car had looped by lazily twice during that time, the last sighting just a few minutes before. It wasn't due back for at least a half hour. Kincade decided to make one last pass before trying to retrieve the trap. He drove at a speed appropriate for the time of day, looking for anyone who might be able to follow his movements. Not spotting anything suspicious, he made a U-turn and pulled his faded, arthritic van up to the bank's night depository.

B.C. sat on the seat next to him, the tip of the dog's tongue protruding happily through its snow-white incisors. "I don't know what you're smiling about; you obviously don't have a clue what the penalties are for violating federal banking statutes."

Summoned by the ancient mission of Border collies, the dog stared back, waiting for an opportunity to please its master. Kincade stared back. "You talking to me?" Suspecting a discernible order was about to be issued, B.C. shifted its hindquarters on the seat anxiously. "You talking to me?" Kincade invited again. The dog just gazed back intently. With one swift motion, Kincade drew a snubnose revolver from somewhere under the seat and pointed it at the dog. As it came to rest within an inch of the animal's dry black nose, B.C. craned forward slightly, halving the distance to the gun's muzzle, and sniffed it objectively. Deciding it had neither nutritional nor sexual possibilities, the Border collie leaned back and awaited further instruction. Kincade shook the small revolver to verify each of its five chambers was empty and then placed it back under the seat. He looked at the dog, trying to stare it down, something he had never been able to do successfully. "Okay, okay."

Kincade pushed open the van's door. As he got out, the mini-van gave a metallic, three-syllable groan. He left his lights on as a legitimate customer would and called to the dog, "B.C., go pee!" The Border collie jumped out the driver's door and ran to the edge of the lot onto a small fringe of grass. Its ears dutifully cocked, the dog raised a rear leg and began urinating as its nose tested the air for enemies. It wasn't anything Kincade had taught the dog but rather its normal procedure. The animal's predatory senses started to ease Kincade's concerns, but then, without warning, it locked into a combat-ready stance, slowly lowering itself to the ground. Kincade froze. Their eyes searched the surrounding area. Suddenly the dog stood up, tested the air for a final time, and then dismissively trotted back to the van. Kincade could feel his accelerated pulse start to slow. "Inside, boy."

The dog jumped up and positioned itself in the passenger seat, its tongue happily askew once again. Kincade walked to the night deposit chute and lifted the lid.

Inside was the trap, a 12- × 24-inch sheet of thin, flexible plastic that had, at each end, an oval slot cut into it as a hand-hold. Experience—and Manning's confession—had taught him that they would aid, not only in the device's installation but also in keeping its removal quick and unnoticed. There was no reason to leave evidence lying around if it could be helped. Conversely, he did not wear any type of gloves to preclude leaving fingerprints. If he were spotted wearing anything over his hands in the still-mild fall weather, it would have created more suspicion than if his fingerprints were eventually discovered on the device. If the lab identified his latents on any of the traps, as the case agent, he would simply be judged a careless handler of evidence—a remarkably common misdemeanor among agents—rather than a suspect.

When the first of his trapping cases was reported to the FBI, the younger agents in the office dismissed it as inconsequential. They considered it such an antiquated and unobtrusive crime that it should be regarded, with some contempt, as a symptom of the "Old Bureau," an organization where "stats" and the tiny cases that produced them could no longer be taken seriously in today's more cerebral, "quality over quantity" FBI. That was fine with Kincade because once the supervisor saw his uncharacteristic interest in the case, he gladly assigned it to him, hoping to get some work out of him, no matter how insignificant the crime might seem. Also, as any subsequent cases suspected of being committed by the same person are traditionally assigned to the same agent, Kincade knew all the trappings would then be given to him to investigate.

Even though this was his fourth time, he again reminded himself not to get lazy. One of the reasons for the unflagging caution was that his second device had been discovered before he could remove it. It had been found on a busy Saturday night when there were so many deposits that the bank bags backed up and a customer could not get hers into the chute. She called the bank. A security officer had personally come out and found the trap himself. Later that night Kincade was shocked to find the chute empty. Fortunately, the bank employee hadn't had the foresight to stake out the night depository. On the following Monday morning, he proudly turned over the device to Kincade.

Before installing each of them, Kincade had spray-painted one side of the plastic sheet flat black to lessen the chances of anyone noticing it sitting down inside. It was another technique developed by his former quarry-turned-mentor, Alfred Manning. On the reverse side, at both ends above the hand slots, Kincade had applied strips of double-sided tape to keep the trap from falling down into the bank's repository. Manning had always used clear fishing line to suspend the trap, leaving the knots anchored semivisibly around the outside of the chute. But the tape modification was one that Kincade had devised himself, and, as it did with all criminals, led him to an assumption of entitlement, that ingenuity would somehow prevent capture.

Slowly his hand started to explore the inside of the chute and almost immediately he felt the coarseness of canvas—a bank bag. After extracting it, he reached in again to pull the trap away from the walls and eased it out. He quickly threw both items on the passenger-side floor in front of the dog.

For the next fifteen minutes Kincade drove randomly, frequently changing directions, driving down one-way streets and then abruptly pulling over, "dry cleaning" himself to make sure he wasn't being followed. Finally satisfied, he pulled into a gas station and had the attendant fill the tank. He leaned over and picked up the bank bag from the floor. Inside was a deposit slip for The Children's Boutique, listing the bag's contents at almost four thousand dollars, $2,132 of which was in cash.

As a seam in the traffic opened up, he pressed the accelerator to the floor. The belching vehicle lumbered on to the street, slowing the cars coming up behind it, and reluctantly gained speed. Before he realized it, the van was doing fifteen miles an hour over the speed limit, which surprised him because the faster his life spiraled downward, the less he found the need to hurry. But then he realized why. His instincts as both an agent and a thief were telling him the same thing: Dispose of the evidence as quickly as possible, all of it. He needed to get back to the game.

# 6

REACTING TO A DELUGE OF CALLS FROM THE MEDIA
and assorted human rights groups, the chairman of the Senate
judiciary committee called the director of the FBI to ask what
was being done about "the mess in Chicago." The director had
been receiving regular updates almost from the moment the
bomb was planted and told the senator that he was sending in
the best man the Bureau had. He called Roy K. Thorne and told
him to be there first thing in the morning, if not sooner. Although his previously mandated transfer to Chicago was not
supposed to take place for another month, being dispatched in
the middle of the night was not an unusual occurrence for him.
When a particularly complex or sensitive problem arose, he expected his phone to ring.

For many years, Thorne had solved difficult cases in impres-
sively short periods of time, but most of his recent missions had
been internal matters, growing in number, that involved employee misconduct, a symptom he attributed to the lack of leadership within the agency. All but gone were the old "Specials,"
heavily manpowered, blitzkrieg-type investigations. These days
no one seemed to expect the FBI to solve every case, maybe not
even the majority of them. The Bureau was more often the tool
of the politicians, illicitly used to calm the day's headlines.
Whether it was an epidemic of carjackings or interstate domestic

violence, both clearly not within federal jurisdiction, the Band-Aid sound bite was the same—*We're sending in the FBI*. It was small wonder that agents didn't know what was expected of them anymore; no one did.

But Thorne knew this case was different. No amount of front office spin could disarm a bomb or make it seem less of a threat. Whoever was responsible for planting it had done his job well. And time would not dilute its urgency. No, this one belonged to the infantry. With retirement visible on the horizon, it would likely be Thorne's last legitimate special investigation, and he welcomed the chance to taste the dusky nostalgia of a career well spent.

After hanging up with the director, he contacted the Chicago office. He was put through to the agent in charge, Al Bartoli, who briefed him. Thorne then ordered the ASAC to set an all-agents meeting for 9 A.M., to be held inside the Cook County Jail.

"Inside the jail?" Bartoli's voice rattled slightly with an elevated pitch. "Do you think that's safe?"

"Absolutely not," Thorne said and hung up.

Thorne's plane landed at O'Hare Airport at 7:20 A.M. In the terminal, he spotted a neatly groomed agent from the counter-terrorism squad who had been sent to meet him. He walked over and introduced himself. The agent seemed slightly embarrassed not to have recognized Thorne, but the new SAC was not what he had expected. His flat gray eyes locked on the younger man, who immediately understood Thorne would not be the first to blink. It was a test, a demand for loyalty. *If you're with me, look me in the eye.* The agent, carefully chosen by Bartoli, now noticed the slightly cruel hook at one corner of Thorne's mouth and let his gaze slip away.

When he looked up, Thorne was already moving toward the baggage claim area. As the agent hurried to catch up, he was surprised that for a short, compact man, the new SAC moved with a graceful fluidity. His navy blue suit had somehow survived the flight without a noticeable wrinkle. And his shirt collar, so stiff with starch, appeared to still be lined with the cardboard underneath. It pinched a fold of skin on either side of his muscular neck. As the agent reached him, Thorne looked over his shoulder to make sure no one was within earshot. "What's the local press saying about this?"

"I really haven't had a chance to watch the news or read the newspaper today."

Thorne's eyes flashed, and the agent sensed he was about to be tested again. "Any demonstrations around the jail?"

"I really couldn't say."

"I thought we stopped cutting out the messenger's tongue when Hoover died."

"I'm sorry, I don't know what you mean?"

"There's a surprise."

Ben Alton pulled up to a Chicago police officer who was one of fifty-two guarding the four-block perimeter around the Cook County Jail. He was wearing a riot helmet with a replica of the CPD badge outlined in black on the front. Its purpose, presumably, was to protect him if the bomb should be detonated, but Alton suspected the flimsy headgear was more useful as a sign of the situation's urgency. Without a word, he flipped open his credentials. He had been an agent for nineteen years and in all that time had never felt comfortable using a phrase like *I'm with the FBI*. Instead, he let his identification, with the large blue initials printed across it, prove who he was. Even though he had never been challenged, the possibility never stopped nagging at him.

Maybe his reluctance came from having grown up in the housing projects of Detroit, where law enforcement was generally considered the enemy. Whatever it was, he knew he would never experience the ease that his fellow agents did when announcing who they were. But then he wasn't really like them, either. He had gone to a community college and then to the least expensive college in the Michigan system. There hadn't been time or money for fraternities, or golf, or any of the other things referred to during his FBI interview as "agent-related activities."

He had to work and when he wasn't, he had to work even harder studying.

The cop checked his credentials a little more closely than expected and Alton resisted the temptation to believe it was because he was black. "You here for the FBI meeting?"

"Yes, I am, and I'm probably late."

"The only parking left is over there." The officer pointed at a small cluster of cars.

"How far is the jail?"

"Three blocks."

For Alton, the thought of walking the quarter mile was as foreboding as running a marathon. Six months earlier, because of an increasing pain in his shin, he had gone to the hospital for some tests that wound up taking more than half a day. Routed from room to room in an open-at-the-back gown, he spent the final hour sitting bare-cheeked on an examining table, its crinkling, hygienic white paper reminding him of the kind used in a butcher shop. The last doctor he saw that day walked in and matter-of-factly informed him he had cancer. There was a tumor on his lower left leg, involving the bone, and its condition was so advanced that the limb would have to be amputated. He was lucky—according to the surgeon, the growth had been discovered before it spread anywhere else. Although painful, he could now walk on what was left of the tibia with the aid of a prosthetic leg. Alton took his foot off the brake. "That'll be fine."

He parked and turned off the engine. An apprehension that had not been there for years grew inside of him. At forty-five, the loss of a limb was devastating, but not nearly as bad as it would have been at seventeen. He no longer expected his life to maintain the assumed perfection of adolescence, but from this point forward, his hope was to conduct his life without any major limitations. And that's why he was here, a month before he was supposed to return to work—to find out if the cancer had taken anything besides his leg.

In no hurry to get out, he sat in the car for a few more moments. Once again, it was his first day in the FBI. Everything had to be proven again. Using the rearview mirror, he notched his tie up a bit tighter, his neck now smaller. Slowly he reached down and touched the prosthesis; its hard indifference frightened him. He hated it. Even after the five months since the surgery, he still could not look at what was left of his leg in the shower. During that time, he hadn't made love to his wife, Tess, either. The urge had never fully struck him. Whether it was physical or psychological, he wasn't sure. He didn't even know if he could still perform sexually. Part of him wanted to find out, but sitting there, reluctant to face the other agents, he understood that failure now, in any part of his life, would have a way of seeming final. For the moment, it was better not to know. He opened the car door and swung his legs out, feeling the foreign weight of the artificial limb.

Leaning back in awkwardly, he pulled his briefcase off the front seat and locked the door. He stood up straight and took a moment to set his weight evenly on both legs. When Tess and his daughter weren't around, he would practice trying to remove the limp from his walk. In a short distance, he could keep the uneven gait to a minimum, but he had never had to do it for three blocks. What was worse, he would have to walk in late, in front of everyone. It wasn't that everyone didn't already know; they did. But he didn't want to remind them.

In the distance, he could see the jail. Waiting inside was everything he wanted—and everything he feared.

Sprawled back in the chair behind his desk, Ike Warbeck was punctuating his sentences with small, intentional snorts, the kind that would be considered ill bred or rude in polite company. They were a tactic the director of Cook County Corrections used to mark his territory. Physically, Warbeck was an intimidating six foot six and 270 pounds. His nose had been broken a long time before and never set. Large and knotted at the break, it sat in a splayed arc, its tip finally sweeping toward the left corner of his mouth. Its unmended condition, like the snorting, provided a warning that the owner had a great disdain for protocol.

Roy Thorne had been through similar initiations with other officials who had interlocking jurisdictions with the Bureau and understood the unspoken message. Still feeling the sting of his handshake with Warbeck and hoping to achieve some level of détente, he massaged his hand openly, informing the man in charge of the jail that if this was a contest, he had won. "Ike, let's fast-forward through the usual BS and stop trying to see who can piss on the most mile markers. This is your turf. I'm not here looking to make headlines, or enemies."

"It's been my experience that those are the two things the FBI does best." Warbeck snorted again.

"That's why I'm here instead of one of my people. I'm willing to let your department take the lead in the investigation. That way you can control everything that is given to the media or anyone else."

Warbeck rocked forward clasping his thick hands on the desk. "You wouldn't be trying to bullshit an old bullshitter, would you, Roy?" A cautious smile softened his face.

"Absolutely not. To tell you the truth, I wouldn't mind sitting one of these out. I've been doing this too long, and my guess is that the pressure in this one is only going to get worse by the minute."

Warbeck laughed. "Offering to step aside—you are good. You know we don't have the manpower to take the lead in something like this."

"Okay, then how about this? Since the bomb does have our name on it, we'll run the investigation to find out who, and you handle all matters that concern the jail."

"Including the media?"

"Especially the media."

"And if something overlaps, and we disagree?"

"Then it will be your call, entirely," Thorne said. "You have my word."

"Seems fair enough. Did you have anything specific in mind you wanted to do right now?"

"Well, since we can't move or disarm the bomb, what about moving the prisoners?"

Warbeck leaned back in his chair. "You seem a little too savvy for that to be your idea. Sounds like someone in Washington has been reading the tea leaves."

Thorne smiled. "Well, the director is getting a lot of pressure from Capitol Hill."

Warbeck nodded his understanding of the politics involved. "Even if there was another detention facility to transfer them to, do you have any idea of the logistical nightmare we're talking about? The transportation. The security. The manpower. Of course there isn't another jail or prison available. Hell, there isn't even another bed available, anywhere. And even though most of the prisoners are serving misdemeanor sentences, too many of them are experienced felons. In the past, we've had to transplant small groups temporarily, and it was an absolute nightmare. There were astronomical increases in escapes, escape attempts, and assaults. It's almost as if they feel an obligation to try. You simply cannot move fifteen thousand animals to a less confining atmosphere. It's like begging them to test you. And what if we did get them temporarily relocated and the bomb was set off and it destroyed the jail. What then? We'd have no choice but to release all fifteen thousand of them onto the streets of Chicago. You think there's political pressure now?"

"I understand. I was just looking for a little breathing room. I don't think it'll take us long to find this guy. I have a suspicion he wants us to. But the whole country is starting to watch every move and that brings out the politicians who, given enough time, will paralyze the entire investigation."

"I know. I'm getting pressure from the bosses, too. But I have an out." Warbeck smiled. "I just tell them to talk to the FBI."

"That's fine. This is primarily our problem." Thorne stood up and reached a hand over the desk. "Thanks for your time, Ike. I'll pass along your insights to my boss."

Warbeck hesitated a moment and then nodded for Thorne to take a seat. "For future considerations, there may be something I can do to give you a couple of days." Thorne sat back down. "I could have it leaked to the press that we're making secret arrangements to move the entire population out of the complex so the FBI can try to disarm the bomb without any risk to the prisoners, but, for security reasons, the entire move is being kept top secret. We'll tell them that it'll take two to three days to set up the logistics. During that time, I'll make myself scarce so I can't be contacted to verify or deny it."

"That would give us some operating room. And what if it takes us longer than two or three days?"

"Then I'll have to issue a statement to quell the rumor and accuse the FBI of starting it."

"And I'll be on my own."

Warbeck stared at him a moment. "I'm going to guess it wouldn't be your first time."

"And in return?"

"Your boys are in here a couple times a year looking to lock up my guards for various felonies, mostly trafficking. Nobody wants a dirty employee out of here more than I do. I just want the heads-up so if possible I can take care of it myself and save my office the embarrassment."

Thorne stood up again and reached his hand across the desk. "I'd offer to buy you lunch, but I believe you've got a rumor to start."

Thorne stood in the front of the Cook County Jail mess hall with his suit coat buttoned and watched as the agents filed in. It was no different wherever he went. No longer was there an us-against-them collective, but rather individuals, each filing his or her own daily agenda; its course set for only a single beneficiary. One agent, with his head shaved and an earring dangling from the left lobe, came in wearing a motorcycle jacket, sending the message that he was *undercover* and far too important for this nickel-and-dime bullshit. There were a few in business clothes, but the majority looked as though they had been rounded up during spring break and herded into this room against their will, their demeanor promising full mutiny the moment the opportunity presented itself.

But the thing Thorne noticed most was the absence of esprit de corps. That was his oldest memory of the Bureau, coming to work before first light, everywhere the smell of scalding, black coffee. The agents, still not having shaken off the night's sleep, but with banter fully lit, would argue about the previous day and challenge one another with the coercion of unwritten competition. Each day promising, on some level, to provide another small, interlocking piece of the fiction they wanted to believe about themselves. But beneath it all was an unspoken alliance, the knowledge that if anything went wrong—no matter how wrong—an agent was never alone. It had always been the greatest benefit of the job. That kind of friendship no longer seemed to exist. This was not the FBI he had joined thirty years earlier. The camaraderie, the result of being united by some greater goal and a shared sense of identity, was gone. But that was about to change.

Thorne tracked another agent as he walked in. He was in his late forties, and middle age had been particularly unkind to him, rendering his stature bulbous and teetering. There was an animated nervousness about him; his head turned in quick, short arcs, searching the building's interior structure. Finally he looked back at the wall that was the closest to the bomb and moved without hesitation to the seat that sat the farthest from it. He took a chair no more than ten feet from where Thorne stood, without seeming to notice his proximity to the man who had ordered him there. Now Thorne could see that he wasn't really excessively overweight, but wearing a bulletproof vest under his jacket. Although the behavior was extreme, Thorne took it as a sign that his plan was working. In such times, fear was an unfailing ally.

At exactly 9 A.M. he ordered the doors closed and asked everyone to sit down in the two hundred and fifty folding chairs that had been set up. A predictable portion of the group took their time seating themselves, and as they did, fired a brief scowl in the direction of their new boss. Most of the chairs in the front rows were left empty. He turned to Bartoli. "How many agents are missing?"

"I'm guessing everybody's here."

In a penetrating cadence, raised to reach more than the ASAC's ears, he said, "If I thought guessing was the way to go, I'd be on fucking Wall Street. I hope this is the last time I have to repeat myself: *How many agents are missing?*"

Bartoli called all the supervisors forward quickly. While Thorne waited, he looked into the faces of as many agents as he could, and, one at a time, held their gazes until they turned away in discomfort. It didn't take long for the rank and file to realize that Roy K. Thorne was not a man interested in making new friends.

Bartoli came back to him and looked down at a 3 × 5 card that he had taken notes on. "There are eighteen agents on sick leave or annual leave. Six are at in-service or other training."

"Everyone else is accounted for?"

"All except one, an RA agent, Jack Kincade. They've been calling his residence and beeping him all night."

"Tell whoever failed to supervise him that when he is located, no one's foot but mine is to be put up his ass," he said loudly enough for much of the rest of the room to hear.

"Yes, sir."

"But everyone else is already here?"

"Ah, there's a few who called and said they'd be late."

Just then a door at the back of the hall opened and two agents walked in. Thorne said, "Up here, gentlemen." He waved at the empty seats in the front row and watched as the two agents, slightly embarrassed, walked forward. He tracked them until they were seated, furthering their discomfort. He then stepped to a more central position to address the group.

He waited for almost a full minute before breaking the silence. "I am Roy Thorne, and I'd like to welcome you *back* to the FBI. I was supposed to arrive here a month from now to become your new SAC, but the director moved up that schedule late last night. I am now officially listed as the Special Agent in Charge of this division, but until this case is resolved, you should consider me someone with the patience and sensitivity of a sixth-century

Chinese warlord. In case some of you have forgotten—and from the look of the way you're dressed, you have—the FBI is not a democracy, especially in this office at this moment. There are no avenues of appeal, no time off because of a death in the family— not even your own. No Constitution, Bill of Rights, EEOC, ombudsman, full night's sleep, family dinners, trips to the gym, movies, shopping, or long pseudosexual discussions of college basketball or football. This bomb," he pointed in the general direction of the loading dock, "is now your entire life. I don't know what you've heard about me, nor do I care. The only thing you need to understand is that I am an existentialist. For those of you who spent more of your time in college trying to get laid than attending class, an existentialist is someone who is responsible for whatever he or she does or fails to do. Before this is over, you will all understand that philosophy far better than you care to."

The door at the rear of the room opened again, and Ben Alton came in quietly, but not unnoticed. Thorne looked up as he started down the aisle, his face sweating, trying with little success to disguise his limp. Thorne turned as Bartoli hurried next to him. "Sir, that's Ben Alton. He's just lost a leg to cancer. He's been gone for months. I don't think he's supposed to be back to work yet."

"The agent who just came in," Thorne said, "I've saved a seat right up here for you."

Alton plodded forward, feeling every eye in the room. Only a few of them had seen him since he lost his leg, and now he felt that everyone was looking at him with that *poor bastard* stare. He collapsed in his seat with a clumsy thud. Thorne looked at him. Here was a better-than-scripted opportunity to demonstrate his intolerance of failure. "Do you know what time this conference was supposed to start?"

"I didn't know I'd have to park so far away."

"There are several spots right in front of the building."

Alton looked up at Thorne, his anger thinly disguised. "I believe those are handicapped spaces."

The answer caught Thorne off guard. A scattered murmur of approval for Alton went cautiously through the room. Someone had put the son-of-a-bitch in his place. The SAC smiled. "My mistake," he said to Alton and took a step back before continuing. "Does anyone know why I chose to have this meeting here?" No one answered. "Well, if you think we're here to prove how brave we are, don't flatter yourself. You're no braver than anyone else in this world. If you were, Mr. Hoover wouldn't have tried to convince the public by making sure the word *Bravery* found its way into the FBI motto." Thorne let his words harden for a few seconds. "The FBI is here simply as a statement of reality. To demonstrate to the world that whether you are prison inmates, Bureau agents, or anyone in between, life contains risk and danger, and sometimes you just have to accept its uncertainties. Now, while you may not be filled with *Fidelity*, *Bravery*, or *Integrity*, until this bomb is neutralized, you're going to work and act as if you were. And when that is accomplished, I will, to your great satisfaction, retire to the SAC's office and, like all ripened bureaucrats, start looking for a retirement job so some unsuspecting corporation can take over my house payments. At that point, all of you will be able to repopulate the world's gymnasiums and shopping malls, and safely confide to your friends, family, and neighbors that you have once again made the world safe, and yes, your press clippings are indeed true."

Thorne looked around; a few pulsing faces glowered back. "This case, like every other case, is going to be solved by talking to people, people who, for varying reasons, are reluctant to tell us everything they know. These people, whether they like us or not, expect FBI agents to look and act a certain way. You'll know them when you see them: They're the ones who have no idea that our competence is a myth. So shave your goatees; cover your tattoos; take out the ear, nipple, and tongue piercings. Dig out your handcuffs and load your guns. And goddammit, break out your business clothes. Don't ever think that if you dress like the people you're talking to, they are going to be more truthful. If they wanted to talk to someone who looked like a bum, they'd turn to their friends. You see, they actually feel important if someone who is college-educated and wearing a suit comes to them for help." Thorne walked over to Bartoli and whispered something in his ear. "Now, if you're wondering what I'll be doing while you're out there actually *earning* your salary, I have only one job and that's figuring out who's not giving me everything they've got. And believe me, I'll know. Let me offer you one shortcut to a happy life: *Don't get on that list.*" Thorne let his threat sink in for a moment. "Are there any questions?" An agent on the left side of the room, with some reluctance, raised a hand. Thorne stared at him for a moment and then said, "Since there are none, let's get to work. If you'll open up your packets and follow along. Lieutenant Elkins."

A rustling of paper rippled through the hall as the agents opened the envelopes that had been placed on the chairs. Ben Alton had already thumbed through his. As the blond CPD lieutenant came forward, Alton took a moment to study Thorne. Evidently, everything he had heard about him was true: old school, extremely capable, and difficult to work for. Sent in to untangle one emergency after another, he had the power to ignore all the pettiness the Bureau increasingly answered to. Although initially embarrassed by him, Alton took it as a positive sign that Thorne was to be his boss. Results were now the currency of the day, and that's all Alton wanted: to be judged by what he could do, not what he couldn't.

"I'm Lieutenant Dan Elkins from the Chicago PD Bomb Squad." Referring to various photos and diagrams in the packet, Elkins described how the bomb had been constructed and then placed at the rear of the jail. Calling for the lights to be dimmed, he showed some slides depicting the bomb from different angles. One was a close-up of the message. That was followed by an edited version of the surveillance camera videotape showing the bomb being placed on the loading dock and then being armed. Finally, the bomber's careful planning and insightful construction of the bomb was discussed in brief but specific detail.

Thorne thanked him and then addressed everyone in a tone that was a bit less combative. "Apparently, this individual has some gripe with the FBI, and I believe he wants us to identify him so he can make demands on us. Why the demands were not made in the first place, I have no idea. I'm sure we'll find out as soon as we discover who he is. But let's worry about one thing at a time. Now, how do we identify him?"

No one answered. "This is where I do want you to say something."

Finally, a hand came up. "We have the video of the truck—it's probably a rental. We could hit all the rental places."

"That's certainly a start. However, I'd be surprised if it's going to be that easy. As indicated by Lieutenant Elkins's analysis, this guy thought ahead. And I'm sure he knows that's how we solved the World Trade Center and Oklahoma City bombings. But you're right, it's something we have to run out. Also, you saw in the video stills that a forklift was used. In case he didn't get it at the same place as the truck, we want to check all forklift rentals. What else?"

Another hand went up. "We've got his picture on the video—give it to the media?"

"He's pretty well covered up, but it's another lead we have to cover. What else?"

There was no further response. Most agents relied on the ease of previously used techniques to solve crimes and were usually not creative in their approach unless prodded. But Thorne did not have the reputation of solving difficult cases merely because he knew how to bully agents; he always tried to use his imagination. The photographs of the bomb and the jail had been e-mailed to him in Washington, and he had spent every available moment studying them. They gave him an idea that he had not mentioned to anyone, wanting to spring it at the right time to make it appear spur-of-the-moment, hoping to encourage the agents to think on their feet. Now seemed to be the most advantageous time. "Lieutenant, the lead sheeting that the casing is lined with, any way to tell how thick it is?"

Elkins thought for a second. "The message he left us was actually cut through the lead. That's the only way the X ray could pick it up. If we photographed it at an extreme angle, we might be able to determine how thick it is."

"And from that . . . what?" Thorne threw the question out to the agents. When no one answered, he continued, "If we know how thick it is, then we might be able to determine its use. It has to have some commercial application. We may be able to track it down that way."

Another hand went up. "How about the sign on the side of the truck? It looks like one of those plastic magnetic signs you could have made up."

Thorne said, "Excellent. We'll cover those shops also." It was another lead Thorne had thought of but not brought up to see if anyone would figure it out. And someone had, which meant that at least one agent was awakening to the chase. "Anything else?" In the short void after his question, Thorne heard several of the folding chairs scrape on the floor; the agents were becoming anxious. "Okay, let me have all the supervisors up here so we can get these leads organized and assigned."

Thorne called Bartoli over. "Let's get our relative positions clear. For now, I'm in charge of this investigation, and I want you to take care of the daily nuts and bolts of the office until this thing is disarmed."

"I understand."

"This guy Alton wasn't supposed to be back for a while?"

"I'm not sure of the exact time, but at least a month."

"As much as I would like someone with that kind of grit out there working on this, he is on limited duty. I wouldn't feel right about him out chasing around after this guy. He seems like the kind who won't like it, but limited duty does dictate that he is desk-bound."

"I'll take care of it."

"Don't misinterpret this as me being a nice guy. My priority is to get rid of the bomb, nothing more. We'll have enough problems doing that with two good legs, understand?"

"I understand."

"And I still want to be the bearer of bad news for Special Agent Kincade."

In a tone more sincere than humorous, Bartoli said, "I wouldn't want to deprive you of that pleasure, sir."

# 7

BEN ALTON WAS TOLD BY THE SECRETARY TO GO right in to the ASAC's office. Albert Bartoli was busy initialing paperwork. "Ben, I didn't get a chance to talk to you at the meeting this morning. How're you feeling?" There was a touch of a New York accent in Bartoli's pronunciation, something he turned on to prove himself one of the guys and off when dealing with a superior. And those of equal rank . . . well, Alton supposed the former acting SAC recognized no such individual.

Still not used to maneuvering in more formal situations, Alton tried to lower himself to a chair but wound up falling into it with considerably less control than he would have liked. "I'm all right."

Bartoli came around the desk and took a chair next to him. "Sorry I didn't get up to see you in the hospital. I've been in charge of the office, and it's had me buried."

"Those five months flew by for me, too."

Alton had never been overly deferential toward Bartoli before his illness, but now his bluntness was signaling some new layer of invulnerability. "You're right, I should have made time. There is no excuse."

"Fine, if anybody asks me, you're one of my closest friends. Now, why am I here?"

Bartoli's mouth lengthened with the slightest hint of arrogance. "No time for bullshitting around, huh, Ben?"

"Cancer does have a way of stripping away the need for high tea."

"Okay, if that's the way you prefer it. You understand that you are on limited duty."

"Which means?"

"Well, by the letter of the law, you're supposed to be working only in the office. But you're the bank robbery coordinator, so that shouldn't be much of an adjustment."

"In other words, I'm not supposed to work the bombing."

Bartoli threw his hands up in a practiced, but still unconvincing, gesture. "Don't shoot the messenger. It was Thorne's idea."

"So if I walk down the hall and ask him, he's going to tell me the same thing?"

"Why would you think I'm not telling you the truth?"

"I came back a month early so I could work this."

"No one expects you to be here. Take the month."

Alton stared at Bartoli and shook his head slowly, not caring how it was interpreted. He was being warehoused, taken out of the daily maelstrom where the only requirement to wander about freely was two good legs. For Alton, the greatest thing about the job was its freedom. To be given a case and let loose. Armed with nothing more than a vague notion that evil could never outdistance hard work, Alton would start, never allowing himself to consider the discouraging odds, that the criminal, known or anonymous, had the entire world to hide in. And then, whether within hours or years, it would happen with a sudden euphoric release from gravity—one of life's small miracles—he would make an arrest. It would be over as abruptly as it had started. But now they wanted to deprive him of all that. It had become his biggest single fear, to be subtracted into a separate, narrowed column on a manpower report. But experience had taught him that the tougher a case became, the more difficult it was for those in charge to ignore someone with a track record. He just had to keep circling the fray at a visible distance.

Briefly, he considered going to Thorne, but after witnessing the SAC's inability to take no for an answer at the jail conference, Alton decided it would be a waste of time. With Thorne so focused on the bomb, individual needs would carry little weight. But if his career had taught him anything, it was that success had little choice but to surrender to endurance. He might not be the fastest agent in the Bureau, but he sure as hell had endurance. He struggled to his feet. "Was there anything else?"

"While you've been away, the bank robbery solution rate has slipped. How about seeing what can be done about it."

Alton gave him a crooked smile. "These things have a way of working themselves out."

The game had lasted all night and Kincade got back to his motel at a few minutes past 11 A.M. Once the last of the dollars changed hands, almost all of which had gone to Kincade, he offered to buy everyone breakfast. When he had returned from the Barrington bank, he was dealt winning hand after winning hand, almost as if being punished by not being able to lose the loot from the burglary. On the few occasions the initial cards were not good, he bet wildly, trying to recapture the rush that such bets normally produced, but only wound up winning larger pots. Even though he had never won that much playing poker before, it gave him little joy. Back in his room, he took out the wad of bills and counted them. There was more than $5,800.

He tossed it on the bed, which was the only item in the room not in disarray. In six months of living at the motel he had never once slept on it following his first night there. That night, his dreams had become so violently animated he was afraid to fall back asleep. *In the darkness, he heard a gentle tapping at the door. When he opened it, a nun asked for a donation. After returning with the little bit of change in his possession, she had stripped away her habit to reveal a thin silk dress. When she saw how he looked at her, she told him his son, Cole, had run away, and then she disappeared out the door. He ran after her, but once outside found himself in Pennsylvania searching for his son. Hurrying from person to person begging for information, he found that no one spoke English but instead an archaic dialect of Dutch, which he had never heard before.*

*He got in his car and drove at a high speed looking for any signs in English. He ran out of gas and in the distance could see someone hurrying away with his son. When he tried to get out, the doors wouldn't unlock. His son, looking at Kincade over his shoulder, kept getting farther and farther away. Then the darkness swallowed him.*

That night, to avoid the recurrence of such terror, he withdrew to the broken recliner in the corner, reasoning that it would be better to sit awake all night than to risk the sweaty torture of sleep. The night had passed in a semiconscious blur, leaving him unsure whether he had slept or not. After that, periodic attempts to use the bed always resulted in his waking up in the recliner the next morning.

Although curious about the phenomenon, Kincade suspected that if its origins could be unmasked, additional demons would likely be added to the mix rather than removed. Sometimes, when no longer able to restrain the analyst inside, he surmised the problem was guilt. The day he had checked into the less-than-fashionable Roman Inn, and the owner asked him whether the nightly rate or the monthly was preferable, without a moment's consideration, he opted for monthly. Later he interpreted this as having subconsciously decided that the normalcy life gravitates toward had, in his case, expired. And since nothing reminds a man of the comforts of a regular life more than eight hours stretched out in a bed, his subterranean gremlins were protesting. His subconscious, infinitely more demanding than his conscious, was dutifully standing watch, not allowing the night to go unchallenged, not allowing the variety of daily damages to be repaired. He had other theories, one of which had to do with the relative position of his head and his heart. In bed, the heart was allowed to rise up to the level of his brain, and emotion, whenever given an equal footing, took over. However, in the chair, the head remained above, clear and unprovoked. While his theory about guilt was undoubtedly Freudian, he suspected the head-over-heart analysis could find its origins in something no more empirical than *The Wizard of Oz*, or even the perils of the helpless characters of Saturday morning cartoons.

The Border collie sniffed at the bag on the table next to the recliner, tactfully reminding Kincade that it, too, had not eaten. Even though all the players had breakfast, Kincade just drank coffee and smoked, half listening to their stories and trying to figure out why his most successful night of gambling was so disappointing. As they were leaving, he ordered a couple of hamburgers to go. Now he opened one of them and placed it on the floor with its wrapping underneath to protect it from the dusty carpet. "Here, B.C." The dog came over, gave it a quick sniff of approval, and then gently picked the meat off the bun.

Kincade slumped back in the permanently tilted chair and opened his burger, staring down at it, trying to arouse some appetite. Exhaustion started to close in around him. Sleep would come easily now, at least for a few hours. He leaned over and placed his sandwich on the floor. B.C. stopped eating for a moment and looked at Kincade to verify its good fortune. "Yeah, it's all yours, pal. Just chew quietly." Leaning back with his eyes closed, he felt himself starting to fall toward unconsciousness, but then buoyancy luxuriously slowed his descent until he was in a deep sleep.

A sharp, insistent knocking came from the door. Not knowing how long he had been asleep, Kincade looked down and saw that B.C. had just started on the second hamburger. As the knocking continued, he freed himself of the chair, more by falling over the arm than athletically gaining his feet.

It was the motel's owner, Jimmy Ray Hillard. "Christ, Jack, have you got the phone off the hook again?" He bobbed a little trying to look past Kincade to the table next to the bed.

"Just got in. I was trying to sleep."

"Your office has been calling all night looking for you."

"All night?"

"*All* night."

"Was it the RA or downtown?"

"Downtown. Please call them so they'll stop aggravating me."

"Sorry." Kincade closed the door and went over to the phone. After reestablishing the connection, he dialed. An older male voice answered. "Yeah, hi, this is Jack Kincade. I got a message to call the office."

"Well, finally. This is Dan Gooding. I'm the duty agent, and Thorne has had us looking for you all night."

"Thorne? What squad does he supervise?"

"He's the new SAC. He just got in this morning."

"That's not Roy K. Thorne?"

"I'm afraid so."

"And I'm already in his good graces."

"You were supposed to be at an all-agents conference at the jail this morning." When Kincade didn't say anything, Gooding said, "You have heard about the bomb at Cook County."

"I've been out of town."

"Out of town? It's been all over the national news. Thorne wants to see you ASAP—actually ASAP was hours ago."

"Why's he looking for me?"

"Mainly because you were AWOL, but I think it also has something to do with the fact that you went to bomb tech school. He apparently thinks you could be useful."

Seven years ago Kincade had gone to the Redstone Arsenal in Huntsville, Alabama, for four weeks of training, most of which was spent drinking and trying to hustle up a poker game with the soldiers who were stationed at the base. "Useful? Boy, is he shopping in the wrong neighborhood."

"I'd get down here as fast as possible, Jack. I think he's looking for someone to make an example of."

"Well, he's in luck. That's one of the things I do best."

The SAC's secretary didn't know Jack Kincade by sight. When he walked into her office, she smiled pleasantly. "Hi, I'm Jack Kincade. The SAC wanted to see me."

Her smile remained fixed, but her eyes darkened with prosecution. Like all bosses' secretaries, she possessed a great deal of secondary power, a large portion of which came from being regularly solicited for a verifying opinion. Part of the secretaries' responsibility, as they interpreted it, was to know who was in trouble. And the more capable ones could even intuit the degree of forthcoming punishment. Even though it was Thorne's first day, Kincade sensed the secretary's eyes were measuring him for a coffin. "Have a seat, please."

As she buzzed the SAC, he sat down in one of a half dozen chairs that lined the walls of the small anteroom. Even though barely ten feet from her, he could not hear anything being said in her low, confidential monotone. She hung up and let the professional smile slip from her face. Pointing at the closed door immediately to the left of her desk, she said, "You can go right in."

Thorne was sitting at a small conference table with three other men at the far end of his rather large office. As Kincade got closer, he could see there were several maps of the greater Chicago area spread out, most turned to the SAC's vantage point. "I want all the dental supply leads called out to the agents as soon as they're developed. And they are to be completed by four o'clock. Any problems with that?"

"Well, it is Saturday. Some of them might not be open," one of the men offered.

Thorne leaned back in his chair and put his hands in his pockets. "Let me present a hypothetical situation to you. If I told you that your next paycheck was going to be held up one day for every minute past four o'clock that a lead wasn't covered, when would you guess it would be covered?"

Realizing that Thorne's narrative was probably not all that hypothetical, the agent smiled contritely. "Four o'clock sharp."

Thorne leaned back over the maps. "What did we find out about the aliases he used to rent the truck and forklift?"

"The name and address he gave were phonies. We're doing some more work on the ID he presented, but it doesn't look like it's going to lead anywhere."

"What about the sign shops?"

"There's only a couple. We've interviewed them all but one, and its owner is on some sort of trip in Florida. We've sent leads down to Jacksonville."

Thorne looked over at Kincade who was standing five feet away. "What do you mean 'sent leads'?"

"We sent a priority communication." Thorne looked at the

supervisor as if to say, Do I have to say it? "I'll call them right away."

The SAC picked up a pencil and made a note in a small notebook. "And I'll call the SAC down there to make sure they understand there are no Saturdays or Sundays this week. Anything else?"

"Not right now."

"Let's take a break. I need five minutes."

Kincade looked at the three other men and thought he detected a trace of disappointment in their faces. They were going to miss the chance to witness a beheading, and by as legendary a practitioner as Roy K. Thorne. They cleared out quickly.

Thorne looked up from his notes, his eyes small, hard dots. "Sit down."

Kincade, instead of opting for the relatively comfortable distance at the far end of the table, sat down next to Thorne. "I'm Roy Thorne. Do you know anything about me?"

"Do you mean aside from wanting to have me for lunch?"

"Yes, besides that."

Kincade said, "In the late eighties, you solved the Representative Fielding assassination in—what—three weeks?" He pinched the inner corners of his bloodshot eyes with his right thumb and forefinger, trying to rub away the exhaustion. "Then in 1994, the Coast Guard cutter *Eloise*, that was just over a week, wasn't it?" He was still rubbing his eyes and noticed Thorne staring at him with some curiosity. Pulling his hand down, he crossed his legs with as much nonchalance as possible but noticed that his trousers were so covered with B.C.'s hair that it seemed to be part of the fabric's design. The urge to brush them off started gnawing at him. "If you gave me a minute, I probably could recall some others."

The corner of one of Thorne's eyebrows rose slightly in surprise before he spoke. "That you know about those cases means at one time you had some pride in this outfit. And because you've been an agent for more than ten years, I'm going to assume you are aware there is a two-hour recall rule. You were out of pocket for at least ten hours. Where were you?"

"Is this about where I was, or what's going to happen to me?"

"So you don't want to offer any mitigation?"

"I wasn't up all night with a sick friend if that's what you're looking for."

"One of the reasons you were called was because the Bureau spent a fair amount of money training you as a bomb tech agent. You weren't available. That's unacceptable." Thorne got up and walked over to his desk. He picked up a file, reading it as he walked back. "Graduate of Dartmouth. First office Philadelphia. Says you were a pretty fair agent once, but also that you were caught drinking and driving a couple of years ago. Looks like you've been heading south for a while. What happened?"

"I guess I'm just not built for distance."

"Then why do you stay? With an Ivy League education, you could find something else to do."

"The truth?"

"This isn't a therapy session. I don't ask hard questions so I can be lied to."

"Because there's a million places to hide on this job."

"By 'hide' you mean collect a check without really doing anything."

Kincade smiled. "I've learned to set modest goals for myself."

Thorne closed the file. "Well, unfortunately for you, I get paid to make sure there is nothing modest about any of my agents' endeavors. And since you appear to at least have the capability of being a productive agent, one whose problem is apparently motivation, I evidently need to provide some. You are now assigned full-time to this investigation, and if you bring to it anything less than a one hundred percent effort, I will interpret that as meaning you need more supervision. The first step of which will be a transfer back to headquarters from your hideout at that cushy resident agency you work out of."

Kincade tried to invoke his *don't give a good goddamn* mantra, but he couldn't release even the first syllable inside his head. Instead a small, neglected fear went to full throttle. If he were taken out of the RA, his bank trapping cases would be reassigned to another agent. Had he covered his tracks as well as he thought? Did anyone? "You've got my undivided attention."

"Your attention? I own everything you jam into those trousers every morning. Do you understand?"

"I think so."

"You *think* so? I'm telling you right now, if you go at this half-assed, you'll be working the Migratory Bird Act in East Orgasm, Utah." Thorne turned back to his notes and took a moment to study them. "Is Wheaton in your area?"

"Yes, it is."

"One of the dental supply companies is out there. I want you to contact them."

"Dental supply?"

Thorne glanced over both shoulders as if someone else were in the room. "What, is this a gag? You came in here knowing that you were in deep shit and you didn't bother to find out about the case? Do you know anything about it?"

"Only that there's a bomb at the Cook County Jail that the Chicago PD Bomb Squad hasn't been able to neutralize."

Thorne handed him one of the information packets from the all-agents meeting. "The casing is lined with lead. Do you know what that means?"

"It can't be x-rayed, so the power pack can't be isolated. And whoever made it is smart."

"Some of the lab people have calculated that the lining is three-tenths of a millimeter thick. The most common industrial application of that thickness is lead aprons used to protect medical and dental patients from X rays."

"So you think this guy got them from dental or medical supply companies."

"We're checking with all of them in Illinois and the surrounding states."

"How many sheets are we looking for?"

"The best the lab could figure is between ten and fifteen."

"More than any one individual should be ordering," Kincade said, coughing the harsh, grating hack of a smoker.

Thorne waited for him to finish. "Apparently, that mind of yours does still work. So if you find an individual who had ordered that many, he's definitely someone we want to talk to."

"Who came up with the thickness idea?" Kincade asked. "Pretty ingenious."

Thorne tilted his head curiously. He was surprised that someone who had depicted himself as having such lackluster desire would make such an inquiry. "Do you know who asks a question like that?"

"Someone who missed the meeting?"

Undistracted by Kincade's irreverence, Thorne said, "Someone whose fire isn't completely out."

Turner Medical Supply was located at the back end of an industrial park in Wheaton, a western suburb of Chicago. Fortunately for Kincade, a twenty-four-hour number had been listed for them in the phone book. After convincing the company's answering service that he needed to talk to someone with access to their records, he was patched through to one of the vice presidents. Once he explained that the inquiry had to do with the well-publicized bomb at the Cook County Jail, the sales manager was dispatched to meet Kincade at the company's offices.

By the time he got to Wheaton, the sales manager was waiting for him in the lobby. Kincade flipped open his credentials and introduced himself. Conducting an investigation on Saturday had an out-of-order obtrusiveness to it. There was none of the populated routine of the work week, a time when people seemed to enjoy being distracted from their schedules by the unannounced arrival of the FBI. But people were possessive of their free time. Kincade knew he was. Not that he had covered enough leads since coming to Chicago to be an authority on anything remotely industrious, but even with Thorne's threat hanging over him, talking to a salesman about lead shields was the last place in the world he wanted to be on a weekend.

Bill O'Brien was overweight and wearing old clothes that suggested the public service he was about to perform might have interrupted his yard work. The shirt and pants no longer fit him, exposing a bulging stomach that was obviously accustomed to being hidden underneath a business suit. He had the round, practiced smile of a salesman who never stopped selling. "That girl swore she was eighteen." He laughed and extended his hand. "What can I do for the FBI, Jack?"

With each passing year, because of legal liability, businesses were a little more reluctant to give agents access to their records. One way Kincade found to bypass the obstacle was to make whomever he was dealing with think that they were being trusted with need-to-know information. The technique, he discovered, had a way of psychologically deputizing them. "Is there somewhere we can talk privately, Bill?"

O'Brien led him to a deserted office. Kincade nodded at the salesman's clothing, and, with the perfect pitch of male sports-bar banter, said, "I hope I didn't take you away from anything important."

"I was trying to get the grass cut so I could watch the game this afternoon."

"Illinois-Michigan?"

"Someone else is playing this weekend?"

Kincade held up his hands acknowledging surrender to O'Brien's partisanship. "Think Illinois is going to win?"

"I'm hoping, but Michigan's favored by ten."

"I don't know if you're a betting man, Bill, but I was talking to some of the OC guys this morning," Kincade lowered his voice, "and they said the word is that Illinois is definitely going to cover." Actually Manny Tollison, a voracious sports gambler, had announced at the card game the night before that betting Illinois was an absolute lock.

"OC?"

"Organized crime. But you didn't hear it from me."

O'Brien became quiet and Kincade could see that he was processing the information. Whether he was a gambler and would do anything with the "inside" information didn't really matter. An act of trust had been demonstrated by an FBI agent, and he was now obligated to reciprocate. "Exactly which records did you need to get a look at."

An hour and a half later, Kincade thanked the sales manager and left with three possibles: a dental clinic; an area hospital, which had just opened a trauma center; and an individual who lived in China Hills, named Conrad Ziven.

# 8

WHEN O'BRIEN GAVE HIM THE DETAILS OF THE orders, Kincade had been careful not to let him see that Conrad Ziven's purchase qualified him as a prime suspect. In fact, he asked O'Brien to continue his search of the records as if Ziven's order had not set off any alarms at all. The salesman continued ponderously, eventually adding the dental clinic and hospital to the list. If he had sensed some urgency on Kincade's part, he might have been tempted to contact the media. It was not likely, but it wouldn't be the first time a leak had occurred in a high-profile case, especially if someone knew a reporter. While such deception, under normal circumstances, took considerably more effort than Kincade liked to expend anymore, he feared that the SAC would condemn any breach of security, whether innocent or intentional, and Kincade's head would be rolled with equal speed and distance.

Ziven had received a shipment of fourteen lead shields almost a month earlier. They were shipped to an address in China Hills, another western suburb. That was all he had, a name and address. Of course, as had been the case for the truck rental, the name could be a phony. But the address had to be valid; the shields had been delivered there. The name sounded foreign, possibly Eastern European, where bombs and coups were longtime acquaintances. But all this was supposition, and he couldn't be sure of anything until he went out to the address and knocked on the door.

Not that he was going to hurry out there and give up home-field advantage to a strong suspect. Valor, he recalled, required considerable investment while returning little a sensible man could use. He wasn't going to rush in thoughtlessly, carrying Roy K. Thorne's snapping battle streamer. Some time would be needed to assess how the information could best be converted to his own advantage. He headed for his motel and a brief conference with Pistol Pete.

As he drove, doubts about having solved such a difficult case so easily started crowding in on him. One simple lead and the bomber had been identified? It was highly unlikely, and anymore, he had much more confidence in his ability to analyze odds than solve major cases. But maybe he had simply lost his ability to judge who was capable of what. He certainly had in his own case.

He decided to invoke his backup mantra: *This too shall pass.* Never in the history of man had the pressures of civilization failed to succumb to that bit of listless wisdom. With every agent in the division working on the bombing, even if his suspect didn't work out, the case would be solved, and eventually he would be restored to his former invisible self.

When he pulled into the Roman Inn's lot, a car was parked directly in front of his room. It looked like a Bureau car and a black man was behind the wheel. Kincade parked across the courtyard, got out, and walked up quietly behind him. He was reading a book. The radio mike was lying on the seat next to him. It was an FBI car. "Winston Churchill's biography?" Kincade said. "Isn't that a little dry?"

Ben Alton marked his place and closed the book. "Actually, it's pretty interesting." While he said it, he diverted his eyes as though unconvinced himself of what he was saying. He got out of the car. "I'm waiting for Jack Kincade." Alton looked at him in a way that indicated he thought he had found him.

"Mission accomplished." Alton introduced himself and they shook hands. "Come on in while I let my dog out." As soon as he opened the door, the Border collie appeared and thrust its nose forward to verify Kincade's identity. After petting the animal, he said, "Go pee." The dog trotted out past the units into a field overgrown with weeds.

Alton had been waiting for over an hour and when he got out of the car walked with more of a limp than usual. "I'm the bank robbery coordinator." "Bank robbery coordinator" had a little emphasis placed on it, as though it proved something, some distinction among agents. Within the FBI, there was always a small number of agents who spent a great deal of energy trying to convince anyone who would listen of how important they were. Generally Kincade found them to be a confused and chronically lonely bunch looking for some way to define themselves. Titles were just one more failed attempt by the Bureau to legislate respect within its ranks, and Kincade, recognizing the quixotic designs of those who tried, avoided them with an unusual energy.

"Where're you from?"

"Detroit," he answered and then, as if he hadn't convinced Kincade of anything, added, "I grew up in the Brewster Projects."

Alton seemed a little old, he guessed somewhere in his mid-forties, to offer such sophomoric proof, but maybe he thought that was the most important thing to know about him. His voice had a thorny pride to it, and he had pronounced his boyhood home prah-*JEKS*. There was something self-conscious and forced about the way he spoke; he took great care to enunciate the last syllables of his words, particularly those at the end of each sentence. "Tough town," Kincade offered.

They walked into the room. Clothes and newspapers were scattered around in neat piles. Alton was surprised that Kincade didn't seem at all embarrassed by the disarray. "Ever been there?"

"Yeah, only we called it Philadelphia."

Alton gave a short, cautious laugh. "Yeah, I guess there's not much difference."

Kincade noticed that Alton established eye contact only briefly enough to be polite, and then looked away before completing his statement. "Sounds like you're here on bank robbery business. I thought all hands were working the bombing case."

"I'm on limited duty."

Kincade lit a cigarette. "Thought I saw you limping. Anything serious?"

"Just cancer." Alton smiled just enough to let Kincade know that he didn't feel it was really that noteworthy. "I lost a leg."

"Christ, I'm sorry." Kincade pulled the cigarette out of his mouth and flipped it out the door.

"Please—and when I say this I'm serious—don't be. I would prefer you didn't smoke, but if you have to, it's not that big a deal." This time he held eye contact until Kincade answered.

"Fair enough. I thought limited duty meant you couldn't leave the office."

"I think what it means in this case is they're afraid I'll hurt myself chasing the bomber. They gave me the excuse that the bank robbery solution rate declined while I was out getting my leg removed, and if I sit at my desk and light enough candles, it'll somehow rise."

"So you *are* here on bank robbery business?"

"The first thing I found on my desk this morning was a complaint that the night depository at the Barrington Community Savings had been trapped. I haven't seen one of those cases in years. But it's the fourth one in the western area, all in the last six months. They're all assigned to you?"

"The first three are. I suppose this one will be, too."

"You got anything going on them?"

"Nothing worth mentioning."

"Right now there are eleven unsolved bank larcenies, burglaries, and robberies in the division this year. If you could clear these it would raise our average considerably. I thought I'd come by and see if there are any routine leads that I could help you with. I tried to get you at the RA, but they said that you didn't spend much time there, and this was the best place to catch up with you."

Kincade could see that although Alton appeared to be somewhat self-conscious, he had an underlying confidence about the things he was familiar with, and could become tenacious once he picked up a scent. Kincade had seen a few others like him. Once challenged, it became personal, their pride at risk. It wasn't necessarily stylish, but it sure as hell was effective. Kincade didn't want someone like that looking into his business—if trapping night depositories could be considered a business. "I appreciate the offer, but the new SAC has given me some rather explicit directions about spending forty or fifty hours a day working this bomb case."

Alton stopped and raised his nose slightly. "What's that smell, paint?"

Although Kincade had gotten rid of everything he used to make the trap, the smell of the black spray paint evidently still lingered. He had to find a way to distract his visitor. "Could be the dog. He's always getting into something outside. Excuse me a minute while I see where he is." Kincade opened the door and whistled shrilly three times. Within seconds the Border collie trotted in and took up its favorite spot on the floor next to the bed. "Let me run something by you." Kincade opened his briefcase and gave Alton a summary of what he had found at the dental supply company.

"What could one man want with fourteen lead shields?" Alton asked.

Kincade could see that Alton understood Conrad Ziven was a worthy suspect. Slowly, his eyes dilated with the possibilities. "I was going to call the RA for some help before I headed out there. Want to save me the dime?"

"I was told in no uncertain terms I was not to work this case."

"I was told in no uncertain terms that my ex-wife would love me in sickness and health."

Alton laughed easily and after a few moments of contemplation said, "Sure." Although he was careful not to give any indication, Alton was aware that Kincade had skillfully diverted his attention away from the paint smell. He didn't know why, but made a mental note of it for future reference. Right now it didn't matter; this suspect was highly probable, good enough to disobey orders for. The opportunity to get back into the bombing investigation had arrived circuitously; it seemed once again that he had been chosen. "Why don't we go see what Mr. Ziven needed all that lead for."

Conrad Ziven's house was a modest Cape Cod that sat back from the street under the shade of two round red maples that appeared to have been planted around the time of its construction and now, in full growth, surrounded the corners of the structure. Next to it, painted the same white with Colonial Blue trim, was a detached two-car garage.

Alton pulled into the driveway and both men got out. There were three stairs leading to the porch. Kincade rang the bell. After thirty seconds, he knocked loudly on the door. Alton said, "The grass hasn't been cut in a month."

Kincade looked at the lawn and then at the other homes on the street. He knocked on the door again, even louder. After a few moments, he leaned over the railing and tried to see past the edge of the window shade into the house. "I'm going to take a look in back." He disappeared around the side of the house, and then Alton heard pounding on the back door. A few seconds later he returned. "It doesn't look like anyone's in there."

Alton walked over to the garage and discreetly tried to pull up both of the overhead doors, but they were locked. There were three small, square glass windows in each door. He cupped his hand to one of them and looked in. Returning to the porch, he said in a low voice, "There are welding tanks in there."

"That's a helluva coincidence."

"You know what the law calls a 'helluva coincidence'?" Alton asked.

"I hope you're not going to say *probable cause*."

"Probable cause. And in this case, with exigent circumstances."

"Do you know what the law calls the misinterpretation of probable cause?" Alton just stared back at him, trying to figure out his priorities. "Burglary."

"I would have thought that working in Philadelphia would have given you a little more creative approach to law enforcement."

"Well, if you, the *bank robbery coordinator*, are not worrying about tainting this case, who am I to object."

"Wait here." Kincade watched as Alton went over to the side door of the garage, and after a quick scan of the neighborhood to determine if any of his movements could be observed, tested the door. It, too, was locked. Checking for witnesses one last time, he took a short step back and, pushing off his good leg, threw his shoulder into the door. It gave a little under his weight but held. Alton rubbed his shoulder as if the collision had been more punishing than he expected. After glancing at Kincade, he backed up four feet from the door and with a quick, hobbled gallop, threw his entire weight onto the door, which exploded from its casing and fell into the garage with Alton landing on top of it.

Kincade walked over to him casually. "Until now, I never did understand the comedy of a 'one-legged Indian in an ass-kicking contest.'" Kincade offered him a hand and pulled him up.

"I'm glad I could clear that up for you. And it's 'one-legged Negro.'"

"From the projects."

"From the projects," Alton said, smiling.

Being careful not to touch anything, Kincade started looking around. One of the first things he noticed was the welding tank Alton had seen through the tiny window in the overhead door. Scattered around it on the floor were several scraps of sheet metal and the ends of steel reinforcing rods that had been cut with a torch. He picked up one of the silvery pieces of galvanized metal. "This is the same material as the bomb casing."

Alton walked over to the workbench. "There's a soldering gun and some wire here."

Kincade dug through a cardboard box and lifted out a handful of toggle switches. "If this guy isn't the bomber, he's missing a great opportunity. But there's not enough to tell how the bomb was built, nothing to help us diffuse it. We need a diagram. It's probably going to be in the house. We should have enough for a search warrant now."

"Fruit of the poisoned tree, Jack. Fruit of the poisoned tree."

"Well—and I hate to ask this question—what do you want to do now?"

One of the ways Alton had extricated himself from the projects was by following rules, no matter how ridiculous they became. Even when no one was looking, the rules kept him from looking over his shoulder and allowed all his energy to be focused forward.

But if he stopped now, he would, in all likelihood, be eliminated from the investigation yet again. Breaking into a garage, especially after spotting the welding tanks, while illegal, didn't seem nearly as felonious as breaking into a residence. People didn't live in garages, at least not this one. But someone's home—that was much more difficult to justify. Littered about him was every indication that Conrad Ziven was the bomber. Alton made the decision that an agent hates to be faced with: He would break into the house and later, if there was a price to be paid, so be it. "Oh, I think you know what's next, Jack."

Kincade shook his head earnestly. "Okay, but why don't we wait until it gets dark. I need to get something to eat first, someplace decent, because I have it on good authority that prison food stinks."

Inside Paulie's Beef Stand, Ben Alton sat uncomfortably at the edge of the hard square booth, and with some relief, extended his artificial leg into the aisle. Kincade was up at the counter waiting for his Italian sausage sandwich. The smell of french fries submerged in hot, roiling oil filled the tiny restaurant, the tanginess of cooked sweet peppers and roasting pork rising through the thick air. Kincade set a plastic tray on the table and handed Alton a Coke. "Sure you don't want something to eat?" Some of the cooked peppers had fallen off Kincade's bun and he started stuffing them back in with his fingers.

Alton looked over at the cook who stood behind the counter, shoveling orders together. His beard was two or three days old and the apron he continually wiped his hands on appeared to be equally truant. "While it's tempting to be able to claim that I survived cancer *and* a heart attack in the same calendar year, I'm going to pass."

"Paulie's owned this place for thirty-five years, came over

from Sicily," Kincade said. "I thought when I left Pennsylvania, I was never going to be able to find anything to replace those Philly steak sandwiches, but these come awfully close."

"I'm sure neither state has any cardiologists applying for unemployment." Alton took a swallow of his drink and crushed some of the chipped ice between his molars. He lowered his voice, which suddenly had a trace of excitement in it. "So, what do you think?"

Kincade took a large bite off the end of the sandwich. He chewed for a moment. "It's good." Alton stared back at him, still waiting for an answer. "Okay, okay, my vote is that it's got to be him. I just hope we didn't screw anything up by not getting a search warrant. I got the feeling that Thorne would love me to make the first mistake in this case so he could turn me into a horror story he could use to keep the troops in line."

"And what would we have put in the affidavit for probable cause—that all this incriminating evidence was found in the garage? 'Oh, yes, Your Honor, we did break into the garage. That's not a problem, is it?'"

"I'm just saying we could have gotten a telephonic search warrant. They don't take long."

"When's the last time you got a search warrant?"

"It's been a while."

"Then you've probably forgotten how reluctant prosecutors are to go out on a limb. Without the stuff from the garage, they would never give us a green light. There's a bomb and thousands of inmates, not to mention the jail staff hanging in the balance. Exigent circumstances. If I have a problem later, that's the way it goes." Alton looked out the window. "It's dark enough now; you ready?"

Kincade had just taken a second bite of his sandwich. He dropped it back on the tray. "Yeah, I'm stuffed."

"You know, you don't have to do this."

"And what, let you go alone? You might not get in enough trouble without me."

When they got back in the car, Kincade held up an unlit cigarette and asked, "Mind if I burn one?"

"Ah, yes, the old nicotine-trumps-cholesterol medical procedure, go right ahead and save yourself. Just crack the window."

Kincade did as Alton requested and then lit the cigarette. As
the car slipped through the suburban neighborhoods, the cool-
ing autumn air pulled Kincade's attention toward the endless
rows of houses that flickered by. Soft interior light seeped from
them into the gathering dusk. Every area of the country he had
ever been in had its own distinctive architecture, identifiable to
even his untrained eye. Chicago's was like its people, largely unadorned, comfortable, welcoming. Whether brick or frame, new
or old, a sense of community seemed to link the neat homes. For
most, a good place to raise a family. Kincade took a last drag and
flipped the cigarette out before rolling up the window tightly.

As soon as Alton parked up the street from Ziven's house,
Kincade got out and walked through the tree-lined darkness,
turned up into the driveway, and entered the garage through the
side door. Moments later one of the overhead doors slid open
quietly. The Bureau car drove up into the garage with the lights
on as if Ziven was arriving home. Once inside, Alton turned off
the engine and Kincade pulled down the door. Alton said,
"How'd that back door look?"

"Easier than the front, but then when I went through college
they had stopped teaching the advanced burglary classes." Alton
snapped on a flashlight and selected a small crowbar from
Ziven's extensive supply of tools.

Quietly, they skirted the house. Alton snugged the curved
end of the bar between the door and the jamb at the point of the
deadbolt. A quick pull and the door snapped open with little
noise. Once inside, they stood completely still listening for a sign
that anyone might be there. Then, using Alton's flashlight, they
stepped up two stairs and found themselves in a clean, unclut-
tered kitchen. Beyond it was a small living room and against the
far wall was a fireplace. Taped above the mantel was a poster-size
black-and-white photograph. It was of a girl, probably in her
early to mid-teens. Her features were American, but no more removed from Europe than one or two generations—they lacked
the blended symmetry of third or fourth generation Americans.

Her hair, pulled back in a disorganized ponytail, revealed ears large enough to be considered targets for schoolmates. Her long eyebrows were thick and spidery. Teenage vanity had not yet dictated the need to begin sculpting them. There were suggestions that later in life, the shadows lining her features would fill in and settle into those of an attractive adult. She was not beautiful, but her face emitted an overwhelming joy, the slender innocence of youth.

The oversize photo turned the wall into an altar. Entering the room had only one purpose: visiting her memory. "What's that?" Alton said. There was an envelope standing upright on the mantel in front of the photo.

As they moved closer, he said, "It's addressed to the FBI."

"Now it's time to call the SAC," Kincade said.

"And confess to two felonies? I'm going to be in enough trouble with Thorne for just coming along with you."

"With *me*? Once again, the search for the guilty party has been swift and sure."

Alton ignored him. "Whoever this guy is, he's been expecting us. Let's see what the note has to say and then, if we've got to throw ourselves on our swords, we'll know at which angle. We're going to need some evidence gloves. I've got some in the car." Alton hobbled toward the rear door. "I'll be right back."

When he returned, Kincade had turned some lights on and was sitting in a small bedroom in the back of the house that had been converted into an office. In front of him on a desk were a bottle of vodka and a half-full glass. Kincade read the look in Alton's eyes. "I don't suppose you want any. It's Polish."

"I have this hang-up about being drunk at work."

Kincade took a healthy swallow. "We'll have to work on that." He started searching the drawers in the desk. "It doesn't look like there's anything here that's going to help us with the bomb. I suppose if he's smart enough to get us here, he's smart enough not to leave anything like that lying around." Alton handed Kincade a set of latex gloves and pulled on a pair himself. He went to the kitchen and selected a filleting knife from a wooden rack.

Kincade was already in the living room studying the girl's picture, which seemed more prominent with the lights on. He picked up the envelope and slit it open on the short side to minimize the damage to its surface from which latent fingerprints might be developed.

To the FBI,
 You are looking at my beautiful daughter, Leah.
 If the individual reading this is not familiar with her case, she is the reason you have found your way here. The bomb was set on the third anniversary of her kidnapping. After your initial investigation, your agency has done nothing to find her. Now you will have to if you want the combination to the bomb. In my office you will find a telephone. Hit the redial button.
                                                        Conrad Ziven

"Leah Ziven? Do you remember the case?" Kincade asked.

"Ziven, yeah. I was down at Quantico at the time for a three-week in-service. I heard about it when I got back. I should have remembered the name. Most of the office worked it. After a month or so, all the leads fizzled. The ransom was lost, too, her father's stamp collection."

"I remember something about that case. We had leads on it in Philadelphia to contact stamp shops. She was never found, was she?"

"No, a few months before she was grabbed, her father was profiled in the Sunday magazine section in one of the suburban papers. You know, immigrant makes good, talked about how he had even managed to acquire this extensive stamp collection. As it turned out, he made one mistake: He told the reporter that it was worth over a hundred thousand dollars. We figured that's why he was targeted."

Kincade looked at the photo over the mantel. "And that's her."

"Yeah, I remember her now. Well, let's go see what her father wants." Alton led the way into the office, picked up the receiver, and hit redial.

After three rings, a calm voice answered. "Good, you have found me quickly." Although there wasn't much of an accent, Alton noticed that "good" had ended with a slight *t*. "May I have your name, please."

"I'll be glad to give you my name, as soon as I know who I'm speaking to."

"I think by now you know I am Conrad Ziven, Leah Ziven's father."

"This is Special Agent Benjamin Alton, FBI, Mr. Ziven. And I am sorry about your daughter."

"Are you alone?"

Alton glanced at Kincade. "Yes, I am. Is that important?"

"If you are being truthful, it is."

"Because . . ."

"If you are alone that means that you have broken into my house. If you had a search warrant others would be with you. Now, are you alone?"

"I told you I was."

"Then you are the one FBI agent I will deal with."

"Why only me?"

"If these three years have taught me anything, it's that justice is only as good as the man pursuing it. And because you found me so quickly, you obviously are a capable investigator. And since you did not hesitate to break into my home, you are—shall we say—resourceful. Which probably means you are a man who is willing to do what must be done to accomplish your goal."

"And you're about to tell me exactly what that is."

"I am glad that you understand. Your goal is simple—find my daughter's kidnapper."

"A lot of agents worked on that three years ago. Sometimes these things can't be solved on a timetable. I am willing to give you my word that I'll do everything I can to solve this case."

"*Are* you giving me your word?"

Alton rolled his eyes. "Yes, I am."

"And now I am supposed to give you the combination needed to disarm the bomb. You can go get a pat on your back, and I can go to prison. Which I will gladly do, but not until something is done to find whoever killed my daughter."

"I understand that we've failed for three years and that is not acceptable, but you have to understand that the FBI cannot allow itself to be taken hostage. There's got to be some sort of compromise on both our parts."

"I have gone to a great deal of trouble to create the situation that you find yourself in. I did not do that just so I could give the advantage away for nothing more than a meaningless promise from your side."

"I'll let the people in charge know your demands. How can I get ahold of you?"

"You'll excuse me for being a bit paranoid, but I think it would be better if I contacted you. Give me your work and home telephone numbers. And I hope you will have enough respect for me and not try to trace my calls. As you will discover, I am an engineer by training and have had three years to learn from my daughter's kidnapper how to evade the FBI."

"I'll give you my numbers, but will you let me ask one question if I do?"

"Yes." Alton gave him his number at the office but gave him a phony home number. "And now your question, Agent Alton."

"The bomb, does it have a countdown timer? Do we have a deadline?"

"I don't think answering that question would be in my best interest."

"You said you would answer."

"You asked me if you could ask one question. You did. I will call soon. Right now you have more important things to do." The line went dead.

"Goddammit!" Alton said and hung up. He picked up the phone and hit the redial button again.

A recorded voice came on the line. "At the tone, the time will be eight forty-one and fifty seconds."

"Goddammit! He somehow erased the redial memory and reprogrammed it." He turned to Kincade. "Well, Jack, are you in or out?"

There was nothing more Kincade wanted than to walk away, but he thought of the SAC's threat to bring him back to head-quarters, and if that happened, he was afraid that Alton would eventually start working the trappings himself. In the back of his mind, he could again see Alton throwing himself recklessly at the garage door. "You want to call Thorne, or do you want me to?"

Alton suddenly felt very tired. He had been up since 6:00 that morning. During the previous five months he had slept whenever the urge struck him, which was fairly often. "I guess it really doesn't matter, does it?"

"Although we did commit two break-ins, you are guilty of a far more serious crime—disobeying the emperor's orders not to get involved. I'd better call."

# 9

WITH THE ARRIVAL OF THE SAC AND A SQUAD OF agents, Conrad Ziven's modest home and the grounds that surrounded it became a crime scene. As members of the Evidence Response Team fanned out through the house and across the property, Thorne, with an impatient wave of the hand, signaled Kincade and Alton to follow him. He led them into the bedroom used as an office and closed the door. He took a moment to look at Kincade with objective curiosity before turning to Alton. "I pegged you as someone who would follow orders."

Kincade said, "It's probably my fault—"

"I can speak for myself," Alton interrupted, his voice rimmed with defiance. "I knew what I was doing."

"If I were a suspicious person, Ben, I would think that you orchestrated this from the moment you were told not to get involved."

"Believe me, Boss, you'd be giving me way too much credit."

Thorne had not been called "boss" in a long time. The expression's use, too reminiscent of the Old Boys network, had fallen from grace in the new "managed" Bureau. "Okay, I'm going to take your word for it." The way the material of Alton's trousers was lying against his shin, Thorne could see the juncture between the artificial limb and what was left of his real leg, a reminder that despite the odds against him, Ben Alton was right in the middle of the investigation. "But irregardless of intent, you are now the connection between Ziven and the bomb being disarmed. From what Jack told me on the phone, he will deal only with you."

"That's what he said," Alton answered.

"Okay then, you're back in. Don't get the impression that I like being outflanked, I don't. We'll just chalk this one up to *circumstance*, and trust that everybody has turned all their cards face up. But if I hear you've taken even the tiniest chance, you'll become my personal driver, and I get the feeling you're not the kind of man who would like that."

"I understand."

"Right now I want you to go call AUSA Martin and tell her exactly all the things that led you to break in. Feel free to embellish the exigent circumstances. I called her on the way here and after she finished screaming about my storm troopers hobnailing their way across the Bill of Rights, she said she could probably spin off enough probable cause to justify the entry."

Alton stood up to go. "I'll take care of it." Then, sensing the SAC wanted some privacy, he closed the door behind him.

Thorne now stared at Kincade, silently demanding an explanation.

"Legally, we may have been a little impatient," Kincade said, "but even if everything here was admissible, I don't think it would go very far toward prosecuting him. The only thing we found out by our little search is that Conrad Ziven is in fact the man who placed the bomb at the jail. I don't think he'll ever deny that; in fact, I'd say he feels it was his duty as a father."

Thorne studied him for a few seconds. "I'm curious, do you think this has gotten you off my hook?"

"I sure as hell was hoping."

"Believe it or not, I *am* going to give you a reprieve—temporarily. Do you know why?"

"Me? A commendation, *and* an incentive award? Am I surprised? Well, you always dream something like this will happen, but—"

"*Becauuuse*"—Thorne dragged the word out to drown out Kincade's monologue—"I've been doing this long enough to know that, more times than not, it's the mavericks who wind up solving these things. I have never been able to figure out why. I suppose it's some metaphysical genie's sense of humor. Whatever it is, right now the only thing that matters is getting the bomb disarmed. Every rights group in America has called either me, or Bureau headquarters, or the Department of Justice demanding anything from me personally throwing myself on it, to releasing every prisoner in the jail. So, Jack, I'm going to keep you on this. You'll work with Ben. Now, any ideas how we can find this guy Ziven?"

"I suppose the usual stuff: relatives, phone and credit card records, the media. But I don't think that just because you catch him, he's going to disarm his bomb. I got the feeling you could chain him to it and he wouldn't give us the combination. He expects to go to prison no matter what. The only way he'll let us up from under this is if we solve the kidnapping."

"You may be right, but we have to do everything we can to get him in custody. In the meantime, do you know anything about the kidnapping?"

"Not really, but Ben does."

"Okay, I want the two of you to talk to the case agent. See if there're any leads that weren't covered. It's been my experience that the answers to ninety-nine percent of old dog cases are somewhere in the files. Get in there and review everything. If you need more help, let me know."

"Wouldn't the kidnapping case agent be in a better position to do that?"

"Don't try to back up on me, Jack," he said. "If the answer is in the file, whoever the case agent is, he hasn't found it so far. I want you and Ben to handle it. Until it's finished. And make sure you don't drag him in harm's way."

"In order to drag someone, you have to be in front of them, and when it comes to harm's way that's certainly never been my position."

Thorne just shook his head and walked out.

Kincade went over to the desk, sat down, and pulled open the bottom double drawer. With some precision, he reached into it and took out his half-finished drink. He took a mouthful of the Polish vodka and lit a cigarette. Using his standard full-hand pinch test, he remeasured the overhang of his stomach. It felt slightly smaller. Speaking out loud as he always did when admonishing himself, he said, "I knew I should have finished that sandwich."

It took less than an hour for one of the technical agents to reroute Alton's incoming calls to the major-case room. As Kincade and Alton carried in some of the Ziven files, the agent was installing reel-to-reel recorders, throwing their cords to the floor before getting on his hands and knees to make the final connections. Arrangements had also been made for the line to be trapped and traced. When he finished, he turned on one of the recorders, picked up the phone, said a few words, and then played them back. After resetting the tape footage counter to zero, he left.

Kincade sat down next to him as a clerk piled the rest of the Leah Ziven kidnapping file in front of them. It was seven volumes, each about as thick as a plump phone book but, as they soon discovered, not nearly as informative. The fifty agents who had been assigned to the case in its first thirty days had written most of the reports, filling five of the seven volumes. During the remainder of the three years, the investigation took up only the latest two volumes, an indication that not much work had been done during that time to find the sixteen-year-old or her kidnapper. There was also a file of evidence collected at the time, the majority of which, like in most major cases, was meaningless and collected out of desperation rather than any forensic logic in the hope that someday it might mystically become significant during prosecution.

By 1 A.M., Kincade had worked his way through the first two volumes and was in the middle of the third. Alton was on the telephone with the fourth and final agent who had been in charge of the case during its relatively brief but agonizingly en-during history. "Come on, Pete. There must be something . . . what about the stamps . . . You covered all the local shops. What about outside the division . . . well, call me right away if you do." He hung up the phone roughly.

"Anything?"

"Nobody knows anything. I'm starting to side with Ziven."

Kincade set the file he was reading upside down to mark his place. "No one could come up with one decent lead?"

"The first case agent was transferred to San Diego around the time the case broke. He was gone before some of the agents got their corrections back from the steno pool. And you know how most agents are when they're *re*assigned a case like this. They're just looking for a way to pass it on to anyone they can. After the first month, it doesn't look like much was done. But to be fair about it, from what I heard at the time, I don't know if there ever was a decent lead."

"What about the ransom?" Kincade asked. Alton didn't an-swer and rubbed his eyes hard with the heels of his hands. He looked gray and hollow. "Why don't you go find a couch some-where? First days back are a monster even without something like this."

"Yeah, I probably should. I'm having trouble remembering what year this is." He opened his briefcase and took out the Churchill biography.

"I guess you like to read."

"I try to get through a book every week or two."

"Then you do like to read."

A tiny crack of anger crept into Alton's voice, directed as much at himself as Kincade, suggesting that honesty had forced him to make the same confession too many times before. "I was never a great student, so I guess I'm trying to make up for it now."

"Let me ask you something." Kincade's tone became almost accusatory. "Why are you doing this? With your leg, you could go out on a disability."

Either Alton didn't like the question or he didn't care for the way it was asked. He straightened up in the chair and his eyes narrowed. "That you would ask something like that means you wouldn't understand the answer."

"I just don't understand why you're putting yourself through all this."

"That's because you and I are completely different. The answer wouldn't make sense to you."

Kincade smiled lightly, the charm returning to his voice. "If I didn't know better, I'd say that sounds like you think you're better than me."

"You're better than you."

Kincade hoped that Alton wasn't making a veiled reference to the bank burglaries. "So you think there's two of me?"

"We're all two people—the one we'd like to be, and the one we settle for. Maybe in your case the gap's a little wider."

He searched Alton's face, trying to determine if the statement was intended as a hint of some discovery. But Alton stared back comfortably, the heat of challenge missing from his eyes. Kincade decided he'd meant it as a philosophical observation, its meaning broad and vague—ambiguity, the lifeblood of philosophers and fortune tellers. But intentionally or not, Alton was right: an ever-widening abyss existed between Special Agent John William Kincade and Trapper Jack.

Alton looked at his watch. "What about you? You'd better get some sleep, too."

"Ah, I'm kind of a night person. I don't sleep much anyhow. I'm going to see if I can't get through the rest of this file tonight."

Alton stood up and tucked the book under his arm. "You'd better be careful, Jack. You don't want to narrow that gap; it might raise someone's opinion of you."

# 10

IT WAS JUST AFTER 8 A.M. WHEN THE PHONE IN FRONT of Kincade rang, waking him from a light sleep. "Jack Kincade." He was still in the major-case room, his legs propped up on the desk. Fighting his way upright and into consciousness, he cleared his throat, trying to eliminate the evidence of sleep. "Yes, hello."

"This is the reception room. I've got Mrs. Alton here. She's looking for her husband."

Not knowing where Alton was, he said, "I'll be right there."

On the way, he found himself trying to guess what Alton's wife might be like. Within a small point spread, men and women were usually closely matched. They had a tendency to look like they belonged together, and on the rare occasion they didn't, it was usually an indication that one of the parties had brought considerably more money to the table. Since Alton was, aside from his rigidity, a fairly good-looking guy without a lot of money, Kincade expected his wife to be in the same range of attractiveness. He supposed his curiosity had been provoked by Alton's refusal to provide additional insights into himself. If Tess Alton fit into his theory, Kincade could congratulate himself on making a small, unauthorized entry into the interior of Ben Alton, *bank robbery coordinator*. Coming through the door, he said, "Hi, I'm Jack Kincade. I'm working with Ben."

Tess Alton's hand came forward with balletic restraint and

precision as she introduced herself. Her skin was dark, smooth and flawless, her eyes, the color of cognac. She wore tear-shaped black eyeglasses that were slightly out of fashion—if they had ever been in—which, coupled with a no-nonsense stare, gave her a subtle air of independence, a flicker of hardness that one suspected came from not having a husband around when the occasional heavy hand was needed. She seemed regimented, as though being married to Alton did not come naturally to her, but was something she had worked at over the years and had changed her far more than him. The young woman with her was somewhere in her middle teens and obviously her daughter, although Mrs. Alton didn't look any more than eight or ten years older. The girl had the same delicate bone structure as her mother; her fragility seemed both beautiful and prohibitive. Her skin, like her mother's, was dark with a deep glow to it and her hair, short and natural. The thing that most distinguished them chronologically was their demeanor. Tess was in charge, but protective and nurturing. The daughter—like most cops' daughters—seemed sheltered, secure, and obedient. "This is our daughter, Sarah." She held out her hand.

"I assume you want to see Ben."

"Is he not around?"

"He's around, I just don't know exactly where he's bedded down. But let's go find him."

"Thank you, but that's not necessary. He called late last night and told me he wouldn't be home. I just wanted to bring him down a change of clothes and something to eat." She turned around and picked up a garment bag from one of the chairs. Sarah was holding a green nylon container with a zippered lid that Kincade assumed held food. "Will you see that he gets these?"

Kincade could tell she wanted to ask how her husband was feeling but that was too personal a question to ask of someone she had just met. Or maybe, because of the way Alton was so reluctant to talk about himself, discussing family business with an outsider at any time was considered a violation of the house rules. "Are you sure you don't want me to go find him? There aren't too many places around here to lie down."

She lowered her voice. "He told me a little about the case, so I know he's going to be busy."

"You're sure."

She held out her hand to Kincade. "Thank you."

Sarah extended hers again, imitating her mother's smile.

Ben Alton had not opened his eyes yet. He could hear someone moving around him, and, it seemed, deliberately making noise. The sounds echoed with a strange, dense clatter. Realizing he was not surrounded by the soft, textured furnishings of his bedroom that normally absorbed the noises that were now irritatingly transferring night to morning, he remembered that he was in the ASAC's office, stretched out on a vinyl couch and covered with the only blanket available, his raincoat. With some effort, he blinked away the rest of the slowly receding stupor of sleep. Kincade was seated at the desk directly in front of him, eating a sandwich and examining Alton's artificial leg. It stood stiffly at attention in the middle of the ASAC's blotter. With the thumb and middle finger of one hand, Alton slowly rubbed the inner corners of his eyes. A vaguely familiar smell floated through the room. "What are you eating?"

Kincade peeled back one of the slices of bread and examined what was underneath it. "I think it's a salmon patty sandwich."

"My wife's here?"

"She was. I offered to bring her up here, but she said it was better that you slept." Kincade took another bite and nodded at the device directly in front of him. "Is this thing comfortable?"

"I suppose it's more comfortable than walking around on the stump. How come you're eating my sandwich?"

"She brought you four. Also some pills and clean clothes. She's like one of those in-flight refueling planes. You never have to land. If I had a wife like that—"

"If you had a wife like that you'd still be divorced. Can I have my leg please?"

Kincade walked over and handed it to him. "She said your razor and stuff are in the bottom of the garment bag."

Alton pushed the end of his left leg into the prosthesis and adjusted it. Then he stood up and pushed his full body weight into it. Finding his raincoat behind him, he put it on over his underwear. Kincade gave him an amused look. Alton picked up his bag of toiletries and turned toward the door. "I'm going to—"

"Flash the great white whale?"

Alton tried not to laugh. "I'm glad to see that my misfortune hasn't gotten you down."

"Sorry."

"Did you find anything after I left last night?"

"Maybe. Let me ask your opinion on something. What do you see as the biggest problem with this case?"

"That it's three years old?"

"That's what I thought, at first. But the more I look at it, the more I think that's where the answer might be. After three years, patterns form."

"This isn't going to be the short version, is it? There's a shower up here somewhere. I'll be back in a few minutes for the rest of the seminar."

"I think I'd better clear out of here before the ASAC gets in. I'll be in the major-case room."

A half hour later Alton walked in wearing the suit his wife had dropped off, looking significantly more energetic. "No coffee?" he said.

Kincade tossed him one of his sandwiches. "We can get some on the way."

"The way *where?*"

"Let's not forget what we get paid for—we've got people to threaten and intimidate."

"I would have never dreamed that enthusiasm could be so frightening."

"The sooner this mess is resolved, the sooner I go back to being Jack *Who?*"

"Okay, okay, I got it. Where exactly are we going?"

"My patterns theory. Remember?"

"Apparently I was a little too subtle when I changed the subject." He took a bite out of the sandwich.

"It's either my patterns theory or more amputee jokes."

"Why do I have the feeling there's going to be no stopping either?"

"You know what the best thing about this job is—the camaraderie."

During the drive to the Roman Inn, Kincade slept and Alton listened to the news on the radio. Most of it concerned the bomb. One reporter was interviewing people on the street who either worked or lived close by. Yes, they thought the FBI had to do something about the bomb, but no, they certainly didn't want any criminals released because of it.

Conrad Ziven, he suspected, was having a very good day.

It was almost 9 A.M. when they arrived at the motel. "Jack, we're here."

Kincade awoke instantly and seemed fully alert. "You want to come in while I get cleaned up?"

"Just leave the door open, I'm going to get that coffee. How do you take it?"

When Alton got back to Kincade's room, B.C. met him at the door, sniffed him briefly, and then raised its nose toward the bag that contained the coffees. "Sorry, boy, I didn't bring you anything. Next time." He put Kincade's cup on the desk, which sat crammed into the corner of the room. The top was so badly warped, he didn't know whether the tall container would sit on it without tipping over. Then he noticed that something large and rectangular had apparently been spray-painted on top of it, leaving a trace of its shape in the flat black residue. Moving a newspaper off one end, he could see an oval-shaped hole had been cut into whatever the object was. He bent over and sniffed at the thin coating to determine if it was the smell from the first time he had been in the room, but the strong smell of the hot coffee was masking it. He took both cups to the windowsill and was about to go back and reexamine the desk when Kincade came out of the bathroom. The towel that covered him wasn't large enough and he had to hold its ends together at his side. Alton could see that at one time Kincade had been an athlete. His shoulders were wide and still muscled, but everything below his chest had surrendered to disuse and turned soft, especially his waistline.

"Give me two minutes." Alton handed one of the containers to Kincade. "Thanks. Now that you have your coffee, are you ready for my patterns theory?"

Clumsily, Alton climbed onto the broken recliner. "As long as it doesn't involve you waving that towel over your head."

With one hand Kincade removed the lid from the cup and took a sip. "You see, while most people would think that the three years is the most difficult obstacle to overcome, I see it as possibly the key to solving the kidnapping. After that much time, patterns emerge, human patterns."

"Like what?"

"I'm not exactly sure." Kincade started getting dressed. "Take the stamps. Everyone was checking with the shops and known fences right after the kidnapping, but maybe the kidnapper decided to let them cool off. So why don't we recheck the shops now or get their descriptions flashed on the Internet?"

"Not a bad idea. We could give it to Thorne. He'll get some manpower on it."

"That's an even better idea because then we could go and look at the drop route. After all this time, there may be some detail that has become more obvious."

"Like what?"

"Again, I don't know." Kincade picked up a shirt from the bed. It appeared to have had at least one previous wearing. "We've got the luxury of looking at it more objectively. Back then with the heat of the chase—I don't know, things are missed, or don't seem important at the time. Hopefully we'll be able to see if anything was missed. The surveillance logs should have everything we need." Kincade loosely knotted his tie and cinched it up to an inch below the collar, which he left unbuttoned. Slipping his jacket on, he asked, "Mind if we take B.C. along? He's always cooped up in here."

Alton looked down at the dog. "Don't be thinking that you're getting any of my salmon patties, boy." The Border collie stood up and wagged its tail twice, testing Alton's resistance to canine appeal. Alton appeared to relent slightly. "I read an article once about how you can judge a person by how their dog behaves."

"Until this moment, I never thought it was possible to read too much."

Alton ignored him. "This dog knows how to work a room."

"If you're saying that B.C. is *charming*, I'd say that was a pretty accurate article."

"I guess bullshit artists, by definition, have to describe themselves as charming."

The kidnapper had called Ziven at home and told him to go to a phone booth in Bellwood, a good twenty-five miles from Conrad Ziven's house in China Hills, to await instructions. While Alton drove, Kincade sipped coffee and read the surveillance log. Three years earlier, with unusual alacrity, the technical people from the FBI and their pals at the phone company placed a trap on the line before Ziven could drive the forty minutes it took to get there. But the kidnapper had anticipated their reaction and taped a cell phone to the back of the stand. Once it started ringing, Ziven located it and pulled it loose. A voice he described as frighteningly calm but barely audible, asked him, "Are you wearing a wire?" Although he was, he said no.

The caller, still without any noticeable emotion, said, "If you lie to me again, I'll hang up this phone and shoot your daughter in the head." Neither man said anything for a moment.

Yes, Ziven confessed, the FBI had strapped a transmitter on him.

"Turn it off, now." Ziven reached under his shirt and disconnected the mike from the body of the device. "Now take it off and drop it on the ground. Put the cell phone next to it. I want to hear you crushing it with your foot." Ziven did as he was told and then picked up the phone again. "Good. Now drive east on the Eisenhower."

Ziven was then instructed to drive through a series of narrow one-way residential streets that the FBI's ground surveillance could not possibly follow without being seen. Forced to give him a wide margin of safety to prevent detection, they eventually lost the father's car. But the Bureau plane still maintained visual contact.

The directed route ended on Lower Wacker Drive, an underground street in Chicago's downtown. At that point the plane could no longer observe Ziven's car. He was then ordered to a specific location and the final instruction was to place the ransom, his stamp collection, and the cell phone under a red Toyota that had a HONK IF YOU LOVE JESUS sticker on its rear bumper. Ziven had the presence of mind to write down the cell phone's serial number and to note the license plate of the car he left everything under. Both the cell phone and the Toyota had been stolen the night before, and subsequent investigation failed to reveal any connection of either to the kidnapper.

When they reached Bellwood, Kincade said, "Looks like it's about two blocks up here on the right." Alton pulled the Bureau car into a small parking lot, stopping within ten feet of the pay phone where the cell phone had been secreted. Both men got out and the Border collie looked at Kincade expectantly. Alton opened the back door and the dog jumped out, testing the warm air with its nose.

"What do you think of all the hoops this guy put Ziven through?" Alton asked.

"Pretty sophisticated. He knew an awful lot about how we do these things."

"He also knew that Ziven would be wired."

"Don't forget the pay phone. Even though it was never used, he knew we'd be kept busy getting it trapped when we should have been concentrating on other things."

"And the drop. Lower Wacker. He had to know we used a plane."

"That's not common knowledge," Kincade said.

"He knew way too much for an amateur."

"And was a little too disciplined for your average felon."

"Meaning?"

"I'm not sure what that means."

Alton called to the dog and opened the rear door. As he started to get in himself, he saw that Kincade was slowly scanning the area. Alton walked over to him. "What?"

"I was just going over the call Ziven got here. As careful as this guy was, would he take a chance that Ziven was actually destroying the wire? Put yourself inside his head. If you devised a plan this elaborate, would you let its success depend on the sound of what Ziven *might* be destroying?"

"No, I wouldn't. What are you getting at?"

"He had to be watching. To make sure the wire was destroyed. Otherwise Ziven could have constantly told the surveillance crew where he was and what was going on. The entire plan hinged on making sure Ziven was alone when he got to the drop on Lower Wacker."

"And if he was watching, we know it wasn't from a car because the surveillance crew was still on Ziven at this point. It's right in the logs that they watched him hat-dance the transmitter," Alton said. "They had four units on him and combed both sides of the street looking for anyone trying to be too casual."

"Again, this guy knew a lot of procedure," Kincade said.

"So if he was watching, where from?"

"Not much around here. No residences." As Kincade checked the neighborhood again, his eyes stopped on a bank across the street. Someone was walking in the front door. "That bank, it has a lobby with an ATM."

They entered the front door of the bank and searched the area immediately above the teller machine. There was a surveillance camera. Alton said, "Could we be this lucky?"

"Let's find out."

After introducing themselves to the branch manager, Kincade asked, "Your surveillance camera above the ATM—how long do you keep the tapes?"

"Ninety days."

Alton asked, "Three years ago, how long did you keep them?"

"I've only been here about a year, but I think it's always been ninety days. You're from the government, you should know that the Privacy Act restricts us from keeping things of nonevidentiary value any longer."

"Is there anyone you could ask to be certain?" Alton said.

"Let me call upstairs to security." He picked up the phone and dialed. After a short conversation, he placed his hand over the mouthpiece. "Sorry, the tapes are long gone."

"Well, it was worth a shot," Alton said.

The manager started to hang up when Kincade said, "One second. Your ATM booth, it takes a card to get in the door after hours?"

"Yes."

"Does it record the cards used on any given day?"

The manager asked the question into the phone. "Yes, it does."

Cautiously, fearing another dead end, Alton said, "How long are those kept?"

The manager asked the question. "He says that because they are simply coded numbers, the privacy laws don't require their destruction. The computer's got them all the way back to the day the machine was installed."

Alton stood up. "Who do we have to talk to?"

Kincade found it amazing how once Alton locked onto a target, interdicting obstacles no longer seemed to exist. Evidently, driven by some developed instinct, he could now see all the steps to the end of the case. And his momentum gave off sparks, infecting those around him. At first, Kincade supposed it was all that he had overcome that made him so resolute, but then he realized he was confusing cause and effect: Ben Alton recognized no barriers because he was so determined. And right now, he had the scent.

Bob Newman was the head of security for the LaGrange Savings and Loan, a relatively small bank with only three branches. He was six feet tall and while not overweight, his face was heavy with wrinkled flesh. Kincade held out his hand. "Jack Kincade, Bob. This is Ben Alton."

"Good to see you. Whatever you want, you got. I did twenty-three years with Chicago at Area Four Violent Crimes."

Kincade said, "We really appreciate it." He then told the retired detective that they were investigating the Ziven kidnapping, but didn't tell him how it was related to the bomb at the jail.

"Yeah, I remember that case. Never found the girl, right?"

"Right, but our luck may be changing. We would like to see the ATM access records for the day the drop was made."

"No problem." Newman swiveled 180 degrees in his chair to a computer behind him and typed in the date that Kincade gave him. A list of numbers appeared on the screen. Newman put his finger to the monitor and started counting them. "Seventeen used their cards to access the outer door, which would indicate after-hour use."

Kincade was flipping through his notes. "The surveillance log says that they were at the phone about 8:15 P.M. Anything around then, or most likely a little earlier?"

"Sorry, there's no time on these. And I don't even believe they're in time sequence. Sort of a digital arrangement."

"Then I guess we'll need a list of the customers," Alton said.

"Want addresses, too?"

"Yeah, and you'd better throw in their dates of birth and Socials."

"I told you I'd give you whatever you needed, but most of that stuff is confidential."

Kincade said, "This is just to generate leads; no one will ever know where it came from."

"That's all I needed to hear," Newman said.

As he turned back to his computer, Alton said, "Seventeen—that's not too bad. I'll call the SAC and get him to roll out the troops. He can put seventeen teams on the street and get them covered in no time."

After a few minutes, Newman clicked the print icon and turned back to the two agents. "That'll just be a minute, but there's one number here I can't help you with. It's not from this bank, so I don't have any info on him or her."

Both Kincade and Alton sensed something. "What bank is it?" Kincade asked.

"Let me check the coding symbol." Newman lifted his desk blotter and scanned a long list of names and numbers. "Looks like Iroquois Bank and Trust in Wheeling."

"Wheeling," Alton said. "That's a lot closer to Ziven's than here."

Kincade said, "Bob, do you know anyone at that bank?"

"Not personally, but most of us belong to ASIS. If they have anyone there who's a member, I can make a call." Newman opened his bottom drawer and took out a small, blue-cover directory with the title *American Society of Industrial Security* printed on the front. "There are very few banks whose security people aren't members. With all the credit card and bank fraud, you have to have people to call, otherwise investigations would take forever to go nowhere." Within minutes, Newman's contact had provided the information requested. After hanging up, he leaned back in his chair, his face congratulatory, that of an experienced cop hearing the first heartbeats of an impossible case being solved. Both agents understood his expression. "The name on the account is William Sloane." He handed them a sheet of paper on which he had written Sloane's personal information and then grinned. "The account was opened six days before the kidnapping, but there hasn't been any activity on it since."

Alton, his eyes dancing, looked over at Kincade and was disappointed that he didn't appear to be feeling the same rush. For Alton, there still wasn't anything like it—of the seven billion people on the planet, they had narrowed it down to one.

He called the SAC and told him what they had found. "Okay," Thorne said, "I'll get some people out on those names as soon as you can fax them to me. I assume you and Kincade are going to work Sloane."

"As fast as we can drive to Wheeling. Could you transfer me to NCIC? I want to run him for criminal history."

"Keep me posted. I've already had two more calls from the ACLU and neither was to nominate me as Libertarian of the

Year." Thorne transferred the call and after a few minutes the NCIC operator told Alton that Sloane did have a criminal record, the most prominent entry being a three-year sentence for burglary. After using the bank's fax machine to send the list to the SAC, they thanked Newman and told him they'd let him know how everything turned out.

It wasn't easy to find the address that they had been given for William Sloane. Wedged between an old, abandoned furniture factory and a fifteen-foot-high railroad berm, it was the only house on a dead-end street, a one-story wooden frame that appeared to have been built at least a half century before. Its windows and doors were boarded over. There was no longer any paint on the siding but the roof was in surprisingly good shape, probably having been replaced in the last ten years. Both men got out of the car and B.C. followed uninvited. "You know, Jack, this house would remind me of you if the roof wasn't in such good shape."

Kincade ran his hand through his hair. "Is that a shot about my hair getting thin?"

"What kind of person would make fun of another person's physical defect?"

At the front of the house, Alton wrapped his fingers around the end of the sheet of plywood covering the door and pulled on it to see if it was secure. "Nobody's been through here in a while."

Kincade and the dog went around to the back, returning a few minutes later. "The back is the same way. Where was Sloane's burglary arrest?"

"Right here in Wheeling."

"Let's try the locals; maybe they know where we can find him."

As Kincade got in the car, Alton stared at the unremarkable house. Its construction, squat and perfectly rectangular, had been intended to last and gave it a weighty solidness, a place where dark secrets could be well hidden. He had covered thousands of leads, the vast majority of which, by their nature, turned out to be unproductive. Sometimes the bad-to-good ratio was twenty-to-one, during some stretches even a hundred–to-one, and sometimes the connection never surfaced no matter how doggedly pursued. But this tiny, unnoticed house was now signaling him like a suddenly sun-struck island in a fog. Everything felt right, his brain making the million subconscious calculations that, when correct, were routinely underestimated as a hunch. Right now, he knew they were close, very close. He got in the car.

Kincade was looking at a map, trying to locate the police department, and did not seem to care that the solution was at hand. A great wave of disdain for Kincade broke across Alton. Kincade didn't even realize that he had gotten them this far. He had not only figured out that the kidnapper used the bank lobby to watch Ziven destroy the wire, but he was responsible for every step of logic that led from three years ago to the present moment. But in spite of his indifference, Kincade's mind continued to fire away, emitting an intelligence that Alton had to reluctantly admire. A gift from the gods, which, no matter how contemptuously squandered, they were apparently unwilling or unable to revoke.

## 11

ALTON SAID, "WE'RE LOOKING FOR WILLIAM SLOANE, used to live over on—"

"Billy 'The Kid' Sloane. That's what I used to call him. Why you looking for him?" Detective Dan Lansing sat behind the desk in his cramped office. His meaty hands were folded in front of him forming one large, knobby cube. They strained against each other as he spoke. He was in his late thirties, and despite a receding hairline, wore his hair in a gouged crew cut. His thick shoulders and arms were made more obvious by a tight short-sleeved shirt over which hung a thick brown leather shoulder holster. A Beretta nine-millimeter angled out of one armpit, handcuffs and two magazines brimming with hollow points sat under the other.

"*Used* to call him?" Kincade said.

"The boy is tits up." With startling speed, Lansing pivoted in his chair and jumped up to the front of his filing cabinet, which was within a couple of feet of his desk. He located a file and opened it. He scanned it for a moment. "He was found shot to death on the west side of Chicago. I don't know if they ever found out who pulled the trigger. At least they never called me if they did."

Alton asked, "When was this?"

"Ah"—Lansing ran his finger down the page—"in two days it'll be exactly three years."

Kincade and Alton looked at each other. "Where was he living before that?" Alton asked.

"As far as I know, the only place he ever lived besides prison, over on Baltimore Street next to the old furniture factory."

"He was living there at the time of his death?"

"Yeah, it was his mother's place until she died, ah . . . maybe five years ago. He never did pay the taxes on it. I don't know, maybe the city owns it by now."

"Would it take long to find out?"

Lansing closed the file, stuffed it back in the drawer, and sat down. He leaned back in his chair until his head hit the wall with a small crisp thud that he didn't seem to notice. Folding his arms across his chest, he said, "I know you boys have got to play it close to the vest, but it seems like all the information passing over my desk is going in one direction here."

Alton started to say something when Kincade interrupted. "We're working the Leah Ziven kidnapping."

"You're shittin' me! Little bitty small-time Billy Sloane. Are you sure?"

"Not a hundred percent, but you can help us find out," Alton said. "She was kidnapped three years ago the day before yesterday. Four days before Sloane was killed. We just came up with his name today."

"So why the interest in the house?"

"Well, if that was where he was living at the time of the kidnapping and he died unexpectedly, maybe he didn't have a chance to get rid of all the evidence that might tie him to it."

"I'll be right back." Lansing hurried out of the office.

Alton got up and inspected the cinderblock wall where the detective's head had hit it, rubbing his fingers across the spot. "Ol' Dan's kind of intense, isn't he?"

Kincade sank farther back in his chair to emphasize what he was about to say. "Unless I miss my guess, we're about to head into another one of those legally gray areas you seem to like so much—Sloane's house. And if I've learned one thing in the Bureau it is when there are people's rights to be violated, look around for the most enthusiastic cop you can find and get out of his way. Then if everything works out: *We're the FBI, of course we led this investigation;* and if it doesn't: *Those goddamn locals.*" Alton had to laugh. It was true. Unlike the police, agents rarely decided on any action before testing it against how their careers might be impacted, but until now, he had never heard anyone admit it.

When Lansing returned, his face was slightly reddened, and small beads of sweat dotted the puffy half-circles under his eyes. "After Sloane's death no one came forward to claim the property so the house was seized by the city for back taxes."

"Gee, Dan," Kincade said, "what do you think we should do?"

As Lansing's unmarked police car sped toward Baltimore Street, the Border collie, even though equipped with the bio-mechanical refinements passed on by centuries of sheepherding, had trouble keeping its balance. Alton held on to the dry-cleaning handle above the window in the backseat. The car stopped abruptly in front of the house. Since the street was a dead end, Lansing didn't bother to park next to the curb. He hit the trunk release, got out and retrieved a large chrome-plated pry bar from the trunk. "Front door all right?"

"Hold on a minute," Alton said. He took out evidence gloves retrieved from his car before leaving and handed a pair to each of them. "Just in case."

Lansing struggled to get his on. By the time they were finally in place, he was sweating even more, and both plastic palms had been ripped open. He grasped the pry bar with both hands and held it in front of his chest as though someone had just given the command to "fix bayonets." The plywood panel was nailed tightly enough that it took him four or five wrenches at different points to free it. The door behind it was locked, but took just one long pull to open.

Alton stepped in with the beam of his flashlight leading the way. B.C.'s nails began striking the hardwood floor behind them with a cautious patter. Everyone stopped for a moment, letting their eyes adjust to the dusty light. The dog, suddenly alerted, lowered itself slowly to the floor and began a barely audible whimper. "What's he doing?" Alton asked.

Kincade had never heard the Border collie whine before. He searched its two different colored eyes for a clue. "I'm not sure."

The house smelled of mildew and an unidentifiable mixture of the other sour odors that accumulate during decades of lethargic ownership. There wasn't much furniture: a couch upon which a pillow and blanket lay rumpled and a grimy console TV with one of its large knobs missing, a pair of pliers on top. Alton started toward the kitchen, which was at the back of the house. Lansing, turning on his own flashlight, headed off to the right to what appeared to be the only bedroom, his foot strikes quicker than Alton's. Almost immediately the detective said, "Nothing in here," and was back in the living room.

That left only the kitchen. The sink was brimming with dirty dishes, and a blackened frying pan full of green-gray mold sat crookedly on the stove. Kincade asked, "Is there a basement?"

"This place is so small, I doubt it," Lansing said.

"How about a crawl space?" Alton asked.

"As low as it sits on the ground, I don't think that's possible."

The dog whimpered again and as soon as the three men stopped, lowered itself to the floor.

"How about an attic?" Kincade asked. "The access is usually in the bedroom closet. Did you see one, Dan?"

"I didn't look."

They walked into the bedroom. The ceiling was cracked with age and settlement and mottled with darkened stains, a sign of water damage, which explained the house's newer roof. Kincade opened the closet door and, taking Alton's flashlight, shined it at the ceiling. A square wooden access panel sat flush against its frame. He could see fingerprints smudged on it and around the edges. Alton stepped in and pushed the few items of clothing hanging from a rod to one side. A twenty-gallon gas can, painted military green, sat on the floor. He rocked it on its edge. "It's full." As soon as he twisted the cap open, the small room filled with the odor of evaporating gasoline. Carefully tightening the lid back down, he said, "Looks like there was going to be a fire. I guess somebody's got to go up."

Kincade said, "Okay, Dan, for once the Bureau is not going to steal local thunder. Let me give you a hand."

"I'd go, but I'll never get through there."

Kincade examined the detective's girth carefully and then with fleeting hope considered the width and breadth of the opening. He looked at Alton. "And I suppose you're going to claim having only one leg disqualifies *you*."

Lansing looked genuinely surprised by the announcement. Without a hint of subtlety, he inspected both of Alton's legs, trying to decide if it was true, and if so, which leg was not real.

Alton said, "Oh, that's right, send the black guy up there; that way, if anything happens, you won't be losing a *real* FBI agent."

Kincade said, "Then you'll go?"

Alton turned around, and leaning against the closet wall, cupped his hands on his good knee. "Come on, I know you know how to step on the black man."

Kincade, flashlight in hand, put his foot in Alton's hands. Reaching up, he pushed the overhead panel hard enough to flip it out of the way. "You'd better not forget you owe me one when they start picking teams for the three-legged race." Kincade was surprised at the ease with which Alton lifted him up through the opening.

The attic's trapped air was hot and dry; immediately it became harder to breathe. A musty organic odor was thick in the air. The joists were covered with scrap lumber, some of which was nailed down to provide wide surfaces for storage. Next to the opening, sitting on a small square of plywood, was a cardboard box. He opened it. Inside was a stack of plastic display sheets, each containing a number of stamps. Without a word, Kincade handed down the box through the opening. He heard Lansing say, "Damn, that's got to be the ransom."

"Anything else up there, Jack?" Alton asked.

He felt like screaming, If you want to know so badly, why don't you get your black ass up here, but he settled for, "Isn't that enough?" He didn't expect Alton to answer, and he didn't. Defensively, as if fearing some kind of macabre attack straight out of the movies, Kincade swung his flashlight in a sweeping arc. At the far end of the space, something with a cloth cover over it was pushed up against the rafters. It was the shape that he had hoped not to find—long, with a familiar, undulating profile, about the right size for a small body. Like all retired Catholics—although, at this moment, he was sure that they never *really* retired—Kincade decided that he was up there due to past sins. Because of stealing, and missing roll call—he wasn't sure which commandment covered that—he found himself in league with a man with a missing limb whose intensity had brought him to the point where he was now: inching toward the object at the other end of the attic. And why had he exploited this poor detective? Thou shalt not . . . whatever. Half crawling, half sliding, he moved over to it.

Defensively, his mind floated away from the form in front of him. There was something just too neat about this investigation, too easy. They had come so far in one day. Too far. If there was one thing the past few years had taught him, it was the undeniable presence of entropy, the measurement of disorder in every system. The less energy contained therein, the more disorder. His life was certainly proof of that. If it wasn't chaotic, it couldn't be true. This case had not taken all that much energy so it should have been rife with chaos, but here they were, led to this location one quick, simple step after another. He then remembered that he just wanted his involvement in this case to end, and the sooner the better. If the solution was imperfect because of its neatness, why should that be his problem? "DON'T . . . GIVE . . . A . . . GOOD . . . GODDAMN," he mumbled as he moved to within a foot of the object, its odor now prohibitive.

He looked down at what appeared to be a dirty, worn bedspread, its edges tucked up under whatever it was hiding. His blood suddenly felt too thick to flow through his heart. He inhaled the stifling air, and the single breath he wanted came in two spasmodic, disconnected jerks. He threw back the cover.

"Jesus Christ!" he said in an oxygenless whisper.

Staring up at him was a dark brown, leathery mask that was too large for the skull it covered. The eyelids and nostrils were no longer openings. The process that had mummified the body in the dry heat of the attic had sealed them. The mouth was open slightly and pulled to one side, revealing five lower teeth, all wrapped carefully in silver braces, each bright white against the coffee-brown parchment. Her thick dark hair, pulled back in a ponytail, was only slightly mussed. It was the only recognizable feature from the girl above the mantel.

Carefully, Kincade lifted the cover completely off the body. She was wearing a sweatshirt and dark skirt. Her hands appeared to be wearing thin, papery brown gloves except that they were tipped with fingernails. Between the bottom of her skirt and the top of her soiled white gym shoes, the skin appeared as dark brown, baggy stockings. He looked at her face again and compared it to the poster-size photograph of the sixteen-year-old girl. Maybe someone could see a resemblance but it wasn't going to be him.

With a reverence that was uncommon in him anymore, he slowly pulled the cover back over her and turned off his light. For a moment, he sat there. An anger he had not felt in years pulsed through him in the choking darkness. He was angry that Billy Sloane was dead, that some unsuspecting dope-dealing scum had killed him so routinely, not realizing the justice of what he had done. He was angry that Sloane had died a junkie's death, that half-expected end to life for which they have more contempt than fear. His death should have been the final loop of justice, but instead, he died without the defining and eternal damnation for what he had done to this child.

Kincade's mind, like that of many cops in these situations, started toward his own son, but he wouldn't allow that. He had become adept at detaching himself from the daily realities that streaked by him at the speed of light. This, he reminded himself, had nothing to do with him. Slowly, he crawled back toward the square of flickering light and the Border collie's muted whimpers.

# 12

FOUR FBI CARS PULLED UP TO THE SLOANE HOUSE. As soon as the lead vehicle stopped, Roy K. Thorne was the first one out. Kincade, Alton, and the Wheeling detective stood out in front waiting for them. Because the girl had been found, the two agents realized that they had to tell Lansing about the connection between the kidnapping and the bomb at the jail. Initially, the big detective felt slighted but once it was explained to him that he was about to stand center stage with the FBI, his objections faded. Alton introduced him to the SAC.

"Are you sure it's her?" Thorne asked quickly.

"The ransom was hidden with the body in the attic," Alton said.

Thorne looked at the small house. "In the attic? That seems a little unusual."

Lansing said, "The last couple of years that Sloane was alive, he was a suspect in some arsons for profit. Any arsonist worth a damn knows that if you want some evidence destroyed, the ceiling area burns hotter and longer than any other area of a building; it has its own burn, which is basically nothing but dry, unpainted timber, plus the burn from below. Besides, there was no basement or crawl space to hide the body, so he had little choice if he wanted to get it out of the way temporarily."

"What makes you think he was going to set this place on fire?"

"There's a twenty-gallon can of gasoline inside," Alton said.

"And burn the stamps, too?"

"They were right on the edge of the access opening, probably just being hidden there until he could unload them. He was probably going to set the fire and grab them on the way out."

Thorne called to a tall, slender female agent who was too well dressed to be searching a murder scene. "Beth, how soon can we expect the media?"

She came over to the group. "I've called everyone; they should be on their way."

"I don't want anything said about how the kidnapping connects to the bomb at the jail, but we've got to get the word to Ziven that this case is solved. Let me know when they're all here and ready to go." He turned back to the others. "Dan, you've done a hell of a job here. We're in your debt. Please stick around for the press, I want to let them know your part in this. But please remember, other than your chief, I don't want anyone to know how the two investigations are tied together."

"I understand, sir."

"And you two . . . thank you," the SAC said with a sincerity that gave Kincade a quick, forgotten chill of pride. Instead of embracing it, Kincade invoked his backup mantra: *This too shall pass*. "But we're only halfway home," Thorne continued. "We've still got to neutralize the bomb. I want both of you to get back to the office as quickly as possible. You're going to have less than an hour before this hits the radio and TV. I'm going to tell them that we have found the victim and have a strong suspect, but I won't identify him or why he's under suspicion. Hopefully, that will make Ziven call you for details. But remember, while he deserves a great deal of sympathy over finally learning the fate of his daughter, you cannot give him any slack. We've done what he's demanded, now he has to uphold his end. The deal has to be enforced. You've solved the case, now he owes you the disarming sequence. And until you get it, what you've already accomplished is incomplete."

Alton, heeding the SAC's call for haste, drove intently, pushing the Bureau car eastward along the expressway. Kincade said,

"Ben, what does your family think about you coming back to work?"

The night before the conference at the jail, Alton had told his wife he was returning to work. She just nodded her head, suggesting confirmation of something that had been long feared. She wasn't thinking about anything that might happen to him, but rather their marriage. They had a son who had gone off to college and a daughter in high school. With their home soon to be empty, the complicated shield of family, which keeps couples from admitting distance, was being lowered. She thought because of the cancer, he would develop some sort of dependence on their marriage, but with his announcement of going back to work, and a month early at that, her fears were confirmed. She had always been quick to rationalize the relative importance of his job, but that was no longer possible. In a voice that seemed to have already surrendered to the futility of what she was about to propose, she reminded him that he was eligible for a rainbow of governmental disability options. He didn't answer. As she had done throughout their marriage, she tried to understand some of what he was going through, and concluded that now more than ever he needed to be a special agent of the Federal Bureau of Investigation in order to be emotionally whole again. Aware that this interpretation was probably allowing a new branch of denial to flower, she also knew that marriages without such tangled bouquets were rare and all too often doomed. "Don't think because you've eaten one of my wife's sandwiches, you've been asked to dinner."

"That sounds like they don't like it."

"You know, my whole life when I wanted to get someone to stop asking me questions, all I had to do was insult them. That doesn't seem to work with you."

"Okay, no more." There was an unusual timbre of surrender in Kincade's voice, as though he hadn't intended to be confrontational, just communicative. He motioned the Border collie to come forward and lean its head over the back of the seat to be petted. B.C. readily obeyed, and Kincade silently rubbed an index finger along the black and white divide that bisected the animal's nose. The sensation appeared to be as soothing to Kincade as it was to the dog. Alton then understood that what Kincade had seen in the attic was starting to take a toll on him.

Keeping his eyes on the road, Alton said, "I never thought to ask them. I've always assumed that *I* am my kids' most important lesson. And what better way to teach them how to get up off the canvas when something knocks them down."

Kincade's only response was a distant, appreciative smile.

In the major-case room, with B.C. lying between their chairs, Kincade and Alton watched Thorne's televised news conference. He seemed a little out of sync. While most people who wound up in front of a camera appeared to be suited to its illusion, as glossy and self-marketing as the medium itself, Thorne emitted an above-the-fray dignity. As he spoke, a hidden restraint prowled under the surface of his words, suggesting he was capable of much more than he presented, that he was prostituting himself in order to achieve some greater good. He stood outside the Sloane house explaining that a body, believed to be Leah Ziven, had been found inside. And, yes, a suspect had been developed. With timing that seemed too dramatic not to have been planned, the body, encased in a black synthetic bag, was brought out on a stretcher behind the SAC. Kincade rapidly switched channels and all the stations had the same shot. The camera left Thorne's face and zoomed to the body bag, its dimensions tragic. When he finished, there was a flurry of attempted questions, mostly concerning the suspect's identity. His only comment was that the investigation was ongoing and to comment further at this time would not be in the best interest of justice or the Ziven family.

Before the reporter could summarize what the SAC had said, the phone in front of Alton rang. Kincade said, "I think that might be for you."

Alton reached over and picked it up. "Ben Alton."

This time there was emotion in Conrad Ziven's voice. "Is it true? You have found my Leah?"

"Mr. Ziven, I'm very sorry. We can't be positive until the coroner verifies it, but the body we found was wearing clothes that matched the description you and your wife gave us three years ago."

"How can I know that this is true?"

"Mr. Ziven, I'm going to put this on the speakerphone." Alton hit a button and hung up. "This is the other agent who was with me when we found her, Jack Kincade."

"I'm very sorry for your loss, sir."

"How can I be sure you're not staging this?"

Alton said, "Mr. Ziven, I could never do anything like what you're suggesting. The FBI has greatly disappointed you once, and I would never intentionally do it a second time."

"Agent Alton, these are noble words and if I knew you personally, I might be able to believe them, but I don't know you."

Kincade said, "Mr. Ziven, do you still have your television set on?"

"No."

"Please turn it on and wait while we try something." He went to a different phone and dialed the radio room. "Get anyone on the air who is with the SAC and tell them to have him call me immediately." Less than a minute later another phone rang. "Kincade." He talked loud enough so Ziven could hear him over the speakerphone. "Yes, sir, we've got him on the line, but he's not convinced that this is real. Are any of the TV crews still set up . . . good. Can you get them to shoot a close-up on the stamps . . . You'll have to flip the pages slowly so Mr. Ziven can see that it is his collection." Kincade hung up and then spoke into the speakerphone. "Mr. Ziven, it's going to be on Channel Two."

"I will call you back" was Ziven's only response.

Kincade turned to Channel 2. Thorne, wearing evidence gloves, was carefully taking the clear plastic pages out of a large bag. He held them up to the camera one at a time. The phone rang again. Kincade answered it on the speakerphone. Ziven sounded as though he might have been crying. "This could still be a trick. The FBI knows what stamps were stolen."

Kincade picked up the phone to eliminate the impersonal hollowness of the speaker and held it so Alton could hear. "Mr. Ziven, you have my word, this is not a trick."

"I just don't know."

"Mr. Ziven, if it helps, it doesn't look like she was assaulted . . . I mean . . . sexually."

He could hear Ziven sobbing now, as if some unspeakable, looming fear had finally been slain. Kincade waited: Ziven had to speak next. Finally, he did. "What about the person who has done this?"

"He's dead, killed in an unrelated crime. That's why your stamps were still with her."

"I have your word as a man that this is all true."

"You do."

"Then you have upheld your part. At five o'clock, I will meet you at my home."

Kincade hung up and gave Alton a just-another-day-at-the-office shrug of his shoulders. Alton made no response; instead he just sat there again admiring Kincade's ability to think on his feet, which now seemed even more impressive because of his apparent lack of commitment to anything having to do with being an FBI agent.

By 4:30, a half hour earlier than Ziven had instructed, they were parked outside his China Hills home. On the way, Kincade had dropped B.C. off at the motel, feeding him an entire can of dog food—twice his normal portion—his reward for helping find the girl's body.

When they radioed the SAC to tell him that Ziven was surrendering, he was reluctant to let them go alone. Not because of any physical danger, but because of the possibility Ziven might get cold feet and try to take off, two agents not being sufficient to interdict all escape routes. Alton argued that having his cooperation was as important as having him in custody. Any overkill tactics might give the impression that they were worried he wouldn't live up to his end of the bargain. Raising doubts at this point would only make his cooperation that much more tentative.

Once they had him in custody, there would be no need to abide by such protocols, but they wanted to make sure they did indeed have the cuffs on before introducing him to the unpleasantries of his immediate future. One of the reasons Thorne had been successful was that he allowed subordinates to make decisions as long as they understood they had to live with the consequences. After he reiterated this, the two agents were permitted to go alone.

Kincade said, "Can I ask you something?"

"No."

"It's about your cancer."

Alton sighed. "You know, right about now I should be getting some satisfaction from all this, but you're sure sucking the joy completely out of it."

"Does your leg matter? Well, I know it *matters*, what I mean is are you the same man without it?"

Alton stared at him. "That's what I'm trying to find out."

"And what if you're not the same?"

"Then I'll work harder until I become better." There was a flat chantlike quality to the sentence, as though it was something that had thrummed through his head his whole life, a simple, but well-trained device capable of holding failure at bay until it could be outflanked and then overrun. "How about you, Jack, are you better today than yesterday?"

Kincade's face switched to the engaging look of amusement that always seemed to surface when the conversation became the least bit serious. "If I am, I'm sure it's just a temporary setback."

Alton opened his briefcase and pulled out a new book, *Days of Grace*, the memoir of tennis star and activist Arthur Ashe. He also took out a sandwich, removed half from its plastic wrapper, and handed the rest to Kincade, who asked, "Does this mean we're having dinner?"

"Fuck you."

At a couple of minutes before five, a freshly washed green sedan drove slowly by the house. Alton slapped his book closed. "That's probably him. Think I should go after him?"

"He didn't come here *not* to surrender. Give him a minute, he'll be back."

At precisely 5:00, Conrad Ziven came walking up the sidewalk. Short and ghostly thin, he wore a dark suit which hung on him as loosely as if it belonged to another person. Inexpertly cut, his hair had a military look to it, the sides not much more than patchy stubble. The way he walked was a strange mixture of weighted sadness and overriding determination, his arms swinging with a stiff precision, while his hands remained knotted apprehensively. There was no satisfaction in his eyes. For three years, he had been driven by hope, and more recently by the need for vengeance. But now with full revenge struck, its cost, the final death of hope along with its gauzy promises, had left him empty. His daughter was gone, and with her, a man's greatest responsibility: the preservation of his family. When he turned up the driveway, Alton got out with strained nonchalance. "Mr. Ziven?"

"Agent Alton?" There was a slight hesitation in Ziven's recognition indicating that he was surprised that Alton was black. Kincade could see that this seemed to please Alton.

"Yes, sir." With a sense of confusion, Ziven extended his hand in a manner that indicated he didn't know whether it would be shook or cuffed. Alton took it in his hand, shaking it firmly, a complicated mixture of emotions being unleashed. "Why don't you get in the backseat."

"Aren't you going to handcuff me?"

"You're not planning to jump us, are you?"

Ziven smiled thinly. "No."

"Well then, I think we're pretty much going to run this on the honor system."

Both men got in the car. "This is Jack Kincade, you spoke to him on the phone."

Kincade turned around and shook his hand. "Again, I'm sorry for your loss."

"Thank you. I want to thank both of you. And because of that I am reluctant to ask you for something additional."

"Go ahead," Kincade said.

"I would like to be able to go to the funeral. If that is possible."

"Well, since you'll probably be in custody, it's not very likely."

Ziven's eyes sunk back into his head. "I understand. This is only fair."

"Unless . . . ," Kincade said. "Unless, you refuse to give us the disarming sequence to the bomb until we guarantee that you can go."

"I would not do this. We have made an agreement."

"Well, since you won't give us the combination unless you can go to the funeral, we have no choice but to agree."

Finally understanding, Ziven smiled gently, his eyes moist. "Thank you."

"Our boss has instructed us to take you to the bomb location. I hope you don't have any objections?"

"Will he be there?"

"Yes."

"Good, I will give him what he wants."

Alton drove with the red light flashing and Kincade got on the radio to let Thorne know they were en route. Within forty-five minutes, they arrived at the Cook County Jail. On the command side of the sandbags were a small number of Chicago police officers and FBI agents, less than a dozen in all. Procedure and common sense dictated that the area be cleared of all nonessential personnel during any disarming attempt. As Alton's car pulled up to the group, Thorne stepped forward.

Kincade said, "Mr. Ziven, this is the special agent in charge, Roy Thorne."

Thorne nodded curtly.

"Mr. Ziven has had one small additional request," Kincade said. "He'd like to attend his daughter's funeral."

Thorne said, "I assume we have your word, sir, that there will be no problems if we agree to that."

"I am willing to pay for what I have done. I am just grateful that it was not in vain. These two men have at last provided justice for my family. To do anything other than follow their orders to the letter would bring dishonor to myself and my family."

"Then of course you may attend."

A deep, involuntary breath caught in Ziven's throat. "I am sorry to tell you this, but . . . there is no combination."

Kincade said, "Are you saying there is no way to disarm this?"

"No, no, that's not it at all. This is not a bomb."

Thorne glanced over at the device. "But the dogs alerted to explosives."

"There are four very small pieces of plastic explosive packed against those drilled openings. Their only purpose was to give a positive reading to the dogs. They are not connected to anything. There is no battery or blasting cap. I didn't want anyone to get hurt; I just wanted someone to find my daughter."

"What about the surveillance tape? You used a screwdriver to arm it through that hole in the top."

"I knew about the camera. I did that only to convince you that it was in fact a bomb, and to be such, it had to appear that I was arming it."

For the briefest moment Thorne's eyes flashed dark. Then he remembered Ziven's daughter being taken out of the house in the anonymous black bag, and how, after Kincade's description, he decided not to look at the mummified body himself. "Then this was all for nothing."

"Only the FBI could have brought my family this justice. And they did. If you consider that *nothing*, then you are not the man I think you are."

Thorne's first impulse was to be furious with this seemingly meek individual who had held the city hostage. He supposed it would prove embarrassing that no one had figured out the bomb was a hoax, but now that the pressure was off, it was a little easier not to take himself too seriously. Besides, he wasn't sure he didn't admire the little man in the dark, baggy suit.

Alton said, "Mr. Ziven, are you telling us the truth? Because someone is going to have to find out. You don't want to cost anyone their life."

"Do you want me to prove it? I will flip all the switches if you like," Ziven said.

"Let's just slow everything down for a minute," Thorne said. He walked away from Ziven and signaled Kincade and Alton to follow him. Once out of earshot, he said, "Do you think this guy is suicidal?"

"I don't think so," Alton said.

"Maybe now that he knows his daughter is dead, he wants to take everyone with him who failed to save her," the SAC suggested.

"I'm not reading him like that at all," Alton said.

Thorne said, "You must realize, we can't let him near the bomb."

Kincade lit a cigarette and blew the smoke away from Alton. Then, matter-of-factly, he said, "I'll do it." No one responded. "I'm the bomb tech agent. And I agree with Ben, I think he's telling the truth."

Thorne called over to Lt. Elkins from the CPD Bomb Squad and motioned for him to join them. "Dan, Jack is volunteering to go rattle this thing. What do you think?"

"This may sound a little cold, but sooner or later, someone has to."

Thorne tugged at his ear reflectively while he stared at Ziven. "Okay, Jack, suit up."

It took almost ten minutes for Kincade to put on the protective gear. Inside the jail, the prisoners had been moved as far away as possible from the walls adjacent to the device. While the bomb squad lieutenant helped him, everyone was cleared from the immediate area. Eventually, they were the only two left at the site. "Okay, Dan, you'd better get out of here, too."

"Here's our radio. Any questions, I'll be close by. Before you try anything fancy, I'd just hit one of the switches. If that doesn't set it off, chances are he's telling the truth."

"What's 'anything fancy'?"

"Do you know how to operate a forklift?"

"I suppose I could figure it out."

"Come on," Elkins said and guided Kincade around the wall of sandbags. Up on the loading dock, five feet in front of the bomb, was a white forklift with the City of Chicago logo on the back. Between the fork and the driver's seat, four sandbags had been stacked high enough to give an additional shield of protection to the operator. "If the switches don't set it off, get it on the forklift and raise it a couple of feet. If it is a dummy, maybe we'll be able to look up inside." Elkins placed a flashlight on the ground next to the radio and then went over the forklift controls briefly. "Good luck."

Giving Elkins time to clear the area, Kincade walked around the device, his eyes locked on the toggle switches. "Pick a number," he said out loud. "Any number. One to ten." He took a moment to light a cigarette and inhaled deeply. "This sure seemed like a better idea fifteen minutes ago. You're not trying to buy the pot, are you, Conrad?" He took another deep drag and flicked the cigarette away. "But then does it really matter?" He leaned across the top, and with the flair of a concert pianist, flipped all ten switches with a single sweep of his hand.

Nothing.

Elkins had left the forklift running. Kincade looked at it and realized there was no way he could climb up or fit in the driver's seat wearing the armored suit. Now that he had thrown the switches, its protection no longer seemed necessary. With as much speed as possible, he shed the suit, leaving it in a pile next to the quietly rumbling machine. Once in the driver's seat, he eased the machine forward. The two heavy steel blades contacted the sheet metal box along the ground and pushed it back almost a foot before catching underneath. The box's movement was much rougher than he hoped. "That should prove there aren't any mercury switches." Slowly he elevated the rectangular box until it was more than three feet off the ground. He then turned off the engine and climbed down. With the flashlight in hand, he leaned under the device and examined its underside. Just as Ziven had said, it didn't contain a bomb. The frame was made of steel reinforcing rods like the ones they had seen in the garage. Dozens of extra rods along with slabs of steel plate had been welded into the structure simply to give it a convincing weight. In each of the four corners was a six-inch-long wooden triangle upon which sat a small wad of explosive molded into the corner. Kincade stood up shaking his head. "A hell of a bluff, Conrad. Good thing this wasn't something important like a poker game."

He picked up the radio. "All units, the device is safe. You can return to the rear of the jail."

Jack Kincade saw the relief on everyone's faces as they cautiously reappeared through the opening in the wall of sandbags. It wasn't only because a physically dangerous situation had been put to rest but also because a major pain in the ass was over. Two cases, one old, one imminent, but both significant, had been solved. And the agency's reputation, at least to the outside world, had been reestablished.

The first agent through the wall was Ben Alton; he was smiling broadly. "Well, look who turned out to be a hero."

"You may be confusing heroism with a moment of incredible stupidity."

Thorne came through the wall and went straight to the fake bomb. After looking up under it, he came over to Kincade and put a hand on his shoulder. "I know it turned out to be empty, Jack, but that took some balls. And you have no idea how much pressure this takes off of me."

"You mean trying to find something nice to say about me at my funeral?"

Tolerantly, Thorne laughed. "And Ben, I appreciate you coming back early to help out. You know I didn't want you involved in this, but fortunately you were too bullheaded to respect my wishes."

"Thanks, Boss."

Thorne turned back to Kincade. "And now I suppose you'll want to go back to being AWOL."

Kincade gave him an infectious smile. "A man has got to go with his strengths."

# 13

CONRAD ZIVEN AND HIS WIFE SAT BETWEEN KINCADE and Alton in the second row, a few feet from the center aisle at the front of which their daughter's closed coffin stood in stark defiance to the aphorism that parents should never have to bury their children. A framed $8 \times 10$ photo of her, the same one that had been poster-size above the mantel, sat on top, the image less grainy, rendering its colors warmer and more natural, her loss more inexcusable. Throughout the church, the women could be heard mourning, while the men, including Ziven, sat in stoic silence. Alton, sitting shoulder-to-shoulder with him, could feel the rigidity of his body and suspected he was filled with as much anguish and rage as a human being could be.

The majority of those in attendance were relatives and friends. Kincade glanced over at Ziven and could see that his eyes were locked on his daughter's photo, as if commanding her, through sheer force of will, to rise up and end this long, black, suffocating dream. Kincade suddenly realized he was the only one in the church who knew what she looked like under the perfectly polished coffin. He picked up a missal and started reading the copyright page to distract himself.

When the memorial service was over, the two agents stood next to Ziven as everyone filed past him, shaking his hand and embracing him. He had defied the government, but he had become a man of great honor to this small, patriotic subculture. A number of them had appeared at his arraignment, another impenetrable bureaucratic frustration. Ziven asked to plead guilty, to which the federal magistrate had no choice but to refuse, explaining pleas were not the purpose of the hearing, and appointed a federal defender to represent him. The lawyers who worked for the Federal Defenders Office were known for their dedication to the underdog and, like all people who selflessly helped those without hope, were paid accordingly. The individual appointed to represent Ziven was dressed in a dark, shapeless suit, which had faded to the lifeless gray of barn siding and could have easily been confused with those worn by the former communists who filled the back rows of the courtroom.

Appearances aside, he was an experienced lawyer and had been hit-and-run by enough FBI cases to know when he had a loser. Admissions made by Ziven to both Kincade and Alton were irreversibly damning. Ziven himself had gone to where the bomb was located and told agents that it posed no real threat. When painted into such tight corners, defense attorneys have only one option—to plead their client not guilty by reason of insanity. As an exemplary father, Ziven had been distraught over the loss of his daughter, so he made a hoax bomb, and so on and so on. As a capable attorney, he would quickly fill the jury with empathy and then convert that emotion into indignation as he unmasked the real villain—the FBI. It was they who, through apathy and indolence, had forced him to find a way to "motivate" the uncaring agents to simply do their job. Was it not true that the fabled agency was able to solve the case within a few hours when it became necessary? This man's only child had been taken from him, and then his wife lost to drugs because of the tragedy. So he found a way to maneuver the government, to get them to do what they should have done in the first place. And hadn't he immediately surrendered when the FBI finally did their job, just as he had promised, offering to disarm the bomb himself? The government is angry with him because he made them look foolish with a device that didn't have enough explosives in it to blow out a candle. Ladies and gentlemen of the jury, isn't that something we would all like to be guilty of?

The assistant United States attorney knew that the insanity plea would not hold up, but on the other hand, she also knew that the obvious defense would have a lot of jury appeal, in fact, far too much jury appeal. She was going to have to pare down the amount of punishment offered as part of any plea agreement. And, depending on which judge handled the case, she could see Ziven winding up with some sort of long-term probation. That didn't seem all bad to her, but she would like to see some sort of jail time, if for nothing else than to save a little governmental face, and right now the only way to ensure that was to get Ziven remanded to custody. The usual arguments ensued: "upstanding member of the community" versus "devastating disruption of law and order." The federal magistrate who, except in the case of the ridiculous, had a reputation for granting the government's requests, ordered a psychological evaluation and that Mr. Ziven should be held without bail. Alton asked the assistant United States attorney to query the judge about the defendant's attending his daughter's funeral, which the magistrate authorized without hesitation.

As soon as people started leaving the memorial service, Kincade and Alton hustled Ziven out a side door to their Bureau car. An hour later, they were standing at the entrance of the federal lockup checking their weapons with a U.S. marshal. Ziven said, "I appreciate you keeping your word. Being there today was very important." Both agents acknowledged him with a nod of their heads. "May I ask you something?"

"Sure," Alton said.

"This William Sloane, was he a big person?"

Sloane's computerized criminal history had listed him at five foot seven, 135 pounds. "Not especially," Alton answered. "Why?"

Ziven looked at him with an expression that indicated his question was going to be deliberately naïve. "I suppose it's the engineer in me, but I can't see how anyone, unless they were seven feet tall, could get a body up through the ceiling by themselves. Even with a ladder. I assume there was a ladder."

Alton didn't want to tell him that everyone was too busy taking bows to wonder how the girl had been put in the attic; he'd already been asked to suffer too much because of incompetence. "You'd be surprised what these people are capable of when they do something like this."

To Ziven, the response was intentionally nonspecific and ribboned with the insinuation that Alton's experience made him a better judge of the facts than an engineer with a detailed knowledge of physics. It was a more polished version of the answers—or lack of them—he used to receive in response to his weekly queries from the various kidnapping agents. Alton stepped up to the lockup window and knocked again to expedite their entrance. Conrad Ziven smiled to himself. He had seen something in the black agent's eyes—he had armed another bomb.

After returning Ziven to the marshal's custody, Alton drove Kincade back to where he had parked his minivan. As Kincade started to get out, he said, "Are you going back to work, or are you going to give your wife a break and take that last month of sick leave?"

"What is it that makes you think my personal life is your business?"

"You said I'd have to get to the point where I'd understand your answers. I think I have."

Alton thought about it. "Okay, let's give it a try. Right now, I'm going back to the office and find out what's going on. What do you think of that?"

"You know, Ben, nobody's keeping score."

"I am."

"Because of the cancer?"

"I've always kept score. Maybe a little more closely now."

"Is there any time in all that to enjoy yourself?"

"Six months ago a doctor told me if I would allow him to take my leg, I had a fifty-fifty chance to see snow again. Do you know what fifty-fifty is? Throw a coin up in the air, if it comes down tails, you're dead. Do you have any idea what that does to your outlook? So you get your leg cut off, something you've taken for granted for forty-five years, and then you start taking these poisons for months, which, if they don't give you the antidote, will kill you. And you know what—it's so bad that you think maybe you don't want the antidote. Inevitably, you ask yourself, Why am I really here? And you know what I came up with, Jack? Sure, my family is important, but the thing I couldn't get out of my head was I didn't want to find myself lying on my deathbed and figure out that I had lost."

"Lost *what?*"

"That life got the better of me, that I let it defeat me."

"That sounds a little hard to measure." Kincade tried to sound cynical, even dismissive, but Alton could tell that, like any man suddenly asked to contemplate his own obituary, he was asking because some part of him wanted to judge himself.

"Not really. Not if you look at yourself honestly. Just ask yourself, do you accept defeat after a few tries and write it off as 'just one of those things,' or do you push yourself to never concede? Do you roll with the punches, or do you do the punching? Do you take what life offers you, or do you do the ordering? If this cancer overwhelms me, so be it, but if I let it overwhelm my life then I've lost. A perfect example is Ziven. He's a winner, a big winner. They say you can't beat city hall—hell, he humiliated it."

"If you really believe that, then, right now you've got to see yourself as sitting pretty high up in the winner's circle."

"At the moment, I may well be, but there are other considerations. Do you know what the scariest thing in my life is? It's the phrase 'in remission.' It means that this disease sitting inside me could be triggered by something so minor it could never be detected. It may not happen, but the doctors, if pressed, will tell you the percentages are that it will. And every moment I don't occupy my mind with something else, it races back to that fact. So I constantly have to ask myself if I am still sitting in the winner's circle. The scoring—the real scoring—starts right now. And everything counts. Before I could put off certain things because they appeared too difficult, rationalizing that I could make up for it later on. But now I don't know if there is a later on. I can no longer allow myself to pass on the tough ones, because I suspect in the end, they're the only ones that will really count."

"Well, Ben, that is admirable, it really is, but for me, he who doesn't have the most fun loses."

"If that's what works for you, so be it. I'm not saying mine is the only way or even the healthiest. I suspect it's not, but for right now, it gets me through the night."

Kincade got out of the car and gave him a formal, but left-handed, salute. Alton watched as he drove off in his ridiculous minivan, three of its hubcaps missing, the tattered ends of the thin, plastic wood-grain appliques that had once decorated the sides of the vehicle flapping to the beat of the wind. It was a full-time job trying not to like Jack Kincade.

Alton had just finished reading the files for the first three bank trap cases. In an act of dispensation he would grant no other sinner, he smiled. He could see why they were still unsolved. There was practically no investigation reported in any of them. Kincade, true to his personal philosophy, was apparently having a good time, and in that pursuit, not expending his energy on anything as counterproductive as his cases. Considering Kincade's quick, logical mind, Alton wondered if he would trade his plodding, worn successes for possession of that hard, gleaming tool, even if it meant, because of some transcendental design flaw, allowing its potency to go fallow most of the time.

One of the files listed a bulky exhibit, an item of evidence too large to be kept in the file itself and therefore maintained in a secured room. According to the inventory sheet, it was one of the traps that had been recovered when a customer couldn't get her deposit to fall down the chute. It had been sitting in the evidence room for months, and Kincade still hadn't sent it to the lab for latent fingerprint examination.

Alton took the elevator down to the floor where the bulky exhibits were kept. After checking it out, he brought the trap back to his desk. Wrapped in brown shipping paper, it was a rather simple device, a one-foot-by-two-foot sheet of white plastic that had been painted flat black on one side. Oval handles were cut out of both ends. Alton pulled on a pair of evidence gloves and held it up in the overhead light so he could see any obvious fingerprints. It was a fairly common inspection, one most agents did routinely. Several partial latents were visible. Again, he wondered why Kincade hadn't submitted the item to the lab for examination.

Using the same procedure, he inspected the other side for additional prints. There appeared to be several others, including a half dozen partials, which looked to have enough ridge detail to be identifiable. Surely Kincade couldn't have missed all of them. And the file indicated that he had not taken any elimination prints, not even from the customer who had found the device or the security officer who had turned it over to him.

It was the only piece of physical evidence that linked the trapper to his four crimes. It was inexcusable that it hadn't been processed. But then that was Jack Kincade. Alton carefully repackaged the trap and then dictated a letter of transmittal to the laboratory. He also requested that the modus operandi be checked through the Bank Robbery MO database to determine if any banks in other parts of the country had been victimized by the same individual. Both procedures were routine, but Alton reminded himself that Kincade worked diligently to ensure that the word *routine* was never used to describe even the most incidental moment of his life.

Alton double-checked the status of all the unsolved bank robberies in the division. Even though the rate of solution appeared lower than before he had gone on sick leave, after researching the unresolved cases, he saw that it wasn't as bad as he first thought. A number of the cases were solved and just awaiting the case agent's paperwork to catch up with the reporting requirements of the Bureau. In fact, except for the first three trappings, most of the bank robberies were either solved or too recent to have that expectation.

Alton glanced at the clock on his desk. It was almost noon. He took out a sandwich and his Ashe biography.

He read and reread the first paragraph on the page for a few minutes, but Conrad Ziven's question kept forcing its way into his thoughts. How *could* one man have gotten a body up through the small opening in the ceiling? An opening that Jack Kincade, even with Alton's help, had difficulty negotiating.

He dialed the Wheeling Police Department. "Detective Lansing."

"Dan, Ben Alton."

"Hey, how are you? I was going to give you a call. The chief presented me with a letter from your director for the Ziven kidnapping. I've helped the feds before, but this is the first time I got anything out of it. Thanks."

"We couldn't have done it without you, Dan," Alton said. "I'm calling about the girl's autopsy. Did you attend it?"

"Yeah, what do you need?"

"Was there any bruising on the body, maybe from ropes?"

"She died of ligature strangulation. The coroner thought maybe a belt because the marks were wide, but that was all. What do you mean 'ropes,' like was she tied up?"

"No, possibly under the arms, something to help pull her up through the ceiling."

"No, nothing like that."

"Do you remember seeing a ladder anywhere around Sloane's house?"

"No, why?"

"Ziven asked us how one man could get the body up through the ceiling. It's been bugging me, that's all."

"Maybe she was alive when he took her up there."

"I doubt it. Ligature strangulation is usually an upright act; you need your feet firmly planted on the ground, especially if you're using a belt. In that attic, he would have been bent over. If she decided to fight she could have wedged herself in those rafters and given him a helluva go," Alton said. "It just doesn't feel right that he would have killed her up there. Did you ever know Sloane to work with anyone?"

"He was pretty much a loner, but you know he did time so I'm sure he knew a lot of assholes. You think there was somebody else involved?"

"I think the simplest explanation is usually the right one. And the simplest explanation is that he did this alone. If somebody else was involved, why wouldn't they have taken the stamps? No, it's just that since Ziven asked that question, it's been rattling around in the back of my head. I guess I just needed to see how it sounded out loud. Thanks, Dan."

Alton nibbled at his sandwich unenthusiastically. He opened his book, but read less than a sentence. Was there really someone else involved or was he just looking for a way to keep the kidnapping investigation alive so he could continue to prove himself? He rewrapped the sandwich and tossed it along with the book into his briefcase. If others were involved, he wasn't going to find out sitting there. And if Sloane acted alone—well, maybe he had earned the right to be wrong once in a while.

# 14

KINCADE HAD SIGNED IN AT THE RESIDENT AGENCY by phone. He told the senior agent that he had some leads to cover that were closer to his residence than the office. It was not an unusual procedure, but when it happened too often, the employee's explanations became suspect. In his six months at the RA, Kincade had abused it, drawing the initial kidding that usually registered with a conscientious agent as a warning to discontinue the practice. Of course, as the supervisor soon found out, to appeal to Kincade's sense of pride was effort injudiciously spent. The next management technique to be used in vain was a "closed door" session. And finally, an official warning was issued. Kincade, knowing exactly how many links there were in the leash, cut back.

But the solution of the bombing and kidnapping cases had, at least temporarily, left him unbound. The rules were in place, allegedly, for only one reason: to make agents, and ultimately their performances, more efficient while carrying out the FBI's mission. But with the lightning quick solutions of the two difficult cases, Kincade had proven that his own "system" was not to be tinkered with by subjecting him to the rules that were necessary to govern mere mortals. Not that he had solved the cases alone, he hadn't. But one of the nice things about working for the world's greatest investigative agency was that because it had been built on illusions, rumor and misinformation were eagerly welcomed, then embellished and eventually sworn to as fact. If it is good for the Myth, then the Truth is an acceptable loss. At the moment, Kincade knew those around him were greatly overestimating his worth as an agent, and it just didn't get any better than that. He had been thrown into the investigation against his will, but now had a free ride, something he understood better than most. And he was going to ride this gravy train until his supervisor boarded with another official warning.

Right now, though, he had another problem: the bank robbery coordinator. With things returning to normal, it was just a matter of time until Ben Alton aimed his energies at the bank trappings. Kincade had been able to divert his attention from the burglaries before, but now his interest would almost certainly be renewed. And, although they had worked well together, Kincade was certain that he had earned no slack because of it. He suspected, with some surprise, an even greater motivation was that he didn't want Alton, someone he had come to respect, to make that discovery. The first thing he had to do was clean his room. One of the disadvantages of his "condo" rate at the motel was that it did not include maid service, and the room had not been vacuumed in the six months that he had lived there. Generally, it took a small earthquake of personal resolution to get him to move the dust around, but Alton had smelled the spray paint used on the traps. Ever since then Kincade had tried to detect it in the air but couldn't. Between drinking and smoking, his sense of smell had become dulled and unreliable. But Alton had smelled it, and Kincade wasn't going to give him a second chance.

The door to his room was open and the warm fall sun angled in. B.C. lay across the threshold, its nose pointing out into the still air, ready to detect new opportunities. Kincade ran the vacuum cleaner he had borrowed from the manager. Its noise kept him from hearing Alton's car pull up.

As soon as Alton got out, the dog recognized him and, although not caring for the sound or hot-oil smell of the vacuum, trotted inside and stood in its path. Kincade turned off the machine and looked through the doorway. He reached down and scratched the Border collie behind the ear. "Good boy."

Alton knocked on the frame. "Jack, how you doing?"

"I'm a little surprised to see you."

"The RA said you were out covering leads. I thought you might be here." He grinned facetiously. "But vacuuming?"

Kincade sat down on the bed and pulled a cigarette off the nightstand. Holding up the lighter, he said, "Mind?" Alton waved away any objection and Kincade lit it. He motioned for Alton to have a seat in the recliner, but instead he opted to stand next to the desk. Unconsciously, his eyes started tracing the same faint black outline of paint on the desktop he had noticed the last time he was in the room. Its odd symmetry was somehow familiar. Kincade said, "There was a time in my life that I didn't need to vacuum."

"What changed?"

"I got married." He took a long drag on his cigarette. "What brings you out here? I didn't take you for the kind that likes to talk about old times."

"Why's that?"

"You're not a guy who likes to look over your shoulder and reminisce. Too many dragons to slay in the other direction."

"Actually, I am here about the kidnapping. But not to reminisce. Have you thought anymore about what Ziven said?"

"I'm sorry, what did he say?"

"About getting the girl's body up into the attic."

"To tell you the truth, no, I haven't. It's pretty much my personal policy that if they're happy downtown, my time is better spent figuring out what I can get away with before they come to their senses."

"I'm serious. Do you think anyone else was involved?"

"Are you basing this on the difficulty getting her up into the attic?"

"That and the fact that the drop was very smart," Alton insisted.

"These guys sit in prison and dream up ways to commit crimes. It might not have been his idea at all. He just got out and used it."

"It was executed without a hitch. And from everything we've heard about Billy Sloane, that was way beyond his skill level."

"If there was someone else, why didn't they take the stamps?"

"I don't know, but could you have gotten yourself up into that attic without me helping you, let alone a body?"

"Necessity is the mother of invention. And I'm not exactly a gymnast anymore. If someone else was involved, the stamps would be sitting in a private collection by now."

"Maybe they didn't know where the stamps were, and when Sloane got killed, they were afraid to go back to search the house because the body was there and the police might be watching."

Kincade's tone was edged with growing impatience. "There's way too many 'maybe's in that sentence for me to invest any more of my time. I'm sorry, Ben. You may well be right. But this is my stop, and I've already gotten off. If there is someone else, I'm sure you'll find him. You found the girl."

"Don't give me all the credit so you can blow me off."

"Then let me put it another way—no. Thorne had a gun to my head. That's why I got involved, but that's over. So again, N-O."

"You're a selfish person."

"Well, no shit."

"You gave your word to Ziven."

"I gave my word that I would defend the United States against all enemies, too. You've seen some of my files, how do you think that's working out?"

"Your self-loathing is unbelievable."

"That's the difference between us: I'm comfortable with mine, but you, you've created this hero complex to hide yours behind."

"Hero complex?"

"Did you ever ask yourself why you're always reading those biographies, men who history has labeled as heroes? The only thing I can figure is that you're looking for some magical blue-print."

Alton's face locked into a mask of indifference. Without look-ing at Kincade, he walked out and got into his car. To distract himself from the embarrassment of his tirade, Kincade walked over to the bed and picked up a scattering of newspapers. After shuffling them into an orderly stack, he went out the door to a large trash container in the parking lot and threw them in. He glanced at Alton. He had not started the engine, but instead ap-peared to be lost in thought.

Alton knew he had not found the girl. Kincade had uncov-ered almost every critical link in the case, from the ATM in the bank lobby being used as a lookout point to showing the stamps on TV to convince Ziven to surrender. If there was a second kid-napper, he was going to need Kincade's help, but after what had been said, that didn't look like a possibility. Closing his eyes, he tried to let his mind go blank. A geometric figure, an oval with flattened sides, appeared. What was that? Then he realized it was the top of Kincade's desk, the pattern in paint. Where had he seen it before? He had seen the shape somewhere else—today.

That was it—the trap. The desktop pattern was the negative of the handhold cut into that piece of plastic. The first time he had been there he had smelled paint, and Kincade had intention-ally changed the subject. Jack Kincade was the trapper? Could it possibly be? He wouldn't be the first agent to be caught stealing. It would certainly explain why the evidence hadn't been sent to the lab. The more he thought about it, the more it all fit together. And while an agent becoming a thief always seemed like a be-trayal to Alton, knowing Jack Kincade somehow mitigated its severity. He got out of the car and walked back into the room.

When Kincade saw him, he said, "Look, Ben, I'm sorry. Who-dunits just aren't as much fun as they used to be."

Alton went to the desk and took a moment to confirm his suspicion. "Does that mean I shouldn't expect you to ever iden-tify the trapper?"

The question was not only out of context, it was asked with the wrong rhythm. It should have been slightly indignant, or even sarcastic, but instead, it sounded like a pre-checkmate move, carefully worded to place the quarry in the easiest possible location for capture. Did he suspect that Kincade was the trapper? Why had he stared at the desktop before saying anything?

"Unlike the kidnapping, those cases are assigned to me. I'll do what I can, but right now I don't have any promising leads." He looked over at Alton; there was something he wasn't saying. Suddenly the need to defend himself took control. "The only way to catch a guy like this trapper is in the act, so if he doesn't hit again, there's probably not much I can do. You know how these things are solved: Nine out of ten times some cop will catch him in the act." Casually, continuing to straighten up the room, Kincade picked up a book off the nightstand and placed it on the desk. He could now see the black outline of the trap. His heart beat four quick, hard strokes.

"Then you won't mind if I do some work on them."

"I thought you were going to be looking into the possibility of a second kidnapper."

"It's a matter of the best use of my time." Alton's voice suddenly had a double edge to it. "Without you, I don't feel confident that I would be successful looking for a second person."

Kincade now realized that Alton had some degree of suspicion about him, certainly enough to work on him as a suspect. And Kincade had seen his tenacity. Again he flashed back to the black agent, artificial leg and all, throwing himself at that garage door, not once but twice, before taking it off its hinges. Kincade decided he didn't want to be taken off his. He smiled. "Well, since you can't seem to live without me, I guess I can spare you a couple of days."

"Good, I'll call the two prisons listed on his criminal history." Alton took his cell phone out of his briefcase.

"I know a bondsman. He can make some calls and get bail and court information," Kincade said, picking up the ancient black rotary telephone on the nightstand. While Alton's dialing produced a fugue of mechanical tones, Kincade hooked his index finger into the ten-hole disk and pulled it around to the stop, released it, and watched it glide back into place. There was something reassuring about the old phone. He dialed the second number. Its refusal to be rushed. The third. The fourth. Even the weight of the receiver seemed comforting, an anchor to the past.

When Maurice Wharfman answered, Kincade gave him Sloane's name and date of birth. The bondsman said he would check around and get back to him if he found anything. Twenty minutes later he called back. "Jack, I've never written a bond on him, but Paulie Gannon did. About a year before the kidnapping, he was arrested for possession of cocaine. Paulie wrote it for ten grand. Had a little hassle getting it back when Sloane was found dead, had to get a copy of the death certificate and all that."

"The possession—was it enough for distribution?"

"Less than a gram of coke. And it had been cut to the bone, so chances are it was for personal use."

"We're looking for any friends or relatives."

"The only thing listed was a woman, relationship unknown, Laura Welton, with a phone number. Do you want that?"

As Kincade wrote it down, he wondered if she was still there. For the kind of people who would befriend someone like Billy Sloane, four years was a long time to stay in one place. "You must have a contact at the phone company."

"You mean the FBI doesn't?"

"We need a subpoena for everything."

"One of my bounty hunters knows someone."

"You're a real patriot. How long will it take?"

"As soon as I can get ahold of Tex, he has the contact. A half hour or so."

"I'll call you."

Alton was just finishing his calls to the prisons. "There were only three known associates. I called the office; they're running them for CCHs and driver's licenses for current addresses. The only relative listed was his mother. Didn't Lansing say she was dead?"

"Yeah, that was her house. That's why it was boarded up. I

came up with a female associate with a phone number. He's getting me an address."

Alton's phone rang and as soon as he answered, he started taking notes. When he hung up, he said, "Of the three associates, one, Danny Milton, is still locked up and has been for the last eleven years on an armed robbery. Lee John Martin, whose whereabouts are unknown. The third one is Ronald David Bay who was paroled about a year before the kidnapping. His driver's license says he's living on the west side off Halsted, near Division. Sloane's body was found on the west side, which moves Ronald Bay to the top of my list."

Kincade picked up a tie and looped it around his neck and pulled on a shapeless sports coat. "To the Batmobile."

# 15

RONALD BAY'S NEIGHBORHOOD WAS THE KIND THAT agents spent most of their time in. The houses and small apartment buildings were stacked next to one another, separated only by narrow cement walkways, their exteriors in pale disrepair. Generations before, they had been occupied by working-class immigrants who were able to walk to their jobs. In a time before air-conditioning and television, the children played on into twilight as their parents watched from their front porches. But now the residents were generally unemployed and nomadic, following the decaying trail of low-rent dwellings. At night, only the desperate chanced the streets. As Kincade and Alton exited the Bureau car, a young man with long, dirty brown hair and a cracked green leather jacket gave them a quick sideward glance, lowered his head, and almost imperceptibly, increased his speed.

Bay's building was a weathered apartment house whose odor of damp decay and neglect was noticeable as soon as they walked into the vestibule. Alton gave a reassuring tug on the butt of his nine-millimeter and at the same time hitched up his trousers to disguise his apprehension. Kincade then remembered that he wasn't carrying a gun. "You're not carrying a backup, are you?"

For a moment Alton's eyebrows lowered while he tried to figure out the reason for the question. "You don't have your weapon?"

"Sorry."

Alton didn't say anything; he just ran his finger down the tenants' mailboxes until he found R. BAY 3B. "In the basement," he said.

Kincade tried the inner door; it was locked. A large steel plate protected the electronic bolt behind it. There were several gouges in the dark wooden frame revealing the tan oak under the aged varnish where someone had tried to pry it open. Alton pressed the bell for 3B. No one answered.

Kincade pressed the bell and held it. After thirty seconds the door buzzed. He held it open and motioned Alton to go first. "Arms before beauty."

"You're a beauty, all right." As he started to descend the stairs, Alton reached under his suit coat and hit the thumb release on his holster.

The last door along the dark hallway was 3B. Before knocking, they stood off to either side of it. The sound of Kincade's knuckles on the old wooden door rattled down the uncarpeted corridor.

"Yeah?" The voice was loud, barely muffled by the thin door.

"Looking for Ronald Bay," Alton said.

"Yeah, who are you?"

Both agents moved a few inches farther to the side, and Alton answered, "FBI."

Almost immediately, the dead bolt was thrown and the door swung open. "I'm Bay." He was average height with stooped, powerful shoulders. His record indicated that he was fifty-three, and his face had that lint-gray, spent looseness to it, an ex-convict's pallor. His eyes swept across the two men, verifying who they were. "Come on in."

Bay picked a cigarette out of the pack on a wooden kitchen table with two fingernails and lit it with a disposable lighter. He tossed the lighter on the table and then, with intentional irreverence, flopped into a torn, stuffed easy chair, the only place visible to sit down in the tiny apartment. The room had an out-of-place, pathological neatness about it, one that Kincade and Alton had seen before in the residences of ex-convicts. "So, what am I supposed to have done?"

Kincade said, "This is about someone you knew."

"Please close the door on your way out." "Please" was filled with all the courtesy and decorum of "fuck you."

"We're not looking for a snitch; the guy we're curious about is dead."

"Dead? Who's that?"

"Billy Sloane."

"This about that kidnapping?" Kincade glanced over at Alton. "It was in the paper," Bay interjected.

"That's what it's about."

Bay smiled. "I thought that's why you feds pinned things like this on dead guys, so you don't have to do any more work on it."

"Normally, that's true," Kincade said, "but we're one frame short this month, and, what with Christmas bonuses coming up—"

"Okay, okay, what do you want to know about him?"

"The first thing we want to know about him is where were you when the kidnapping happened?"

"When was it?"

"Three years ago last week."

Bay took a long drag on his cigarette, too long for someone who wasn't nervous. "I was down in Houston, working on an oil rig."

"When did you get back?"

"Little over a year ago. Check. I even had a Texas driver's license. Wildcat Petroleum, check it out. I don't do kidnappings, and I sure as hell don't kill kids."

"We'll look into it," Alton said, but didn't have to look at Kincade to know that they both believed Bay. "How about Sloane?"

"We did time together. I assume that's where you got my name because I never had anything to do with him on the outside. He was a punk, always hanging on, looking for someone to carry him. That doesn't make you many friends inside. Outside it makes you poison."

"Were you surprised to hear that he pulled off this kidnapping?"

"Surprised? When I knew him he couldn't pull off a rubber after he came."

"Do you know anybody who could have *inspired* him?" Kincade asked.

"Like I said, I knew him only inside, and he wasn't thought of as solid. Basically, he was a junkie who got in trouble because of his habit. If there was no such thing as cocaine, he'd've been stocking shelves at a Wal-Mart somewhere."

Alton took out a business card and handed it to him. "If you think of anything else; it's always confidential." He could see the hate in Bay's eyes. He had seen it in dozens of other white ex-cons who had survived the daily race wars in prison; they couldn't or wouldn't ever trust a black man. In his own way, he understood. "At least wait until we're out the door to tear it up."

Back in the car, Kincade settled into the seat and closed his eyes. "Where's that leave us?"

"Just Lee John Martin, if we can find him. And the girl—the one you got from the bondsman—what's her name?"

"Laura Welton. Let me see your cell phone." Kincade dialed Wharfman's number. "Wharf, it's Jack." Kincade wrote down an address. "Thanks. Friday? Probably, but I'll have to let you know." He disconnected the line. "She lives in Northbrook."

Alton put the car in gear and pulled out into traffic. "What's Friday?"

"We've got a weekly poker game."

"What kind of stakes?"

"More than a responsible person would think about betting."

Without turning, Kincade could feel Alton's stare, which, if returned, would necessitate an explanation. He just put his head back and closed his eyes.

Laura Welton's neighborhood was surprisingly middle class, not what either of them expected after being to Sloane's house. Whatever her connection to him was, it wasn't based on lifestyle. Her address turned out to be one of a couple dozen look-alike condos in a crisp, well-planned development. It was fairly new construction; the concrete that peeked out at the base of the buildings was still bright white, unstained by time.

When Alton rang the bell, a four-note chime played faintly inside. The door opened with a small, sucking *whoosh* that pulled the storm door closed. A woman in her mid-thirties leaned forward and pushed open the outer door. "Yes?" She was wearing a loose fitting, beige robe with a faded floral design. Her hair was a deep, chocolatey red and her skin had a dark orange freckled hue. Kincade had a soft spot for redheads and found himself wondering what she looked like under the robe. Her face was made up and her hair freshly done, giving the impression that she was about to go somewhere as soon as she finished dressing. There was a sexy confidence about her: She knew who she was, and she liked men who liked her looks.

Alton opened his credentials. "FBI?" she said with the usual mixture of surprise and defensiveness, and a slightly larger amount of awe than Ronald Bay had exhibited. "Well, come on in." As they walked by her, she took an extra moment to look at Kincade. She had noticed how he looked at her. It was something she was accustomed to at work, but she had never had the opportunity to find out if FBI agents were equally as appreciative. "I'm getting ready for work, but can I get you some coffee or something?"

"No, we're good," Alton said and in a light tone started the prescribed transitional small talk. "So, where do you work?"

"La Strada. It's an Italian restaurant in Hoffman Estates. Great pasta. I tend bar." She turned around and looked at a wall clock. "If you don't mind speaking up a little, I can finish getting dressed while we talk." She went into another room.

"That's fine. We're here about Billy Sloane."

Her head and one bare shoulder with a bra strap showing angled around the doorjamb. "That's what I figured, with the kidnapping and all. He was my stepbrother." She disappeared again and Kincade could hear cloth whispering as it was pulled along skin.

"How close were you?"

"Pretty close. You know, when he had a problem, I was one of his top three phone calls."

Kincade heard a zipper being pulled up.

"He never listed you on any of his arrests or prison records."

"He once told me he did that so if anything happened, I wouldn't be connected to him. But then he called when he needed bail, so I don't know what good it did."

"Were you in contact with him around the time of the kidnapping?"

She walked back in the room, checking a tiny, black-strapped wristwatch, and sat down. She was wearing a short black skirt, which exposed a nice length of her long muscular legs and a sheer white blouse that apparently wasn't designed to hide the swell of her breasts. "About the same as normal. He'd call once a week or so, usually to shoot the breeze. I've thought about it quite a bit since I saw on the news that he was involved; he really didn't give any indication that something was going on."

Kincade asked, "Who was he hanging around with at that time?"

She turned her knees directly toward him before answering. "That I knew of? Nobody. He wasn't the kind of person who made friends, and if he did, he'd usually screw them over before long."

Alton hesitated before he asked the next question. It wasn't his method to ask questions that gave out information, but there didn't seem to be any other way to find out what he wanted to know. "If we told you that we thought there might be someone else involved with Billy in this crime, would anyone come to mind?"

She took in a deep breath and then sighed, a little frustrated. "Again, he didn't have any, what you would call *partners*. In fact, about a year before the kidnapping, he was arrested for drugs; that's the time I bailed him out. The judge wanted him to stay someplace that had a telephone so he could be checked on, so I let him stay here for a couple of months. He seemed to be doing okay, and then I got a call from him one night at work. He had been arrested and needed me to bail him out again."

Alton dug into his briefcase and pulled out Sloane's CCH. "That's odd. I don't see any contact with the police after that cocaine arrest you bailed him out on."

"Well, when I got to the police station that night, he comes waltzing out real pleased with himself. Says it was a false alarm. A misunderstanding, only he's laughing."

"Did he ever mention what the charge was?"

"One reason Billy was a lousy crook was because he liked everybody to know his business. Once we got in my car, I couldn't shut him up. Said they had arrested him for arson, and had him good, caught him inside with the stuff and everything."

"Did he say why they let him go?"

"Only that he had friends in high places."

"Where was this?"

"China Hills."

Being careful not to look at him, Alton could feel Kincade's sense of recognition. China Hills was also the home of Leah Ziven. Alton stood up. "We've taken enough of your time, Laura." He handed her a card. "If you think of anything else, please call."

Kincade dug around in his pockets until he found a business card. "Ben, let me borrow your pen." He scratched through the Philadelphia FBI number and wrote down the resident agency's. "I haven't had a chance to get new cards yet."

Taking a moment to read his, she said, "Okay, Agent Kincade."

She stood close enough now that he could smell all the freshly layered fragrances that covered her. He inhaled deeply. "Jack," he corrected.

# 16

THAT WILLIAM SLOANE'S ARREST FOR ARSON DIDN'T appear on his rap sheet was a clear signal to both Kincade and Alton that he had agreed to become an informant for the China Hills Police Department. And having been released without his stepsister posting bail probably meant that whatever he had promised to do for them was significant. The practice was not uncommon in law enforcement, a technique by which good cases were often developed. But neither of the agents had any idea how, or even if, that was tied to the Ziven kidnapping.

Because the China Hills Police Department was small, Alton decided to ask for the chief. If Sloane had been "deputized," the chief would in all likelihood have firsthand knowledge. Besides, rank-and-file police officers, whether they like the FBI or not, were reluctant to identify their sources to anyone, even inside their own departments. Usually the chief understood the "big picture" a little better and, being more of a politician, was likely to see assisting the Bureau as advantageous.

As soon as they walked into Chief Tom McKay's office, they knew their chances of getting the information they wanted had just improved. On the wall was a plaque signifying that McKay had graduated from the FBI's National Academy. The school, nestled in the Marine Corps base at Quantico, Virginia, while thought of as primarily a training facility for FBI agents, had actually been established for the National Academy. Yearly, thousands of rising police officers from around the world went there to learn the latest techniques in law enforcement from Bureau instructors. Anyone possessing the plaque was automatically assumed a "good friend of the FBI."

Alton flipped open his credentials as McKay rose from behind his desk and offered his hand. "Always glad to see the Bureau."

After exchanging small talk about McKay's time at Quantico, Alton said, "Chief, you've probably heard on the news we've been working a three-year-old kidnapping—Leah Ziven." He paused, inviting confirmation.

"Sure, and with some interest. We had a small part in that case when it happened. The family lives here, as I'm sure you know. But she was abducted in Mundelein, at least that's where her car was found, at a convenience store. We gave you guys a hand covering the residence. I saw on the news last week that it had been solved. Congratulations. You got some nice press out of it. Too bad about the father. The little bit of contact I had with him, he seemed like a nice enough person."

"He probably is. I guess he just thought he needed a way to get our attention," Alton said. "But that's not why we're here. This shouldn't go any further, but we think there's a possibility a second person was involved." McKay leaned back in his chair and seemed to be waiting for something that he wasn't going to like hearing. "We'd like to ask you about Billy Sloane." Alton dragged out Sloane's name, indicating that the chief should recognize it from more than the recent newspaper accounts.

"I guess you found out he was a source for us."

"We've kind of pieced that together."

McKay got up and went over to the corner where a sturdy filing cabinet sat. Its top drawer had a combination dial set in it. With a practiced hand, he spun it back and forth quickly. He pulled down on the handle and opened the top drawer slightly, unlocking the rest of the drawers. Out of the third one, he took a manila folder and sat down at his desk. "What did you need to know about him?"

"Any associates, anyone who might have been in on it with him."

"I wasn't the chief at the time, but I know he was caught red-handed at the scene of an arson by one of our patrol officers. When he was brought in, he made some fairly grandiose promises."

"They always do," Alton said.

"Believe it or not, he did start making some cases for us. Nothing spectacular, mostly narcotics, lightweight stuff—" McKay's voice cut off, as if he were about to say, *But then.*

Alton said, "But then . . ."

He hesitated, opened the file, rechecked something, and closed it again. "There were some procedural problems."

Now Kincade spoke up. "Chief, if there is anybody who knows about being embarrassed by *procedural problems*, it's the Bureau."

"It's a little more complicated than that."

"Let me put it this way," Kincade said, "whatever you give us in here, stays in here. If we have to go stumbling around out there to get the answers, we may not be able to control who finds out what."

McKay paused a few seconds, trying to decide which course had the fewest bumps. "He started making some significant burglary and arson cases. Really good cases, the kind of felonies that just don't happen in China Hills. I'm told everybody was getting happy, but when the first case went to court, the defense starts screaming 'entrapment.' Which you know is nothing new for attorneys whose clients are caught in the act. But then it comes out in the pretrial that it *was* entrapment. The detective was picking the targets and getting Sloane to recruit these people. It was an unbelievable mess. There was going to be a huge stink. A couple of the defense attorneys threatened lawsuits. One was actually filed. The prosecutor wound up dumping all the cases. The old chief was fired and so was the detective who had handled Sloane."

"Did the chief know what was going on?" Kincade asked.

"Said he didn't. From what I've been able to find out, most of the problems, if not all of them, were caused by the detective."

"They must have been pretty blatant if everything had to be dumped. Didn't the detective know he was headed for these kinds of problems?" Kincade asked.

McKay laughed. "I'll be kind and say he was overzealous."

In his no-bullshit way, Alton said, "Don't be kind."

"Well, from what I was told, he was wound very tight. Every case became an obsession for him, like it was a personal vendetta."

"I can't imagine anyone being like that, can you, Ben?" Kincade said.

Alton ignored him. "Usually guys like that are closely watched. Evidently no one was bothering."

"Supposedly the old chief loved him. Traven—Alan Traven, that's his name—got the chief, and the department, a lot of ink. Everyone said you've never seen anyone so intense. He'd conduct surveillances on his own time, on the smallest of chances for an arrest on the smallest of charges. He was always out there, never went home. I guess that's how he made detective with just four years in. But he hated to be challenged. Went absolutely nuts on anyone who tried. I guess someone should have seen it coming, but that's always easier to say after the fact."

"We should probably talk to him. Maybe he knows if Sloane had any running buddies. Maybe some of the people he set up decided to get even by leaving him holding the bag."

McKay picked up his phone and told his secretary, "Doris, can you bring me the last address we had for Alan Traven?"

"How long ago was he fired?" Alton asked.

"I was hired almost four years ago. Both he and the former chief were terminated just before I came on board."

The secretary walked in and gave McKay a slip of paper. He gave it a cursory glance before handing it to Alton. "If you need anything else, just give me a call."

Kincade and Alton headed for Alan Traven's last known address just outside Deer Park. It turned out to be a modest neighborhood of small houses isolated from one another on different-size lots. Alton put the car in park in front of Traven's brown brick story-and-a-half. "Think we're chasing our tails, Jack?"

"This is your mystery, Doctor."

That this investigation, which seemed to be going nowhere, was Alton's idea struck a nerve. He looked straight ahead as he started to speak. Kincade had come to recognize the tactic as a prelude to a veiled insult or at least a mild diatribe. The slow, unemotional tone to Alton's voice confirmed that this was of the insult variety. "What do you think would happen if one agent was both very smart and very motivated?"

Intentionally, Kincade let his tone become cavalier. "I doubt if anyone with that kind of potential would stay in this outfit for very long. The FBI has become just another federal agency. Now, defending what we have failed to do is what we do best. The entire system with its rules and surveys and reports has become geared, not for success, but to identifying and managing the rate of failure. I'm afraid your superman wouldn't put up with it for long."

"So by trying to solve this case, I must be wrecking the curve."

"I'm glad you're finally seeing the error of your ways."

"You are one uplifting SOB." They walked up to the house and Alton knocked on the door. He waited for thirty seconds and tried again. "Doesn't look like he's home."

"Well, it is work hours. So if he's not home we can be pretty sure he hasn't become an FBI agent."

"Try the neighbor on that side, I'll get this one."

The men walked across the sparse lawn in opposite directions. The woman Kincade talked to said that she did not know Alan Traven well, but thought he worked construction. He usually didn't get home until after eight o'clock at night. By the time Kincade got back to the car, Alton was already sitting inside. "He doesn't get home until after eight."

Alton said, "I got him at a local gym after work every day. Place called the Oomph Stone. Let's try it."

"A gym? Doesn't anyone in this case ever go to a bar?" Kincade called the radio room and got an address for the gym. It was located in a small, isolated strip mall about five miles from Traven's house.

It turned out to be a double storefront. Inside, one glance told them it was not a place that tried to attract middle-class people who were hoping to shed ten to fifteen pounds before bikini season. It was for hardcore lifters. There were no aerobics classes, bicycles, stair climbers, kickboxing classes, or shapely membership coordinators. Just tons of iron, mostly free weights, with some of the standard bodybuilding machines. The air was filled with the rancid ether of sweat and heavy metal music.

Although fairly crowded, there was only one woman working out. She was dressed in black. Her tank top revealed frighteningly large shoulders and arms, her waist cinched tightly in a thick leather weight belt. She looked at them with complete indifference. Alton said, "I think we've finally found you that date for the Christmas dance."

"I do have low standards, but I never date anyone who can kick a SWAT team's ass." A thunderous weight was dropped somewhere in the back and the shock rippled through the floor. The men were starting to notice the two agents, and they didn't seem any friendlier than the woman. Kincade said, "Now I know what that first day at the Cook County Jail must feel like."

The manager stood behind a small counter. He had glanced up from his newspaper when the two men in suits walked in but immediately went back to reading it, intentionally ignoring them. Alton stood over him and stared down, his quicksilver anger ready to ignite. The manager finally closed the paper. "Can I do something for you?"

"Looking for Alan Traven," Alton said, using the minimum number of words to return the man's rudeness.

"Who are you?"

"You know who we are, Slick."

He looked at both men slowly. Taking a small step back from the counter, he craned his head to the side. "I think that's him on the bench press in the back, in the white sweatshirt and glasses."

As they approached him, Traven was on his back pushing up a weight with relative ease, finishing his last repetition. Kincade quickly calculated that it was over three hundred pounds and had been done without anyone spotting him. Traven dropped the bar onto the bench racks with a metal clank. Then, noticing the two men who seemed to be waiting for him, he got to his feet. He had on a baggy sweatshirt, its sleeves cut off at mid-forearm, and long, tapered black sweatpants. In his late thirties with round, titanium-rimmed glasses and short brown hair, he looked more like an MBA candidate than a former detective. Kincade estimated he was about five feet, eight inches, 170 pounds, not very big to be lifting all that weight. But he could see that the muscles of Traven's forearms were heavily developed. In contrast, he had small wrists and even smaller hands, and his face had a soft, graceful symmetry; its most striking feature was his dark, long-lashed eyes. He held himself erect, not with a weight-lifter's strength but with a dancer's balance.

"Alan Traven?" Alton asked.

He looked at both agents. "Yes." The single word came out quickly, confidently.

Alton opened his credentials. "We'd like to talk to you."

A new song came on the sound system noticeably louder than before. Kincade glanced back at the manager who was just turning back to his newspaper from the receiver, which sat on a shelf behind him. Traven raised his voice. "Sure."

"Maybe it would be better outside," Alton said.

Traven gestured with his hand that they should lead the way. As Alton walked by the manager, he glared at him. "Let's go sit in our car."

Traven got in the backseat, Kincade and Alton in the front. "What's this about?"

Both agents had heard the question hundreds of times before. And when it was asked, they always looked for a trace of discomfort. By arriving unannounced, the hope was to catch the person unawares, and if they were successful, deception would be easier to detect. Traven's response contained none of the stress that they were used to hearing.

Both agents turned around to face him. Alton said, "Billy Sloane."

Traven nodded mechanically. "I thought the FBI had solved the kidnapping."

"Just tying up some loose ends."

Being familiar with the 'loose ends' ploy, Traven smiled warily. "Okay, if that's the way you want to play it, what about Billy Sloane?"

There was a remote effeminacy to Traven's voice that made him somehow more calculating.

"When you were working him, who were his partners?"

Traven considered the question for a moment. "A couple of minor leaguers, no one polished enough to help him with the kidnapping. I assume that's what you're asking me."

Alton and Kincade looked at each other. Normally in an interview, one agent did all the talking. If both agents began firing questions, the person interviewed usually began to feel ganged up on and his or her candor diminished accordingly. Just as important, the second agent watched for the tiny tics of deception that invariably leak out under pressure. Traven's answer had alerted both agents that he was not going to be that easy to read. Having been a detective, he was aware of procedure. Kincade watched him more closely. "That's what we're asking you," Alton confirmed, letting him know that they weren't impressed with his insights.

"No, no one. He was pretty much a loner, not that he wanted to be. Billy was the kind of guy who really needed people. To the point that it usually repulsed them."

"Do you think Sloane could have done this by himself?"

"Not the Billy Sloane I knew."

"Does that mean you think someone helped him?"

"That means I don't think about it at all. I don't have to, because I was fired. But I'm sure you're aware of that."

"We've been to China Hills," Alton said matter-of-factly. "So, how about giving us a hand and thinking about it now."

Traven got a smile on his face that Kincade couldn't quite decipher. Then he realized that the ex-cop was studying them with an equal intensity. "If I had been there three years ago, I could have told you how to solve it."

"Okay," Alton said, "how?"

"From what I read, the key was the cell phone call to Ziven at the phone booth. I would have had the phone company do a Terminating Number Survey to see where the call had been made from." Kincade noticed that while Traven enunciated each word clearly, it was accomplished with some effort. He released his words with precision, one at a time, careful not to allow his tongue to touch any other part of his mouth or teeth. With less of an effort, Kincade suspected a lisp would have been the result. But he had detected something else. There had been the slightest emphasis on the word *read*. It might mean nothing more that he was protesting his firing, only allowed to "read" about the case, or it might mean something more. Like all such tiny flags, it could not be judged by itself; Kincade would have to wait and see if any others surfaced, and if they did, analyze them collectively.

"What's a Terminating Number Survey?" Alton asked.

The crooked smile was back on Traven's face. "To oversimplify it, it's reverse toll records. If you know what number was called and when, the phone company can tell you where it originated."

Alton said, "You ever hear of it, Jack?"

"No."

Traven said, "When I was a detective, I once had an extortion case against the local office of the phone company. One of their security guys did it for me. The FBI never used it?"

Alton cleared his throat, slightly embarrassed, and Kincade thought Traven's smile got a little brighter. "We'll check it out. But that still doesn't tell us if someone else was involved."

Traven appeared to consider something for a moment. "I saw those protective plastic covers for the stamps on the news. Did you have them examined for fingerprints? If there was someone else involved, you might have three sets of prints on them: Ziven's, Sloane's, and your mystery man's."

There was an air of assurance in Traven's tone, as if he knew exactly whose prints were on the stamp sleeves. Alton stared at him for a few moments. "I'm a little confused," Alton started. The phrase, used to get the person to overexplain and possibly tell an irretrievable lie, alerted Kincade to the fact that Alton was about to put some stress on Traven. He didn't know if it was because the ex-cop had embarrassed them or if the black agent, for some reason, had become suspicious. "You've said that you didn't think Sloane was capable of pulling this off by himself, but when I asked you who, you changed the subject. So let me ask you again, who could have helped him?"

"It didn't take long to figure out you couldn't trust Billy Sloane. So to answer your question, I don't know who would be foolish enough to get involved with him."

Remembering what the China Hills chief had told them about Traven hating to be challenged, Alton said, "Didn't you get involved with him?" Kincade knew where Alton was heading and watched Traven for any reaction, but the intentionally misleading accusation didn't seem to cause any noticeable anxiety in him, a characteristic not uncommon in individuals with psychopathic personalities. "I mean when you worked him as an informant."

"I assume we're through."

"I guess you didn't like the question any better the second time." Alton took out one of his business cards and handed it to Traven. "If anything else should come to you, I'm sure you'll give us a call. Jack, do you have anything?"

Kincade wanted to see if lightening the conversation would reveal anything. Controlled individuals can gird themselves against stressful moments and react calmly, but switching gears to small talk is usually too big a change to disguise. "Alan, where are you working now?"

"Tensor Construction. Heavy equipment."

Kincade looked at his smooth pale skin. "You work outside?"

"You mean because I'm not tan. I wear sunblock." The same unreadable smile settled over his face. "Being dark might seem like a good thing, but everyone knows the problems that it causes, so I try to keep myself as white as possible." Traven briefly glanced at Alton for a reaction, then got out of the car and walked back inside the Oomph Stone.

With his mouth slightly agape, Alton turned to Kincade and said, "Am I crazy or was that a racial shot?"

"Racial?" Kincade, who had also been startled by Traven's comment, grinned. "Why does everything always have to be racial with you darkies?"

Alton's only response was to stab his key in the ignition, letting Kincade know he was in no mood for his humor. He started the car with a roar, but then sat there lost in thought. After a few minutes he turned the engine off. "Do you think *this* guy could be the second kidnapper?"

"If he is, and the Terminating Number Survey lead would have solved the case three years ago, that means he intentionally left it for us to follow to Sloane. Which means he would have to make sure that when Sloane was identified, he wouldn't be in a position to give up Traven. And the only way to be sure of that was to personally see to Sloane's early exit from this life."

"But if he didn't take the stamps, what was his motive?"

"From what the chief at China Hills said, that job was his entire life, so if I had to guess, I'd say revenge against anyone and everyone who he thought was responsible for taking it away. And part of that responsibility was Sloane getting him fired, so he would have taken care of all his enemies with one well-planned kidnapping."

"He'd have to be one twisted human being because no one would have known but him."

"I got the impression that he doesn't really care what other people think. He doesn't recognize anything beyond his own needs." Alton picked up his cell phone and dialed. "Who're you calling?"

"The tech room." After a short conversation about Terminating Number Survey with one of the technical agents, Alton hung up. "Interesting. It's an old, little-known procedure. The phone company used to have a specially designed computer run that could determine who was calling a certain number. Three years ago, they had different computers, much less sophisticated, and, to do it, they had to shut down the normal functions temporarily. When I gave him the circumstances of the kidnapping, he said it would have given us the number that called the cell phone at the booth."

"Too bad somebody didn't think of it three years ago."

"It was a costly and time-consuming process, so the phone company didn't advertise it," Alton said. "Anyway, if it had been used, I'm sure it would have come back to Sloane and he would have been written off as acting alone."

"If Traven is the second kidnapper, I'll guarantee you there is a third set of fingerprints on those stamps."

"And you can be sure that none of them will be his."

"I'm sure you're right," Kincade said. "They'll belong to someone else who is dead, or we won't be able to identify, so if this ever did go to trial, there's proof that our 'mystery man,' as he put it, is the real kidnapper and not Alan Traven, who the government is obviously framing. Give the guy credit, not only is the crime perfect, he's already built in an ironclad defense."

Alton started the car again.

"Where we going?"

"This all sounds great while we sit around theorizing, but the fact is, we don't know he's involved for sure. At least we can't prove it."

Alton drove to the front of the gym and up onto the sidewalk. "Maybe if I talk to him nicely, he'll confess," Alton said and started to get out. When Kincade opened his door to follow, Alton stopped him. "Why don't you wait here. Something tells me he's going to be a little more candid if he can get me one-on-one." He aimed a half-serious glare at Kincade. "Me being a darkie and all." Alton got out and, as he always did, let his weight settle on both legs. He pulled himself to full height and threw open the gym's door. Glancing back, his face exhilarated, he wagged his eyebrows at Kincade and went in.

Inside the Oomph Stone, Alton was met by an eerie calm.

The concussive music had been shut off and the manager had disappeared. Even the gym's light seemed to have been dimmed. In the back at the same weight bench, Alton could see Traven's sweatshirt glowing white in the stinted light. He sat with his elbows on his knees, his hands patiently folded. The blood surged in Alton's head as he walked back through a gauntlet of blurred, mildly contemptuous faces. Surrounded by all the overpowering physical ability, he increased his effort to eliminate the hitch from his stride, but with each step, he was convinced that it became more obvious.

Traven appeared to be waiting for him, his smile malicious and far less inhibited than it had been in the car. "I thought you would have to come in here alone." His tone was that of a challenger about to take on an aged champion, the belt far less important than the opportunity to humiliate him.

"What did you tell your partner, that there was a better chance of me doing something stupid without witnesses? But we both know this is really about you proving you're a man. That seems to be a necessity with *African Americans*. And even more so, I would suspect, with gimpy ones."

A controlled smile settled on Alton's face. "Well, not all of us can be real men and strangle little sixteen-year-old girls. But then, I bet that was Billy and not you, right, Al?"

Something vicious flickered at the backs of Traven's eyes, then vanished. "Why don't you admit it—Billy Sloane was just a whole lot smarter than you guys."

"I guess the clues are a lot more obvious when you're committing a crime than investigating it."

"Am I being accused of something?"

"No, but I'm going to make your life miserable anyway."

"You're a little late. China Hills already did that."

Alton leaned in closer. "You don't know what misery is. You're going down for this."

"Better be careful, Kunta Kinte, that might be a little more weight than you're used to. There's no affirmative action out here." Traven dropped back, lifted the massive barbell off the rack, and started pressing it.

Alton grabbed the bar in the middle with one hand and leaned his entire weight onto it, pushing it down toward Traven's throat. After a few seconds of useless struggle, the ex-detective's eyes began to widen with fear. Alton bent over and whispered, "Now you know how she felt, you sick fuck." Alton released his grip, and Traven used the little strength he had left to push the bar up, just high enough to drop it back on the rack. Alton walked out at a comfortable speed, not caring how much he limped.

"Well?" Kincade asked when Alton got back in the car.

"It's him."

"Did he sign the confession?"

"Apparently it is about revenge. He's still pissed off about losing his badge. Whatever demons that job kept at bay were released when he was fired."

"Now the problem is proving it. After three years I doubt he's left any evidence lying around for us to find." Kincade could see a look of confidence on Alton's face. "But I assume there's an evil plan rattling around inside that fevered brain of yours."

"We'll bumperlock him."

Escaping air whistled between Kincade's lips, revealing some reservation. "That's an awful big commitment for someone we have no evidence against."

"That's why it's necessary. Our only hope is to get him to self-destruct."

"Ben, if Traven is the right guy, he isn't your average felon. He killed two people, one a sixteen-year-old girl, out of revenge. And now he's more or less challenging us to prove it. From where I sit that makes him pretty dangerous."

"So we should just go after the easy ones."

Kincade suspected that Alton's race-against-death scorekeeping was responsible for his decision. He was convinced that the more insurmountable a situation was, the more inexcusable its avoidance. Kincade, however, had a healthy regard for caution. If Traven was responsible, it meant he had a great capacity for violence, or more accurately, an unusual control over it. Most criminals used it because they couldn't help themselves, but for him it had simply been a tool to use when necessary. And that made Traven far more evil than any one man was good, even Ben Alton. "If you're asking if I have any problem being a hypocrite, I don't."

Alton's voice gained a new level of authority, reminding Kincade of his likely suspicions about the bank burglaries. "I'm not asking."

## 17

BUMPERLOCKING WAS A TACTIC OF ATTRITION, ONE
that was designed to wear down the opponent, to give him the
impression that justice—in this case the FBI—was going to be in
his rearview mirror for all of eternity. But the cost was manpower. The target had to be followed twenty-four hours a day
and by enough agents that it was continuously obvious so the individual was never able to have a moment's peace. Alton had
gone to the SAC to get his approval for the additional troops. He
explained how Traven had been developed as a suspect and his
reaction when confronted. The Terminating Number Survey
statement had been the clincher. Thorne was a little disappointed that Alton had instituted additional investigation on the
case without informing him, but he understood hunches and an
agent's reluctance to expose them before they harden into probability. And anyone willing to flaunt their crimes in the law's face
was worthy of a full effort, not because it was the FBI's face but
because anyone who had no fear of justice wouldn't hesitate to
kill again should the notion strike them. Alton convinced him
that there was no way to make a case against Traven unless they
went on an all-out attack. But a shadow of concern spread across
Thorne's consent. As someone who had made a career of dealing
with dangerous people, he reminded Alton that the very thing
that made Traven such a worthy target also made him a danger-

ous one. Although Alton said he understood, the SAC saw an urgency in him indicating that caution was not going to be one of his priorities.

Alton immediately arranged for the surveillance squad to follow Traven around the clock. He then told them, in all likelihood, the ex-cop would easily detect their efforts, and if for some reason that didn't happen, they should become increasingly obvious until it did. The unit rarely used bumperlocking, but occasionally, when all other logical avenues of investigation had been exhausted, the counterintuitive technique could sometimes produce unexplainable results, most commonly causing the individual, in one form or another, to give himself up. Normally, the objective of surveillance was to see and not be seen, but after the initial mental adjustments were made, the far less intensive procedure could be a welcome change.

The next morning, Alton picked up Kincade at the motel a little before nine. He walked out with the Border collie at his side. "Okay if we take B.C. along? He's been eating my clothes when I'm gone during the day."

"I don't know what's worse, his taste in roommates or cuisine."

"I think he gets lonely being left all day."

"One of you really should get some codependency counseling," Alton said.

Kincade opened the rear door and the dog jumped in, immediately hanging his head over the front seat to be petted, which Alton did with some enthusiasm. "Thanks, Ben. He won't be any trouble." Alton lowered the rear window so the dog's face could slipstream through the cool morning air. "I knew you had a soft spot for abandoned creatures," Kincade said.

"Don't think of yourself as abandoned; it's more like you're temporarily misplaced."

"I am indeed fortunate to be in the presence of such a compassionate human being," he said as he inspected Alton's silky blue double-breasted suit. "And by the way, I wouldn't be too quick to jump on other people's clothes there, Shaft."

"When's the last time this poor hound ate?"

"You mean a nonwoven substance?"

"I'm certainly not a dog expert, but I'm willing to go out on a limb and predict that if you fed him once in a while, he wouldn't find it necessary to dine on your Blue Light specials. Let me find a drive-thru somewhere."

"So you don't have a dog?"

"No, thank you very much. Even though my daughter has had the full-court press on lately. Tess thinks it's because her older brother, and partner in crime, went off to college this year."

"Think she'd like B.C.?"

"Just like that, huh? It's a real comfort knowing I'm working with someone as loyal as you."

Their first stop was Traven's house. Leaving the freshly fed Border collie to nap in the backseat, the two agents each took off in a different direction to talk to neighbors. The sky was clear and the morning air cool. Kincade took a moment to feel the late autumn sun on his face.

The plan was to ask questions, which while nonaccusatory, would leave those spoken to with the impression that Traven might well have had something to do with the deaths of Leah Ziven and Billy Sloane. The first door Kincade knocked on was answered by a woman in her seventies who was wearing nothing but a sheer yellow nightgown. Her hair was a champagne blond and ingeniously held in place by a series of small buttresses constructed solely of tissue paper and silver pinch clips. Between her long, pendulous breasts, she held an incredibly overweight tiger cat, its green eyes narrowed into menacing vertical slits. She aimed its claws out at Kincade with the defensive authority of a Taser. Once Kincade identified himself, the woman seemed to relax, unceremoniously dropping the big cat to the floor and exposing even more of the shifted planes and shadows of her aged torso. She invited him in for coffee, but with uncharacteristic awkwardness, he declined. With eyes diverted, Kincade ran through the questions about Traven nervously, causing the woman to regain not only her suspicions of the uninvited visitor but also the need for the physical buffer of the tiger, which she retrieved and hoisted back into the lost valley of her bosom. As he was about to depart, she asked him for his card, which he told her he was fresh out of, but if she needed him, she just had to call the Chicago office and ask for him. His name? Gathering his best come-hither smile, he said, "Ben Alton, darlin'."

He spoke to two more neighbors before returning to the car. "Anyone seem like they were going to let Traven know we were here?" Alton asked.

"Maybe, I can't say for sure."

"I had a couple that weren't anxious to open their door for an African American no matter how many badges I showed them. I left my card. He'll get the word."

As Alton pulled away from the curb, he radioed the surveillance crew, but there was no answer. "Wonder where they are." A few minutes later, he tried again. This time, the team leader answered, and Alton said, "I tried you before, any problems?"

"Sorry about that. I heard you, but they're doing some blasting on the site here, and there are signs all over the place not to make any radio transmissions. So I had to drive away from the area to answer you."

"Is he still there?"

"Yeah, we've got an eye on him and his truck."

"Does he have an eye on you?"

"If he doesn't, he has to be blind."

"Okay, we're en route. After we get done there, keep close to him. We're hoping when he sees me spreading the word, it'll provoke something."

"We're ready."

A large tan and green stucco office building, one of the proposed structures, was painted on a large white sign marking the entrance to the construction site. At the bottom was a map showing exactly where each of the fifteen two-story office buildings was going to be located. Alton pulled the car up to a trailer that was the construction office. The two agents asked the same kinds of questions they had of Traven's neighbors, again seeding suspicion. They then got directions to where he was working. Walking through the site, they spotted him on top of a bulldozer. Alton said, "You know, to put the maximum rattle on this guy, as much as he likes me, I think it would be better if he saw me talking to all his pals alone. Why don't you go off somewhere else and start trouble?"

"You sure?"

"With somebody like him, I'm sure." Alton walked on alone, carefully searching the immediate area for just the right coworker. A man in a sleeveless athletic-gray sweatshirt was pounding three-foot wooden stakes into the ground with a small sledgehammer. His arms, aged and fleshy, were completely covered from his shoulders to his wrists with a kaleidoscope of tattoos. Alton quickly scanned the inked markings to see if any of them were of telltale prison quality. The right arm was covered above and below the elbow with an elaborately drawn and colored peacock. In the bright sunlight, Alton could see a dark blue name crudely inked in script hidden underneath the bird's tail feathers, which swept down the forearm just touching the wrist. He could not make out all the letters of the tattoo. The man finally noticed him and turned around. "You must like birds," Alton said, his tone neither friendly nor adversarial. The man just stared at him and tightened his grip on the hammer. Alton opened his credentials and deliberately extended them toward the man's eyes as if he were incapable of reading them.

"I hate fucking birds," he answered, each word delivered with the anger of a knife thrust.

Alton knew he was not referring to the peacock tattoo, or even birds in general. This was the right man. "Do you know Alan Traven?"

For a moment the man held his gaze on the black agent and then with insulting slowness, turned his head to verify Traven's location on the bulldozer. He turned back and stared at Alton before answering, "No."

Alton smiled and with exaggerated naïveté said, "Really? That's him on the bulldozer."

"How about that?"

Alton knew he would be wasting time with subtlety. "We're investigating a kidnapping and a couple of murders, one was a sixteen-year-old girl. Did you ever hear Traven talking about anything like that?"

Again, he turned and looked at Traven. "I already told you, I don't know the guy."

"And you don't like fucking birds." Alton stared at him until he returned to the stake, driving it farther than necessary into the ground.

Alton looked up at Traven. He sat motionless on the seat of his idling bulldozer, watching him. Alton then stopped another worker walking by and began questioning him. Traven went back to work, occasionally turning back to see if Alton was still there. And so it went, through a series of short interviews, for a good half hour. Finally, when Traven turned around, Alton was standing alone, not twenty feet away, observing him. He smiled and waved good-bye. Traven stood up on top of the bulldozer, his arms hanging loosely at his sides, completely relaxed. Of all the possible reactions that Traven could have had to the FBI's full-scale assault, a lack of pucker was not the one that Alton wanted. There was something frightening about the way the former cop was behaving, not with anger but with agreement, as if accepting a challenge.

The last stop was the Oomph Stone. Alton went in alone for "maximum effect." When he came out fifteen minutes later, Kincade said, "I was starting to worry, but then I thought, What the hell, how bad can getting gang-banged be?"

"In case you're wondering where the next Aryan Nation meeting is, wonder no more."

"That bad?"

"One guy spit on my card while I was handing it to him. Surveillance have anything?"

"He's still working." Kincade laughed. "I'm sure after you putting the wood to him today, he's probably looking forward to coming here and blowing off a little steam."

"Not giving him a moment's peace; that's what this is all about. What time did that foreman say he got through?"

"Four-thirty, how about we get some lunch?"

"Okay, but let's head toward China Hills afterward. I want to see if they have any type of informant file on Sloane. Maybe there's something we missed. Besides, we should give the chief a heads-up now that we're zeroing in on Traven."

The China Hills Police Department, according to the chief, Tom McKay, did not keep files on informants "per se." It was a small department and any type of paperwork generated was kept to a minimum. An informant was considered paper-worthy only when he or she needed to be paid, and because the department really didn't have a budget for sources, that was infrequent. Any payment usually came out of the officer's own pocket, which kept the possibility to an absolute minimum. William Sloane, as far as McKay knew, had never been paid. If there were a record of anything, it would be in the prosecutor's file, because, ultimately, Billy Sloane was trying to work off his little problem with them.

"Chief, we thought you should know, we're looking real hard at Alan Traven as being involved in the kidnapping," Alton said.

Something knotted up inside of McKay. "Based on what?"

Alton explained about the Terminating Number Survey and his private conversation with him at the gym when Traven revealed as a possible motive revenge for the loss of his job.

"That seems pretty thin," the chief said.

"It's very thin. That's why we came back out here, to see if there was anything we missed."

"Like I told you, this all happened before I got here."

"Is there anyone else who might know something?"

"Because of the low pay, we have a big turnover. Almost everyone from back then is gone and those who are still here were too low ranking at the time to have any inside information."

"Maybe we'd better talk to the prosecutor. I want to see if there's anything in Sloane's file that might help us."

"Let me call over there and set it up. The prosecutor is a decent enough guy, but I got to warn you, he goes strictly by the book."

As they left the China Hills Police Department, Kincade took off his sport coat before getting in the car. Alton noticed he still wasn't wearing a weapon. "Haven't you found your gun yet?"

"Why, have you heard something about this prosecutor?"

"No, I was actually thinking you might need it in the not-too-distant future."

"I haven't really looked."

"Do you have any idea where it might be?"

"Actually, I've got it narrowed down to two places—Pennsylvania or Illinois. But I can't remember if I took it to Vegas last month."

"If you did, I'm sure some blackjack dealer is now wearing it."

Outside the prosecutor's office, they pulled into a parking space marked POLICE VEHICLES ONLY. Alton reached above the visor and took out a small sign marked FBI OFFICIAL BUSINESS and threw it on the dash.

Mike Hadley was a tall, balding man who was dressed in a brown three-piece suit and a starched blue cotton button-down shirt. His tie was a traditional tan, black, and yellow stripe from one of those men's catalogs that offered suit-and-tie matches so the wearer would not have to risk a clothing blunder. His hair was extremely thin, but somehow every strand was neatly in place. He shook both men's hands in a practiced fashion, but his smile was tense, his eyes skittish, as if he didn't like dealing with the FBI, not because of who they were but because he suspected he was about to be asked to do something unfamiliar to him.

An unspoken division of labor was developing between Alton and Kincade. Alton handled anything that needed intensity. When someone needed to be charmed, cajoled, or just plain lied to, Alton had learned to lean back and, with some wonder, watch Kincade do what he did best. "Thanks for seeing us, Mike. I don't know if Tom McKay told you, but we're working the Leah Ziven kidnapping."

"I thought they said on the news that you two had wrapped that up."

"I guess we just aren't ready to give up the spotlight." Hadley gave a short, perfunctory laugh. "Actually, there are a couple of small things that are bothering us, and to resolve them, we'd like to get a look at your file on Billy Sloane."

"I'd like to, I truly would, but without a subpoena . . ."

Hadley didn't have to finish; Kincade knew the rest of it. "Mike, to keep this simple, we're just looking for anything of lead value. How about you getting the file and looking through it to see if there is anything." Hadley started drumming his fingers slowly on the glass top that protected his desk. "If there is something, we'll come back with a subpoena." Kincade smiled conspiratorially, trying to bring Hadley into the fold. Both agents could see the attempt at camaraderie served only to make him more cautious.

Hadley picked up the phone and asked that the file be brought in. "What am I looking for?"

Alton took over. "Anything indicating that Sloane and Traven were doing more than entrapping people." As soon as he said "entrapping," he saw Hadley wince. "Sorry. Anything that will show they were working on more than what you were looking to prosecute."

A middle-aged woman brought the file in and asked if the two agents would like anything to drink. They both declined. Hadley spent the better part of ten minutes reading the file and finally closed it. His face appeared more relaxed, honest. "I can't see a thing in there, I truly can't, sorry." Kincade noted that was the second time Hadley had used the word *truly* as a proof of sincerity. It had been his experience that when people found it necessary to highlight their remarks with expressions like "To tell you the truth" or "In all honesty," their veracity was usually suspect. These phrases were subconscious "tells," offered to convince themselves as much as others. That he was overemphasizing his desire to cooperate meant, in the end, he wouldn't. Kincade tried again to get Hadley to let them see the file but he fell back on his claim that to do so would not be legal. They thanked him and left.

Kincade noticed that Alton looked tired, so he told him he would drive. "What do you think Traven is going to do, Ben?"

"I really don't know. We put a lot of pressure on him today."

"You mean *you* did."

"Well, if we're going to get anything from him, we've got to make his life miserable. Deep down, people like him hate everything and everyone. And when it comes to anyone different, he hates them just a hair more, so it makes sense that he sees it as my finger pushing the button. It's driving him crazy that we're after him, but it's even worse that a black man is leading the charge. That's why I've got to keep on him."

Kincade got off the expressway two stops before his usual exit. "Where you going, Jack?"

"I'd thought we'd get a drink."

"Isn't it a little early?"

"It's after four, you're not going back to the office now, are you?"

"I guess not," Alton said. "I'm not really supposed to drink."

"Who imposed that sanction, the doctors or Benjamin the Disciplined?"

"It just makes sense."

"It makes sense that you've got to let some of that steam out once in a while."

"Okay, one beer."

Kincade pulled into the parking lot of Roxie's. B.C. piled out of the car and instinctively started toward the door. Both men followed and, once inside, Kincade led the way to the deserted back room. The waitress eventually came in and arranged a couple of white cocktail napkins in front of them. "Hi, Jack. Haven't seen you for a while."

"Blame this guy, he's my new parole officer. Ben, meet Sue."

"Hi, Ben, what can I get you?"

"Any light beer, draft if you've got it?"

"I've got it. Vodka, Jack?"

"Yeah."

"Tabasco?"

"Please."

When she had walked away, Alton said, "Call it ESP, but I'm getting a vibration that you've been here before."

"Everybody needs a family."

"You never told me, do you have any kids?"

"A boy, fourteen. His name's Cole."

"Ever see him?"

"Not much."

"Where does he live?"

"In Rockford with his mother. That's really why I took the transfer here from Philadelphia, so I could see more of him. He's really a good kid."

"Your wife won't let you?"

"No, she's been reasonable about it. When I first got here, I'd have him for the weekend, but you've seen the dump I live in. Eventually, I figured the best thing for him is to see as little of me as possible. I'm not exactly a role model."

The waitress brought the drinks with a bowl of popcorn. Alton took a sip of beer, enjoying the almost forgotten taste. In a flat voice, he said, "You're wrong."

Kincade tapped six drops of the pepper sauce into his vodka, stirred it with the spoon that had been brought with it, and took a mouthful. "You seem pretty sure."

"Where I grew up a lot of us didn't know who our old man was, so it was considered normal to be without a father. Or at least the norm. You feel like you've been thrown away. Kids need parents." He took another sip of his beer and wiped his upper lip with a crooked index finger. "Even if you just drive out and see him for an hour once a week, it makes a difference. Is it because you're embarrassed, is that why you don't see him?"

Kincade took a single kernel of popcorn and carefully chewed it. "Probably."

"And it's not your room; it's the way you live."

Kincade took another piece of popcorn. "I thought this was supposed to be a friendly drink."

"I've been around you enough to know what I'm going to say won't change a thing, but I've got to say it—"

"No, you don't."

"Man, you're destroying yourself. You have all this talent . . . and what do you do with it?"

Kincade knew the statement was, at least in part, another reference to the trappings. And that meant it was time to change the subject. "Desire is a far greater gift than talent. Homeless shelters are full of talented people, but you're not likely to find anyone there with desire, not for long anyhow. And like it or not, that makes you the one to be envied."

"I never thought about it that way. Maybe you're right. Tess always says I do have a tendency to see the grass as greener on the other side."

"Do you know what that adage is really about?"

"I assume envy."

"It's not really about the other side, it's about your side and not liking it enough to see exactly how green it is," Kincade said. "Does that make any sense?"

"Yeah, I guess so."

"Ben, whatever you think is chasing you, you beat to death a long time ago. What you do every day is who you are. From where I'm standing, the grass under your feet is as green as it gets."

Alton took a moment to study the back of his hands. "You know, five years ago, I thought I had finally figured all that out. My father-in-law was dying. Emphysema. He was always a little indifferent to me, as though, by marrying his daughter, I had scammed my way into the family. But a strange thing happened. Like I said, he was on his deathbed and having a great deal of trouble breathing; his heart had slowed to the point where it wasn't going to be much longer. Everybody started going up to him, one at a time, to say good-bye. Holding his hand, they were all giving him a last hug or kiss, everyone crying. I'm standing there watching until it finally got to be my turn. I took his hand. Once he realized it was me, he used the little bit of strength he had left to pull me down to him. And he mumbled something. I couldn't make it out. Within five minutes, he was gone. I thought about that for a long time. My first thought was that, because he was in so much pain, and I was this guy from the streets, that he wanted me to somehow end his suffering. It took me back a little. All I could think about was what a distorted view he must have had of me. I didn't say a word about it to Tess for months. Then one day when we started talking about him, I told her what I thought. She smiled, almost painfully, because I had missed the point. She said, although her father would never admit it, he had a great respect for what I had become and even more so for where I had come from. She told me that when he pulled me close to him, it wasn't to kill him, it was to cure him. It took a while to sink in, but once it did, I realized what I had accomplished with my life." Alton stared off as if reliving some regret. "But when things like that take so long to realize, they can be pretty fragile. When they were getting ready to take my leg, I promised myself that, given another opportunity, I wasn't going to take anything for granted. I appreciate what you've said, Jack, but I've been back to being a *normal* person less than two weeks. I guess I'm trying to find out exactly who I am *now*."

Kincade's glass was empty and the waitress, without being summoned, brought him a fresh drink. She put a basket of french fries on the floor next to B.C. and patted him gently on the head. "How about you, Ben, ready?"

"Yes, maybe one more."

Kincade took a moment to appreciate the swaying cadence of her hips as she walked away. "Do you know who Aias was?" he asked.

"Aias? No."

"From Greek mythology."

"Mythology?"

"Don't laugh. Those old Greeks had an eye for human weakness like nobody before or since. Aias, next to Achilles, was the bravest of the Greeks in the Trojan War. After Achilles was killed in battle, Aias contended with Odysseus for his armor. But Odysseus won. Aias became so enraged that he eventually went mad and stabbed himself to death."

"I know there's a point to this."

"When Achilles was killed, Aias was the best the Greeks had, but he didn't possess the insight to understand that. He thought he needed the armor to prove it, some external identity, something molded in another man's image. All he had to do was look inside and trust himself. In the end he couldn't and wound up destroying his own greatness."

Sue brought Ben's drink and left. Kincade finished doctoring his drink with the Tabasco, and Alton held up his glass. "To green grass."

# 18

SUE SET ALTON'S THIRD BEER DOWN IN FRONT OF HIM. After a quick, experienced glance at his eyes, she said, "Can I get you something to eat, Ben?"

He smiled appreciatively. "No, thanks, I'm fine." He wasn't much of a drinker and the rigors of the last six months had made him even more susceptible to the relatively small amount of alcohol he'd already had. But there was something about being in Kincade's company that made him want to have another, to recline in its languor, to command the stiff business of polishing Benjamin Alton to stand at ease. For the first time he acknowledged his envy for Jack Kincade's freewheeling, fully dispatched course of life, and decided to visit, if only momentarily, its wonderfully undisciplined underworld.

As he was about to take a sip, his beeper went off. He tried to read the number while it was still clipped to his belt. "Who is it?" Kincade asked.

Alton took it off and held it at arm's length. "I don't know. There's a series of zeros after the number. Where's the phone?"

He found the public phone in the hallway and dialed the number. At the other end, a voice answered, "Alton?" It was Traven.

Alton felt his anger rise but allowed himself to answer only with icy indifference. "You beeped me."

"I want to meet with you."

"Come on down to the office in the morning."

"No, tonight. And not at your office. I'll meet you in the parking lot at the Oomph Stone."

"Why are we meeting?"

"I want to talk to you about the kidnapping." His tone was mechanical, without any discernible priority.

"How soon do you want us there?"

"Just you."

"Why just me?"

"In forty-five minutes." The line went dead.

Alton dialed another number. When he was finished, he went back to the booth. "That was Traven."

"Traven?"

"He wants me to meet him at the Oomph Stone. Alone."

"You're not going to, I hope."

"I called surveillance. They're still on him. I'll have plenty of company."

"I'll go with you."

"You can't. According to the crew who's on him, he's already there. On the off chance he is going to say something, it isn't going to happen if I don't observe the rules. Besides, you've been putting that vodka away at a pretty good clip. Come on, I'll drop you off. Anyway, it's Friday, isn't there a poker game somewhere you have to get to?"

Kincade hadn't realized what day it was. It was true, in a couple of hours, the room they were sitting in would be filled with smoke and his pals, gambling late into the night. "I think I'll give it a pass this week."

Alton looked at him in mock astonishment. "Christ, Jack, all this work isn't cramping your style, is it?"

Kincade returned his look of surprise. "I've got style?"

After Alton left Kincade and the dog at the motel, he radioed the surveillance crew that had been following Traven. "Ben, we lost him. After we talked to you, we had him at the gym, but then he took off. He was driving pretty crazy so we let him go, thinking he was going to come right back here to meet you. But that was a half hour ago, and he's not back yet."

"Don't worry about it, he's the one who called the meeting. He should be back there soon. I'm on my way."

Traven's meeting time came and went. Almost an hour later the surveillance crew chief called Alton. "Looks like your boy's a no-show."

Alton was tired. The two beers had drained him and he had spent the hour fighting off the urge to close his eyes. He still wasn't 100 percent, and he hadn't been sleeping that well. "It looks like he's changed his mind. What time is your crew being relieved?"

"We're on to midnight. We've got his house address, anything else you want us to sit on?"

"You have everything. I suppose he'll eventually show up at home. I'll call the midnight crew first thing in the morning." Alton watched as the three surveillance cars left their distant cover and headed north toward Traven's residence. He slipped the Bureau car into gear and pulled away slowly, momentarily disoriented as to the direction of his home. As he eased into traffic, he didn't notice the small dark car a hundred yards behind him, carefully keeping pace.

Even though it was Saturday, Alton got to the office well before 8 A.M. He wanted to catch the midnight surveillance crew in case they were relieved early. He was told that they had been unable to find Traven the rest of the night or even in the morning.

A single cell of a virulent fear started to warm with growth inside Alton. It didn't make sense. Why would Traven ask for a meeting and then completely disappear? Had he finally panicked and was now on the run? But that didn't make any sense either. Panic was a complete loss of power, and Traven didn't seem like someone who would allow that. Alton remembered the hate that had twisted Traven's mouth when confronted inside the gym, the calm challenge in his eyes the day before when he sat on top of the bulldozer. No, something else had to be going on.

Alton busied himself with paperwork until 10:00. He went up to the radio room and contacted the new surveillance team. They, too, were unable to locate Traven. He called Kincade but there was a busy signal. He then dialed the motel office, and the manager said it appeared that Kincade's phone was off the hook. Alton tried his pager, waited ten minutes, and then headed for the garage.

When Alton pulled into the Roman Inn parking lot, he saw a small foreign car parked next to Kincade's minivan. It seemed that he had seen it somewhere before. He checked his watch as he knocked on the door. It was a little after 11 A.M. There was no immediate answer. He knocked again. "Jack, open up, it's me." He could hear somebody starting to move around inside.

Kincade finally opened the door. He was wearing only boxers and his face was creased with sleep. He squinted into the sunlight. "Ben . . . what time is it?"

"It's almost time for lunch, what's going on?"

"Come on in." Alton stepped into the darkened room and could see that the bed had been slept in, and it looked like someone was still in it. Kincade said, "Give me a second," and disappeared into the bathroom, shutting the door. Alton waited for his eyes to adjust to the light.

A woman sat up in bed. "Hi. Ben Alton, isn't it?"

It was Laura Welton, Billy Sloane's stepsister. He smiled. "Yeah, how are you?"

Kincade emerged wearing a robe. "It's after eleven, Laura."

"Oh, man, I've got to get home and change for work."

"We'll give you a little privacy."

When they stepped outside, Alton lowered his voice. "How did that happen?"

Kincade took a pack of cigarettes out of his bathrobe pocket and lit one. "After you dropped me off last night, I was still thirsty, so I headed over to the restaurant where she tends bar, and . . ."

"And . . . ?"

"What, you can't connect the dots? How long have you been married?"

"Obviously too long." He smiled. "I didn't even know you liked women."

"Evidently hanging around with you has made me brazenly heterosexual." A yawn escaped from Kincade's mouth.

"Looks like you finally got a good night's sleep."

Kincade nodded. "Slept in the bed and everything."

"Who knows, maybe she's good for you," Alton said. "Clearly, she's a very charitable woman."

"If there's anyone who can show her the error of that path, it's me."

"I've been trying to call you. Traven's disappeared. He never showed last night. I don't know if he's boogied or what. Surveillance was on his house all night. Nothing."

"And since you're here, I'm assuming that you and I are going to see if we can find him."

Before Alton could answer, the door opened and Laura came out wearing her bar uniform minus the bow tie, which she was tucking into her purse. "Any chance I'll see you tonight, Agent Kincade?"

"If I can find my handcuffs, definitely."

She gave him a brief but sensuous kiss. "See ya, Ben." She got in her car and sped off into the late-morning traffic.

While Kincade got dressed, Alton went for coffee and even brought back a doughnut for B.C. The three of them had just gotten into the Bureau car when Alton's beeper went off. There was a series of nines after his home number, an emergency signal prearranged with Tess. In all the years that he had had a beeper, she never used it. He picked up his cell phone and dialed home. "Tess, it's me."

"I don't know where Sarah is."

Although the panic in her voice was obvious, he didn't want to let it ignite his. "Let's slow down a minute. What do you mean you don't know where she is?"

"Her girlfriend Myra just called me. She drove Sarah to the mall and they split up. Sarah had to return a skirt. They were supposed to meet in a half hour. Sarah never showed up."

"How long ago?"

"About two hours now."

A blinding white panic ripped through Alton, his head suddenly emptied of its balance. His daughter had never been late without calling. "Okay, I'm on my way. Try to keep this line clear."

As soon as he hung up, Kincade asked, "What is it?"

"Sarah's missing. Disappeared at the mall. I hope I'm wrong, but I'm afraid something's happened to her." He didn't want to tell Kincade his worst fear because he didn't want to hear the words, somehow giving them legitimacy.

"She's what, sixteen? Kids that age get distracted all the time."

"Not Sarah. She knows what I see, and how I worry. She would never do this."

Alton glanced quickly at Kincade, then turned away. "What is it, Ben?" But he wouldn't answer. "Come on, what is it?"

"I think I fucked up."

"What?"

"Traven," he admitted. "When he missed that meeting last night, I thought he got cold feet. But it makes sense now. He just wanted to get me to the gym, someplace familiar to him, so he could follow me home."

Neither man said anything for a moment as each tried to find some bit of logic that would refute the possibility. But it was not hard for Kincade to envision Traven doing something like that. After all, he had kidnapped Leah Ziven to take revenge against the China Hills PD. And for what Alton had done to him, Kincade was certain that he hated Alton far more than his former employer. Finally, Kincade said, "Why don't you head home. She'll probably show up before you get there. And just in case, I'll head down to the office. Give me a call when you get to the house."

Kincade and the dog got out of the car and watched as it fishtailed out of the motel lot. He had seen something in Alton's face that he didn't think was possible—bewildered, directionless fear. He put B.C. in his room and then hurried to the minivan.

# 19

BY THE TIME KINCADE GOT TO THE OFFICE, ALTON had arrived home and called the SAC. Sarah was still missing. Thorne was sitting at the small conference table in his office with three other men and a woman Kincade recognized as the media liaison. The only male agent he recognized was the ASAC, Al Bartoli. They were all taking notes as the SAC spoke. "According to Ben, Sarah was driven to the mall by a girlfriend to return a skirt. While she was doing that, the girlfriend, Myra Tonelli, went to a cosmetics counter in another store. They were supposed to meet a half hour later under a clock in the food court. Sarah never showed. I want the girlfriend interviewed in detail. See if she saw anybody following them or anything else suspicious."

"What about the store employees?" one of the other agents asked.

"Let's get some people out to run them down," Thorne said. "And have them check for surveillance cameras throughout the mall. Tom, when they arrive at the house, have one of your people get a recent picture of Sarah and bring it back here ASAP. Also send someone out to China Hills for a picture of Traven. I don't know how he got her, but hopefully somebody saw something."

Kincade said, "I'm sure it would be easy enough for him to

pose as a security officer, those badges are everywhere. He knows how to act and sound like a cop to the point where even an agent's daughter would be taken in."

"Okay," Thorne declared, "we are going to handle this as a legitimate kidnapping." He turned to Kincade. "You've interviewed this guy, Jack. Give us something to go on."

"When we talked to him, he was on the edge. Evidently, he's gone over. We know he's killed before. It appeared to us his real motive for the Ziven and Sloane murders was revenge. He wanted to show the world that he was smarter than the cops who fired him. And now, because Ben has figured it out and gone after him with total disregard, he wants to do the same to the Bureau. He wants to humiliate us and crush Ben at the same time."

Realizing the implications of what Kincade had said, the others around the table sat quietly for a few seconds. Kincade could feel Sarah's hand in his as her mother introduced them in the reception room that morning. This just couldn't be real. All his accumulated sins were now being exacted in the form of this nightmare. He tried to visualize what it must be like at the Alton house. He then realized that Traven wasn't trying to terrorize just Ben Alton, but everyone who would become aware of the abduction: his family, the FBI, and even Kincade; he was getting even with them all.

Thorne said, "Okay, Diane, as soon as we get both photographs, I want massive media coverage, that she's missing and we want him for questioning. Until this is resolved, I don't want to open a paper or turn on the TV without seeing those photos. And the rest of you, I want all agents working staggered shifts, sixteen on and eight off. And if you're off, you're on call. I want every tip that is generated to be investigated within the hour. When you're not covering leads, I want you out there talking to people, developing sources. I want to know everything there is to know about this animal, everything." Thorne looked at each of them for a moment. "Don't get to the end of this and then find out there was something that you didn't do that would have saved her life. Believe me, I've been on these when they have gone bad—you'll wind up second-guessing yourself for a long, long time. Any questions?"

An agent in his thirties with half-lens reading glasses sitting low on his nose said, "As the legal counsel, I have to present a warning: By implying Mr. Traven's possible involvement in the kidnapping—if this is indeed a kidnapping—we will be exposing the FBI to the possibility of a lawsuit."

Thorne turned to the ASAC. "Al, call Quantico and have them send the best available profiler out here ASAP. And find someone to put in that gym as a UC. If someone in there knows anything, I want us to know."

"Yes, sir," Bartoli said as he made a note about the undercover agent.

"And the next time I tell you to round up everyone for a conference about this kidnapping"—the SAC nodded at the legal counsel—"don't include him." The color in the agent's face drained away.

Thorne looked at the others. A quiet sense of purpose that not even the bomb at the jail had evoked was uniting them. What was happening to Ben Alton and his family could happen to any of them. They had felt infallible but now understood what it was like to be the Altons or even the Ziven family. Thorne was aware that their commitment as agents was being redefined. He had always attacked every case as if it had happened to him personally and now they were doing the same. "Is there anything else?" When no one said anything, he said, "Okay, let's get going." Everyone started to get up and Thorne said, "Hold on a minute, Jack."

"Do you want me to stay, sir?" Bartoli said.

"Why?" Thorne asked.

Bartoli seemed to take the exclusion personally. But because someone with his ambition could never find the advantage in faulting a superior, he turned his darkening stare on Kincade as if it were somehow his doing. He shut the door as he left. "Looks like the ASAC could be talked into disliking you," Thorne said.

"I'll take that as a sign that I'm doing something right."

"Don't take him lightly. I try to give him the impression that *I* do, but I never give people like him a clean shot at my back."

"Since I have neither the aspirations nor the lip balm necessary to become part of the Bureau's elite management team, I don't think he can hurt me too badly."

"I just wouldn't go out of my way to poke him in the eye," Thorne said. "What about you, do you have any leads you want to cover yourself?"

"Before I do anything, I thought I'd go out to Ben's and see what I could do for him."

"Go ahead, but I can tell you from the brief conversation I had with him, he's holding himself completely responsible. And you know how stubborn he is, so you're not going to change much of that," Thorne said. "You *know* what the best thing you can do for him is."

"I'll do everything I can to help find Sarah."

"Sometimes in a situation like this *everything* isn't enough. When I get a case like this, one of the first things I do is look around for someone who will do whatever is necessary, no matter the cost."

Kincade stared back at the SAC for a moment to let him know he realized exactly what was being asked of him. "Look no further."

When Kincade got to Alton's house, he parked in the street. A young agent he didn't know opened the door as he walked up the porch stairs. Tess came to greet him and formally shook his hand, thanking him for coming. He could tell she was acting out of an innate courtesy and forcing herself through the motions. He held her hand when she tried to take it back, causing her to focus a little more. "Tess, she's going to be all right." She stared at his lips as if they were speaking a strange dialect, indecipherable but with a lilt pleasing to the ear. "But first, I'm going to need some coffee."

She smiled weakly and turned to go. "I'll get you some. Ben's in the family room."

The space had been converted to a command center. A heavily upholstered couch, love seat, and easy chair were pushed against the nearest walls. Three long folding tables were set up and surrounded by folding chairs. Two agents were sitting in front of reel-to-reel tape recorders checking sound levels. Alton stood with his back to the room, shifting his weight on and off his leg, gazing out a sliding glass door into the backyard. "Ben," Kincade said.

He turned around and for a moment his memory strained to recognize Kincade's face. "Jack. Thanks for coming." He shook his hand warmly. "You were at the office?"

"Yeah."

"I don't suppose they've heard anything."

"You know Thorne—surround Illinois and start shooting anyone who isn't cooperating." Alton nodded his appreciation, but his face quickly retied itself into an anguished knot. "I'm going to get out there myself, as soon as you and I can figure out where I should start."

"I don't know how I missed him following me last night."

"If he did follow you home, he had to sit on this place for a while last night and probably this morning. Has anyone done a neighborhood canvass around here?"

"No, I don't think so. I should have thought of that."

"That's not your job right now. I'll be back in a little bit." Kincade left the house and walked up the block checking for vantage points from which the Alton house could have been watched. He then checked the street in the opposite direction. Once he got back inside the house, he called the major-case room and filled in the kidnapping supervisor. Alton and Tess were sitting in the kitchen, holding hands across the table. When Tess saw him she said, "Jack, your coffee. It'll just be a minute." She got up and started brewing a fresh pot.

Kincade sat down. "Lee Jackson's going to send out a couple of bodies to do a discreet neighborhood. How about the house behind you? Any way Traven could have set up back there?"

"No, unless he got into their house. I saw her out in the yard this morning so I don't think that's a possibility."

"I'll have them check with her anyhow."

Alton glanced up at his wife, who seemed slightly confused, momentarily unfamiliar with the clattering coffee-making equipment. He motioned for Kincade to follow him and led the way down to the basement where there were two stacks of water softener salt bags. They each sat down on one, and Alton asked, "What do you think he wants?"

"To embarrass the FBI."

"How?"

The question, although a single word, held the entire weight of a father's guilt, an ability to trace the cause of any problem, no matter how vague or labyrinthine its origins, directly back to himself. But Alton's "how" had an additional, darker purpose. He was asking if Traven intended to kill Sarah. Kincade had been trying to answer the question since he left the office and decided immediately that he would. The rest of the time had been spent trying to find a reason he wouldn't. Objectively, there were none. The one thing consistent in all Traven's actions was that he never left evidence behind which would incriminate him. And after his abduction of the girl, Sarah's ability to identify him made her evidence. Although Alton had asked the question, he, too, knew the answer, and like Kincade, was looking for something that could provide even the smallest possibility of hope. "I know he's a little crazy, but he's not nuts. I'm sure he's got a way out of this, and to have an out, Sarah has to be all right."

The argument was vague and not completely logical, but in his confused state, Alton decided to trust Kincade's assurances. Even if he could have deciphered the artful curve in it, he was too frightened to try. Kincade's words had suspended his worst fears, and right now that was something he needed more than anything else in the world. But then, uncontrollably, he said, "If anything happens to her, he will have no out because I'll kill him."

Alton's stare then became distant. Kincade guessed he was fighting off some new strain of self-denunciation. "Goddammit, Ben, I can't do this by myself."

Alton looked at him, his attention gathering. "Sorry."

"Come on, we can do this. Now, what are we overlooking? Let's start at the beginning. I need a jumping-off point."

"Well, the first thing we found out about Traven was that he was using Sloane as a snitch."

"Maybe I should go find those burglars the two of them tried to set up."

"They'd know Sloane, not Traven. I'm not sure how much good they'd do."

Alton's eyes started to lose their focus again. "What about Sloane's murder?" Kincade asked. "We haven't done anything with that yet. We know Traven did it, maybe there's something there. Where was his body found . . . Ben?"

"Ah, wasn't it on the west side of Chicago?"

Kincade knew it was. "I think that's right. I'll run it down at the Chicago PD. What was that deputy chief's name, the guy who was there at the bomb site?"

"This is my fault." Alton's eyes started filling with tears.

"Ben—"

"No, it is. I went after him like a maniac . . . so he came after me. I never even gave any thought to my family. First we couldn't solve Leah Ziven's kidnapping, and now it's Sarah."

Kincade stood up and took Alton by the arm, leading him upstairs. "Walk me to the car." When they got outside, Kincade turned him so they were facing each other. "Ben, can you keep a secret?" When Alton didn't answer, Kincade gave him a gentle smile. "Well, can you?"

"Yes, yes."

Kincade leaned in. "We're getting her back."

# 20

THE ASAC'S PRIVATE LINE RANG. WITH SOME RELUC-
tance, he pulled open his bottom drawer and lifted the receiver.
"Bartoli."

"Al . . . Marty Hampton."

"Marty?" Bartoli assumed any private call would be regarding
the kidnapping, but Hampton was the section chief in the Administrative Division at FBIHQ. His area of responsibility had
nothing to do with the investigation of violent crimes. "What
brings me up on your radar, on a Saturday yet?"

"I know you're probably busy with Alton's daughter, but
there's something heading your way I thought you would appreciate knowing about."

Several political subtleties were discernible in Hampton's
briefly stated purpose. The most obvious was the word "appreciate." It meant that at some time in the future, Hampton expected
Bartoli to return a yet-to-be-determined favor, undoubtedly
something that would advance his own career. That he would
call, knowing the kidnapping's priority, indicated he was referring
to an intelligence item of significant weight and probably one
which had a short shelf life. Although an unwanted problem was
about to be dumped in Bartoli's lap, he could see an upside to the
call: Because Hampton, stationed at FBIHQ, the seat of all Bureau buzz, was attempting to "place one in the bank," the deduc-

tion could be made that the price of Bartoli's stock within those hallowed halls must be on the rise. Favors weren't granted to those who were not seen as a good bet to return them in the immediate future. But while such reciprocity was a major currency of Bureau politics, its exchange rate was always negotiable. Bartoli had to minimize the impact of the information he was about to be given, which in turn would decrease the size of the favor owed. "Actually, it hasn't been bad for me. Thorne is running the kidnapping, and I'm running the office, which is not really that difficult." He ratcheted down his tone to sound as incurious as possible. "So, what's up?"

"Ah, I haven't taken this to the director yet, but I wanted to give you the heads-up before I do."

Hampton was trying to drive up the price by implying he was keeping the information from the head of the FBI. Bartoli pressed his secretary's buzzer three times, a prearranged signal they had so she would buzz him back, usually to get rid of an unwanted phone call. One loud buzz was returned. "Marty, can you hold on a minute, I've been waiting for this guy from IRS to call me back." Before Hampton could answer, Bartoli put him on hold. For the next couple of minutes, he read through the latest batch of office mail. Finally he picked up the phone and said, "Marty, I'm sorry, that guy is impossible to get off the line. What were you saying?"

"That you have an OPR problem heading your way." Hampton's voice was now a little injured, a little deflated.

Normally, a call that warned of an impending Office of Professional Responsibility investigation was considered a megafavor, but Bartoli had to be careful not to sound too grateful. "I'm always thankful to anyone who can keep me ahead of the curve."

The word "thankful" satisfied Hampton that Bartoli understood their unspoken contract. "Are you aware that you have four unsolved bank burglaries, all in the western suburban area?"

"What kind of bank burglaries?"

"Night depository traps."

Not wanting to admit that he had virtually no knowledge of

any criminal case within the Chicago Division, Bartoli said, "I know eventually you're going to tell me what bank burglaries have to do with the Administrative Division?"

"You have an agent assigned there, Jack Kincade. He's the case agent on all four burglaries. Do you know him?"

"Yes." Sensing that it was Kincade who was about to become the target of the OPR investigation, and in an effort to continue his tactic of depriving Hampton of the upper hand, Bartoli said, "We've had some problems with him. And there's something about him I've never trusted."

"Well, your bank robbery coordinator recently sent a recovered trap into Ident for latent examination. And as I'm sure you're aware, because agents can screw up anything, the examiner always checks the case agent's prints against any latents of value first. Kincade's prints were found on it."

"I don't understand; you just said agents mishandle evidence all the time."

"The device had a strip of two-sided tape at each end, I suppose to hold it in place in the chute. With a great deal of care, the examiner peeled it back and found a print underneath. It's Kincade's right index finger. The examiner says that no one but the person who constructed the trap could have left it there."

"Marty, that seems pretty thin to me. Maybe Kincade was fooling around with it and pulled it off and then pushed it back down."

"I asked the examiner about scenarios like that, and he said there would have been signs of tape being pulled up; there weren't any. This guy is one of the best we got, and he doesn't feel good about reporting it, but he's willing to testify that there's no question Kincade constructed the trap."

"As much as I don't like him, it still sounds questionable."

"You know he has had his Bureau car privileges suspended because of a drunk driving conviction in Philadelphia."

"I've read his file. But burglarizing banks is a little different than having a couple of drinks and then getting behind the wheel."

"When the bank robbery coordinator sent the trap in for latent work, he also asked the four cases be run through the Bank Robbery MO file. Ten years ago, a subject named Alfred James Manning used almost the exact same device over a hundred times . . . in Philadelphia, Al. And the case agent was John William Kincade."

Bartoli was silent for a few seconds. "That's pretty convincing."

"I'll need to send out a team from OPR and interview him. If he doesn't admit it to them, we'll fly him back here immediately for a polygraph."

"And if he does admit it?"

"He'll be fired, and, I'm sure, with the way things are these days, he'll be prosecuted."

"How long before you have to let the director know?"

"I could sit on it for two or three days, I suppose. If that would be helpful."

"It's just that with the kidnapping being such a priority, I don't think this kind of distraction would be in anyone's best interest right now."

There was a hesitation in Bartoli's voice that made Hampton suspect that the delay was for more personally advantageous reasons. "Sure, Al, I understand. I'll let you know when they're on their way."

Bartoli sat at his desk calculating how best to use what he had learned. When he had asked Hampton to delay the investigation, it was his intention to bring both the news of Kincade's crime and his own intervention in the matter to the SAC's attention, putting one in the bank for himself. Although Thorne had treated him appropriately as his ASAC from the start, he couldn't help but feel that the SAC wasn't a big fan.

Maybe this would turn things around. An FBI agent had committed bank burglaries, and Bartoli was the one whispering it in the SAC's ear, delaying the public disgrace, doing everything he could to keep the division focused on what counted, the kidnapping—a most noble deed on the part of the underappreciated ASAC. He felt a small stab of pleasure that it was Kincade who was going to provide his entrance into the SAC's good graces. Strangely, Thorne seemed to have a growing affection for the ragged agent who had come to his attention by being AWOL. But he got lucky with the bombing case and had redeemed himself. Part of that was Kincade's grandstand play regarding the bomb. But all that was about to change.

Even though it was open, Bartoli knocked on the SAC's door and leaned inside with a just-discernible level of deference. "Sir, do you have a minute?"

Thorne, sitting sideways behind his desk reading a file, looked up. Bartoli sensed the same unwillingness he always did when he approached the SAC. "Sure, but if you don't mind, just one minute."

Bartoli thought about closing the door, but that would have been too obvious. This way he would have to sit close to Thorne's desk and speak in low, confidential tones. In less than a minute, he presented the case against Kincade. Thorne steepled his fingers in front of his lips. "Did whoever you talked to say how long before they made it official?"

Bartoli had come to the SAC hoping simply to be the bearer of bad news, but now he saw an opportunity for additional gain. "He didn't say, but I asked him to sit on it until I got back to him. You know the director's zero-tolerance policy when it comes to agent misconduct, but I think I can have it held up for two or three days." He hesitated for emphasis. "He owes me a favor."

"Since he called to warn you, he must be capable of at least a little bit of conspiracy."

Bartoli assumed Thorne understood that favors within the management food chain, all favors, were subject to complete and unquestioned reciprocity, but since the SAC didn't seem in the least bit appreciative of the information, the young ASAC couldn't be sure. Everyone knew that Thorne could have gone much further had he any patience for politics, but he apparently didn't; he had risen to his present rank by being an extremely effective field marshal, and in all likelihood would be the last one who would ever reach that level strictly because of hands-on leadership.

"I'll take care of it, Roy." He had never used the SAC's first name before. He wasn't doing it to redefine the normal SAC–ASAC relationship but rather to see if Thorne was willing to accept some change in the distance that seemed to exist between them.

He went back to reading the file. "Good" was his one-word answer, which failed to give Bartoli any indication whether he had been successful.

"I'll have him sit on it for as long as I can, but you know the Bureau, when it comes to agent misfortune, the word spreads with great enthusiasm."

Thorne looked up. "Just remember that right now there's only one agent suffering real misfortune."

At the Chicago Police Department headquarters, Kincade sat in Deputy Chief Billy Hatton's office reading the William Sloane homicide file.

"I'm afraid there wasn't a lot of work done on that, Jack. It was more or less classified a drug killing. One problem canceling another. Not an especially high priority around here."

"And Sloane had never been arrested in Chicago before he was killed?"

"Not that our records show."

"Does that sound right to you?" Kincade asked.

"Not the norm, but what is the norm these days? Usually, we would have had some previous contact with the victims of these kinds of cases."

"Can I use your phone?"

"I'm overdue for a meeting with the chief." Hatton stood up. "Take my chair and make yourself comfortable. If you need anything else, my assistant is just outside. And if we can do anything else regarding Ben's daughter, you know all you have to do is ask."

They shook hands, and as the deputy chief left, Kincade picked up the phone and dialed Laura Welton's work number. Once he got her on the line, he asked, "Have you seen the evening news?"

"Not yet."

"Ben's daughter was kidnapped."

"What!"

"And we're pretty sure a former cop named Alan Traven is responsible. We also think he's the one who killed your stepbrother."

"This is unbelievable. Ben must be going crazy."

"He is. Have you ever heard Traven's name before?"

"Never."

"When your brother was staying with you, did he ever have any mysterious meetings or have you drop him off somewhere without telling you what he was doing?"

"No, I think I told you, he was the kind of person you couldn't shut up, but during that time he seemed—I don't know, scared—never said boo about anything."

"When he was killed, how did you find out about it?"

"The Chicago police found my number in his wallet and called. Then they asked me to come and identify the body," she said. "You know that never made sense to me, him being killed in Chicago. He hated the city. He never went there."

"Not even for drugs?"

"I know for a fact that his connection was out here. Before all this started, his car broke down once, and he had me pick him up from his dealer's. He was using heavy then. I could probably go drive around and find the house and call you with the address."

"Thanks, but that really doesn't give me a connection to Traven. I'm sure he dumped your brother on the west side to make it look like a drug deal gone bad. And to give the case to the Chicago PD because an ex-cop like Traven would know they were overworked and wouldn't be able to give it much of a shake, especially since it looked like it was drug-related."

"What does this have to do with Ben's daughter?"

"Maybe nothing, but there really isn't anything to go on. I'm shooting in the dark hoping to hit something."

"Please be careful."

"I heard somewhere that redheaded women don't like careful men."

"I'm serious, Jack."

Kincade's pager went off. He didn't recognize the number, but the exchange was the same as the office. "I've got to go. I don't know exactly when, but I'll try to see you tonight." He dialed the number.

"Kincade, is that you?"

He immediately recognized the brusque authority of the SAC's voice, but with more of an edge than usual. "Yes, sir."

"I've got a problem here that you're going to have to help me with. I need to see you immediately."

A problem? Big enough to draw Thorne's focus away from the kidnapping? Kincade's first reaction was to think it was about the bank trappings. After all, Alton had figured it out, and he hadn't even been trying. And now Kincade was being ordered to the SAC's office, and it apparently had nothing to do with the kidnapping. He couldn't think of anything else that the SAC would have given that kind of priority.

That Kincade could concern himself with his own problems at a time like this caused a small shudder of disgust to run through him. But some part of him buried deep beneath the rubble probably had known from the beginning that this day would come. In fact, maybe that was why he had done it, to sow the slow-growing seeds of his own destruction, to arrange the ultimate conflict that he could not win. "I'm on my way."

Thorne's office was dark. By the ambient light from the hallway, Kincade saw Thorne leaning back in his chair, either asleep or using the darkness to think. Without turning around, Thorne said, "Come on in, Jack."

He switched on a small brass lamp. Even in the low light it gave off, Thorne could see that Kincade knew why he had been summoned. The usual cat-and-mouse games of interrogation would not be necessary. "It *is* about the bank trappings, Jack."

For a few long seconds, a white-hot weight fell endlessly through him, but then vanished with a sense of relief. He now understood that the words he had invariably used to coerce confessions were true: *You'll feel better once you get it off your chest.*

And, if you had to give yourself up, it might as well be to some-one you respected. He smiled. "What about them?"

"Ident found your prints on the trap that was recovered. Some of them were in places they shouldn't have been. They also matched up the MO with your old Philadelphia cases on Alfred Manning."

Kincade shook his head with some admiration. "You've got to admit, Ben Alton is one thorough pain in the ass."

"Goddammit, Jack, this is serious."

"Is there a question you're asking me?"

"I guess there's a question I *don't* want to ask you because I don't want the answer."

"Then don't ask, because I'm not going to lie to you."

"*Goddamn* you!" Thorne jumped up and walked over to the window. After peering out into the darkness for a long time, he said, "I know what I should do; I should call the United States attorney and get authorization to take you into custody." When Kincade didn't answer, he spun around. "Well?"

"You have every right to do that; I deserve it. But I'm not going to run. You can do it in a couple of days when this is over."

"The great Jack Kincade will be noble enough to take his medicine . . ." Thorne barked a single, rifle shot–like *Ha!* "That's very considerate of you. Do you have any idea what something like this does to morale? To our reputation? This is not just about you."

"You're right, what I did was completely selfish, and I have no right to ask this, but I will. Please leave me out until we get Ben's daughter back. Then I'll do whatever you want."

Thorne turned back to the window. "We got a heads-up from the Bureau. You probably have two or three days before it becomes official. As soon as it does, I want you to turn yourself in and give me a signed statement."

"You have my word."

"Do you know why I'm doing this?"

"I'm assuming for Ben and his family."

"That's exactly right. He has enough to deal with right now. Seeing you arrested, I know he'd find a way to blame himself."

"I understand."

Thorne shook his head. "I'll never understand how someone with so much ability can do this to himself." He collapsed into his chair, suddenly looking exhausted. "I'm not the only one around here who knows about this, so make yourself scarce. There are those who see missing the chance to take down a wounded agent as a very poor career move. So stay away from the office until this is over; the fewer people who know where you are, the better. Seeing you might prove just a little too tempting. If I need to see you, I'll do it carefully."

Kincade got the feeling that Thorne had somebody specific in mind he was warning him against, but he had enough to worry about without trying to identify additional enemies. "What if I need to get ahold of you?"

"The number I beeped you to is my private line."

Thorne reached over his desk and turned off the light.

Out in the hallway, Kincade lit a cigarette and started for the garage. For the first time in thirteen years he was alone. No longer was the Bureau's safety net spread beneath him invisibly. Whether an agent was the best or the worst, someone was there to help with any problem, that is, any problem except sedition against the very oath that was the foundation of their fraternity. And now he had found a way to destroy even that bond. Like so many things in his life—his marriage, friendships, his son—he had taken it for granted, never understanding its worth until it was irrevocably severed. He had one chance left—to find Sarah, not to prevent the inevitability of what would happen to him, but to have a starting point for whatever would follow. For the first time he understood Alton's fear of finding himself at the end and discovering he had lost.

# 21

IT WAS ALREADY DARK WHEN KINCADE THREW HIS
only suitcase, containing a couple of changes of clothes, into the
back of the van. Then he opened the compartment in the floor
where the spare was kept. He hadn't kept a tire in it since the
drive to Illinois early last spring when he had to mount it after a
blowout had completely destroyed the existing tire's tread. From
the empty well, Kincade pulled out his holstered Sig Sauer nine-
millimeter. He hadn't carried it since coming to Chicago. It was
funny, when fresh out of training school, the security of being
armed seemed a necessity as he indulged himself in the fantasy
of being ever-ready for the inevitable High Noon Shootout on
the streets of Philadelphia. But over the years, its weight had become increasingly uncomfortable, and he finally concluded that
if he found himself in a situation where a handgun was needed,
he obviously had committed some fairly egregious error in judgment. To minimize that possibility, he simply did not carry a
firearm. But the kidnapping had erased the luxury of such self-
indulgence. Taking it out of the holster, he saw that most of its
metal was covered with surface rust. He tried to wipe it away
but the discoloration was deeper than he hoped and the bluing
had started to pit. After extracting the magazine to make sure it
was fully loaded, he reseated the clip, chambered a round, and
then clipped the gun to his belt. Briefly he considered carrying

the snubnose under the front seat as a backup but then remembered he didn't have any ammunition for it.

Apparently recalling the last time someone had packed their suitcases and failed to take it along, the Border collie waited anxiously next to the driver's door. Once Kincade opened it, B.C. jumped in and assumed the passenger seat, but its stare was unsure. Kincade reached over and petted the dog's head. "Worried about being left behind again, boy? Well, not for a while, at least. But I'm going to be straight with you, when I have to go in front of that judge, I'm going to tell him that those bank burglaries were all your idea." The dog looked at him, panting slightly. "That's what I like about you, pal, you only understand the present, something I can certainly identify with. How about cheeseburgers tonight?" The dog, showing a vague recognition of the noun, shifted happily with anticipation.

After a quick trip to the drive-thru, Kincade pulled over and opened the wrapping on a quarter-pound cheeseburger and reached back, putting it on the seat behind him. The dog sat motionless until Kincade said, "Okay, boy, go eat." In a single motion, the Border collie leapt across the seat and carefully started extracting the cheese-covered patty from between the halves of the bun. Kincade turned around and dumped a carton of french fries on the sandwich wrapper. He then opened a black coffee and lit a cigarette. "Okay, B.C., we're officially homeless."

For the next two hours, through a series of abandoned addresses and blood relatives who initially swore they "didn't know him," Kincade traced the whereabouts of Lonnie Williams, the individual who had found William Sloane's body three years earlier. Kincade didn't hold much hope that Williams would be any help in locating Traven or Sarah, but he had to do something. Besides, Thorne had the rest of the agents in the division running out all the logical leads, and if they were logical, it meant there was a good chance that Traven would anticipate them.

Kincade finally found Williams at a supermarket where, despite his two felony arrests for drugs and two outstanding misdemeanor bench warrants for traffic violations including one DUI, he was employed as the evening security guard. After three years, Kincade hoped Williams might now be able to remember something he had "forgotten" at the time due to his possible involvement in a conflicting criminal enterprise. The night manager directed Kincade to a small office at the rear of the store's warehouse area. Opening the door without knocking, he found Williams sprawled in a chair in front of a small, cluttered desk, dead asleep. Even though Williams's eyes were closed, Kincade could see a chalky hollowness to the black man's face, an indication of continuing drug abuse. This was a valuable bit of intelligence because Kincade knew that drug addicts will do anything to keep from being locked up, even if it's just overnight on some meaningless misdemeanor warrant.

He pulled up a chair directly in front of Williams. "Lonnie . . . Lonnie!" When he didn't stir, Kincade slapped his knee. "Lonnie, reveille." He slapped his knee again and finally Williams started to wake up. For a moment, he stared at the intruder as though his senses, regarding both time and place, had deserted him. Kincade opened his credentials and held them within a few inches of Williams's face. Suddenly, his eyes started darting around the room and finally locked on the open doorway, giving the impression he expected the rest of an arrest team to come crashing in, serving a warrant for who-knows-what dimly lighted felony from his past. He tried to get to his feet but Kincade caught him by the front of his shirt. "Whoa there, Lonnie. I come in peace."

As Williams lowered himself cautiously into the chair, he searched the agent's face for hidden motives, his peripheral vision still straining toward the door. "I'm alone. Just need to talk to you about that body you found three years ago."

"You think I had something to do with that?"

"Man, you've got to lay off that pipe, it's like smoking pure paranoia. I know you didn't have anything to do with that body. I know who killed him. I've just got some routine questions."

Williams used his long, gangling hand to wipe away more of the sleep from his face. "Ain't you supposed to give me my rights or something?"

"Lonnie, try to keep up. You're not a suspect. I know who killed this guy and, in case you don't remember, it wasn't you. I just want to know the circumstances of you finding the body."

"I think I should call my lawyer."

"Stand up." When Williams didn't move, Kincade snarled, "Stand up, goddammit!" Williams stood up and stumbled slightly backward as if he expected to be hit. "Empty your pockets on the desk!" Slowly, Williams complied, placing a couple of crumpled dollar bills on the desk along with a bus transfer and pocketknife. Its blade had been sprung so its tip caught on the side of the casing. It was a street technique used to open it with just one hand by catching the tip against a piece of clothing. Kincade picked it up and put it in his pocket. Then he patted Williams's pockets to make sure everything was out. "Now, let me see if I've got this straight: You don't have a wallet, you don't have car keys, you don't even have a house key, but you've got a lawyer. Does he take bus transfers?"

Williams gave him an angry victim's glare. "I don't remember anything about it."

"You know the greatest obstacle to my job, Lonnie? It's the inexplicable loss of witness memory. The scientists call it Retrieval Failure, and in certain cases its cause is referred to as Motivated Forgetting. That's brought on by conscious or unconscious desires. You with me so far?"

"No."

"Good. Now, doesn't it seem logical that if I can reverse your motivation I can restore your memory?"

"Man, I don't know what the fuck you're talking about."

"A little too theoretical? Sorry. Let me be more concrete: If you tell me everything you know about finding that body three years ago—without once telling me you don't remember some detail—I'll allow you to sleep through the remainder of your shift and not have you locked up on those two warrants, which I'm sure you're about to tell me you don't know anything about, or you've already taken care of."

Again Williams gave Kincade his victim's glare, but then said, "What do you need to know?"

After another painfully tedious half hour, Kincade came away without a single lead. Back in the van, after rechecking his notes, he realized he was close to where Sloane's body had been dumped. Evidently, even after three years of covering his tracks, for whatever reason, Lonnie Williams couldn't muster the resolve to flee his neighborhood, a universal characteristic of junkies. Kincade drove to a gas station and checked their map to make sure of the address's exact location.

On both sides of the street, newly vacant lots were interspersed with modest single-level houses and small four- and eight-unit apartment buildings, a few of which were boarded up. Seeing that the even-numbered houses were on the north side of the street, he counted the houses from the corner and then turned at the end of the block, pulling into the alley behind them. Just as he made the turn, he could see taillights moving away. Once they reached the cross street, the car turned north and vanished from sight. Counting as he idled along, Kincade located the apartment building behind which William Sloane's body had been found. The ground was littered with the refuse discarded by the residents as they had left. He drove over an old muddy mattress and looked up at the building.

Suddenly, B.C. barked; the dog lowered its head and pinned its ears back. A second bark came off-key, distressed. Kincade turned off the engine and got out as quietly as the van's creaking door would allow. The unfamiliar weight of the nine-millimeter pulled on his hip. After a moment, he smelled smoke. It was coming from the apartment building. The windows and doors were tightly boarded over, but thin wisps of smoke were starting to escape from around one of the windows on the first floor. It didn't make sense that a fire could start on its own in a structure so tightly sealed. Fires in abandoned buildings were not uncommon, but this seemed like a hell of a coincidence.

He eased his automatic out of the holster. The side door was not sealed like the other openings. The board that had been nailed around the frame was lying on the ground next to it, and the door itself was ajar. A large "3" had been spray-painted on it. With the tip of his index finger, Kincade touched it. The paint was still wet. He pushed the large wooden door open with his foot. Smoke filled the hallway and its origin seemed to be one of the front apartments. He started up the short staircase into an intensifying heat and the fire grew louder. Taking a step back for momentum, he lunged forward, kicking the apartment door open. More smoke and flames gushed out as he tried to see past it. "Anyone in there?" he yelled. Starting to cough now, he called out a second time, louder but in choked syllables. When no answer came, he backed out down the stairs. Then it hit him—the car in the alley.

He ran back to the van and jumped in. Speeding off in the same direction as he had seen the taillights, he checked the street in both directions. Nothing. He drove up a couple more blocks and then in widening circles, looking for any car, but it was midnight and there were very few in the neighborhood.

Now he could hear a fire engine's siren getting closer. He drove back to the apartment building and got there about the same time as the firemen. A few minutes later, a Chicago PD car arrived. The officer went over and consulted briefly with one of the firemen. Once he noticed Kincade sitting close by in his tattered van, he approached him with some caution. Kincade held up his identification, but for an instant it didn't seem to convince the cop. He got out and pulled his suit coat as if adjusting it so his gun could be seen. The cop noticed it but still didn't appear to be sure. "What are you doing here?"

"The agent's daughter who was kidnapped," Kincade said, hoping the media had done its job. The cop nodded knowingly and seemed to finally accept Kincade's presence. "I was following up a lead at this address."

Like Kincade, the cop seemed to understand that this was too much of a coincidence. "Let me go talk to these guys for a minute," he said with some reservation, apparently knowing more than he was saying.

The firemen worked efficiently, containing the blaze to the front apartment and hallway. After about twenty minutes, the cop came back to Kincade's van. "There's a body inside."

"Man or woman?" Kincade asked, his words clipped by fear.

"They said they can't tell, it's too badly burned. But it's small like a woman, or a kid."

For the next ten minutes, Kincade searched the west side streets for a phone. Once or twice he thought he had passed one but couldn't seem to bring himself to double back. He had to keep moving; the bumpy speed of the van felt comfortable, its rising clatter reassuring. Hypnotically, he stared straight ahead as the city's geometric shapes blurred and then dissolved into the corners of the windshield. No longer was he looking for a phone. Long before Sarah Alton's abduction, flight had become a necessity of Jack Kincade's survival, its comfort his real addiction. But now its reassurance began to unravel.

The air inside the van felt as though it was warming, and with it, a smell started to rise. He was in Sloane's attic, carefully trying to gain his breath and at the same time deny the stench that burned his nostrils. Involuntarily, he threw back the soiled bedspread, and this time Sarah was the one who lay beneath it. A fire started around them. He grabbed her, but where his hands touched, she started to burn. To smother the fire, he threw the cover back over her, but it, too, burst into flames. He crawled backward, retreat his only defense, his only means of self-preservation. But there was no longer a lighted square to escape through.

Kincade slammed on the brakes. B.C. slid off the seat and onto the floor. He pulled the Border collie up next to him and started stroking its head. If only he had gotten to that apartment building five minutes sooner, Sarah might have still been alive. And what about the start of this whole thing: insisting that Ben have a drink with him, undoubtedly the cause of his missing Traven following him home. Or letting Ben go to meet him alone. He should have been the one to confront Traven and become his target rather than Ben and his daughter. All Traven could take from Kincade was his life, not exactly a commodity on the rise.

Directly across the street was an all-night convenience store. He went to the public phone and dialed the SAC's private number.

After Kincade explained the details of what had happened, Thorne asked, "Do you think it's her?"

"I don't even want to guess."

"We're going to need dental records."

"You asking me to tell Ben?" Kincade said, as if pleading not to be the one.

"Okay, I'll drive out and tell him," Thorne said, sounding exhausted.

"No, I'll go."

"You sure, because it's not going to be pleasant. We're going to need those X rays tonight."

"I'll go."

"Thank you. And then, if you can, have him call me. In the meantime, I'm going to arrange for a forensic dentist."

Kincade felt all the strength drain from him as he hung up.

During the drive, he forced himself to focus on his own problem, hoping self-indulgence, an always reliably selfish companion, would displace what had happened, and what he now had to do. But the taste of the apartment fire, at least psychologically, had become lacquered to the inside of his throat, his thoughts of Ben and his daughter refusing to be dislodged. For Jack Kincade, his own future had become inconsequential.

It was almost 2 A.M. when he pulled into the Alton driveway. A few dim lights were visible inside. He knocked on the door and almost instantly one of the agents who'd been there earlier opened it. "Is Ben still awake?"

"Yes, he's in the kitchen."

When Kincade walked in, Alton was sitting at the table with a young black man in his late teens. He had Alton's broad nose and low hairline. Alton looked up and saw the uncertainty in Kincade's face. To prevent the delivery of any news, he stood up and said, "Jack, this is my son, Darian." The young man stood up, too, and shook hands, attempting to smile. "You want some coffee, Jack?"

"I need some equipment from your car," he said solemnly.

Alton's shoulders seemed to lose their rigidity. He understood that something had happened and Kincade didn't want his son to hear what it was. "Let me find my keys." As they walked out of the kitchen, Kincade glanced at Darian. He had his father's instincts—his eyes were widened with fear.

Alton also saw his son's apprehension. "Darian, get to bed. I'm going to need you clearheaded in the morning."

As Alton walked out to his car, Kincade noticed that he was limping more than usual, apparently too drained physically and emotionally to disguise it. He leaned against the Bureau car for support, waiting for Kincade to speak. "Ben, I went out to the west side to take a look at the location where Sloane's body was found. It was behind an abandoned building. Just before I got there, somebody started a fire. The fire department found a body inside."

Alton seemed to stop breathing. "Was it Sarah?"

"It was too badly burned to tell."

Alton's face remained unchanged, but a single tear fell down his cheek. "You'll need her dental records."

"Just to cover the bases. But let's not jump to any conclusions. It could just be a coincidence."

Alton looked at him skeptically. "Let's not tell Tess until we know for sure."

They went back into the house. While Alton went through the family's phone book, Kincade pulled one of the agents aside and filled him in. "You're going to have to get the dentist out of bed. If Ben doesn't have his home number, check the phone book. If it's not listed, one of the tech guys will have a contact who can get it for you. We need those X rays right away."

Alton came in and extended a slip of paper from his hand. The young agent took it and left the room. Alton said, "You want some coffee?"

"Yeah, I could use some."

Alton made a fresh pot and they sat at the kitchen table drinking it in silence. Another agent walked in, talking quietly into a cell phone. He handed it to Kincade. "The SAC wants to speak to you."

Kincade took it. "Yes, sir."

"Jack, when the body got to the medical examiner, one of the technicians gave it a preliminary exam. All the victim's teeth had been pulled out."

Kincade wanted to ask if the body was a man or woman, age, and height and weight, but he didn't want to pronounce those words in front of Alton. He started to get up to go into another room when Alton reached over and pulled him back down into his seat. Kincade finally looked at Alton and could see that he was ready to hear the worst, that it was now better than not knowing. "Did they provide any physical description?"

Thorne said, "It's a woman, believed to be black. They can't tell the age without some further tests. The height and weight can be deceptive when the burning is this extensive." He then gave Kincade some questions to ask Alton.

When Kincade looked over at him, Alton said, "What do you need to know?"

"Do you know her blood type?"

"If you have dental X rays why would you need to know that? What aren't you telling me?"

"Please answer these questions, and then I'll tell why we need to know."

"It's the same as Tess's, O positive."

"Has she ever had any broken bones?"

"No, she never has. Wait, I take that back, she broke her"— Alton held up his own hand to recall the injury—"right index finger playing softball."

"Did she have any spinal abnormalities or problems?"

"Not that I know of."

Kincade passed the information on to Thorne and hung up. "The body, when they got it to the ME . . . they found that all the teeth had been pulled out."

"So we wouldn't know for sure," Alton said, and then his voice, almost apologetic, started to crack. "Is there any way to tell"—he turned away from Kincade and wiped his eyes, sniffled and turned back, fixing his stare over Kincade's shoulder—"was it done while she was alive?"

"Don't do this to yourself, Ben."

"I'm sorry, but I need a minute to feel sorry for myself before I go and tell my wife and son that I got my daughter killed." Alton opened a sliding glass door and stepped out into the backyard, closing the door behind him.

Kincade went out to his van where the dog greeted him with its usual exploratory sniff. He wanted to leave, but he couldn't get himself to put the key in the ignition. The emotion inside the house had been suffocating, but here, in the solitude of the van, his thoughts tracked more normally. Rolling down a window, he lit a cigarette and forced himself not to think about Alton or his daughter for a few moments. Laura Welton was the easiest distraction. He took a deep drag and closed his eyes. Along the tips of his fingers, he could feel the dry, warm satin of her thigh, the muscle and bone underneath.

Then it came to him: The burned body in the apartment was not Sarah. He jumped out of the van, and without closing the door, ran up the stairs and into the house. Alton was back in the kitchen washing dishes. "Ben, she's still alive. Sarah's still alive."

Alton looked up. "How" was the only word he could get out.

"Think about it. Traven knows that the victim's teeth would identify her, so he pulled them, not so Sarah couldn't be identified, but so we would assume it was her. But if he really had killed her, he would want you to know right away."

"You're saying that he killed some other poor girl just to scare the hell out of me?"

"He killed Leah Ziven just to embarrass China Hills," Kincade said. "Don't you see, this way he can punish you more than once. Torture you with the uncertainty."

"Jack, you don't *know* how much I want to believe this, but the only thing I can be sure of right now is that I cannot possibly be objective. I'm . . . I'm going to have to rely on your judgment and hope to God you're right."

"I understand you having some doubts. If I had never met Traven, I'd say I was probably making this up as I was going along. But think about the way he set Sloane up for the Ziven kidnapping. And then as much as told us how we could have solved the case three years earlier, just to humiliate us. This is something his twisted mind would dream up."

"When will they know . . . about the body?"

"There are other tests that can determine age. They have to do mostly with bones. A pathologist has to do it. I would imagine sometime during the next twelve hours. But for now let's assume I'm right."

"I want to, Jack, but I just don't know."

"Trust me, Ben. I let you down once. I won't do that again."

# 22

THORNE COULD TELL THAT STEVE TRASS WAS USED
to working independently. Agents who had been in the Bureau
for a while became marked by an underlying regimentation as
they fell into step with those around them. Because he was a
criminal profiler and spent most of his time outside the Bureau,
Trass found it advantageous to shun such conformity, to distin-
guish himself from the pack. He wore his hair slightly longer and
his somewhat-more-expensive suits with tastefully matched
shirts and ties. But the most telling marker of Trass's independence was the speed at which he worked. He read Alan Traven's
personnel file from the China Hills PD with no more urgency
than if he were on a commuter train rather than in a SAC's office
filled with a score of agents, most of whom would have out-
ranked him had anyone really believed that title, and not competence, was the criterion for authority.

Thorne saw all these as positive signs. Trass spent most of his
time working with local police departments across the country
just long enough to convince them of their latest monster's most
telling and traceable characteristics. He had only a few hours to
impress upon them that where they were being told to look was
worth their time. Working outside the constraints of the FBI had
left him with an ability to remain uninfluenced by the inchoate
opinions of superiors, no matter how hard-pressed with their "in-

sights." And while his objectivity was maddening because he refused to get caught up in the fever of the hunt, it was also reassuring because his opinions were not distorted by emotion.

When Trass finally closed the file, he seemed surprised that everyone was waiting for him. "I assume most of you have read the file." Like students in a lackluster classroom, most of them turned their eyes away. Thorne said, "I've skimmed most of it."

Tactfully Trass said, "Well, for those of you who haven't had a chance to read it yet," he held up the file, "it might be worth your time. When Alan Traven became *overzealous* and they wanted him out of the department, someone came up with the idea of letting the shrinks get rid of him. Three different—and as far as I can tell—competent psychologists and psychiatrists examined him. Without going into what most field agents refer to as the psychological mumbo jumbo of what I do, let me bring up a few of the more important subtexts which might give us some insight into where he's heading. His childhood, which seems even more excruciating than those of most sociopaths, began with an abandoning father and an alcoholic mother. She incessantly reminded him that men were no good, and like it or not, he was just a smaller version of that subspecies. Many times, when feeling the need for an evening of relaxation, she would lock him in a darkened closet while she went to a local bar. Usually when she returned to their one-bedroom apartment, she brought a man with her. The neighborhood they lived in was mostly black and so were the men she brought home. Not only did he have to listen to their lovemaking, but he was not allowed out of the closet, sometimes forced to spend up to sixteen hours in there without food and water or toilet facilities. Once when he started crying, one of the men let him out temporarily to beat him. Understandably, he never protested again. The next morning, his mother, still in a drunken stupor, would let him out. Many times he went to school with the stench of urine on his clothes. According to him, his classmates were less than kind."

Trass leaned forward, picked up his coffee cup, and took a sip. "Although his intelligence was substantially above normal, he did poorly in school. Similarly, although strong and quick, he could never master the accompanying psychological necessities of sports, apparently lacking the social wiring to dedicate himself to the concept of *team*. As a result he grew up with overpowering feelings of inadequacy, a confusing push-pull of talent versus underachievement."

Trass stopped talking and everyone looked up at him. "What I'm about to say is never well received by police officers or agents, but please don't let it be the cause of any narrow-mindedness on your part." He hesitated again before going on. "Many men gravitate toward law enforcement due to similar deep-seated inadequacies. They hope that by having this control over everything wrong in the world, they will be able to overcome those feelings in themselves."

Despite some grumbling around the table, Trass continued. "I've found that the only people who are offended by that statement are the ones to whom it most closely applies." The room became deadly still.

"I'm kidding," Trass said, and smiled. Thorne suspected this was not the first time the tactic had been used to refocus his audience. "Growing up, the only thing that seemed to like Traven back was weight lifting, where his sheer will could overcome almost all resistance. It was something in his life he could control and early on, he became obsessed with it. It gave him power on more than one level. Although he didn't become a bully—at least not according to him—he started feeling a hidden power that he could crush anyone he chose, sort of a secret identity not unlike a comic book superhero. When he finally became a cop, all those years of holding back were unleashed, producing his completely over-the-top style of law enforcement. His superiors at the department described him as the first person you thought of if you needed someone to kick in a door, and the last if you needed the smallest amount of good judgment or restraint once you were on the other side. The three men who analyzed him all felt there was a great potential for violence bubbling just beneath the surface."

"So how does someone like that go from being a cop to becoming a kidnapper and murderer?" Thorne asked.

"You've got to look at it from his perspective. For the first time in his life, as a police officer, he had power. Not weight-lifting power, but the kind that could be exerted over people. And that, left unchecked as it is with some cops, eventually becomes unlimited power. He could right all the wrongs in the world, which meant righting all the wrongs perpetrated against Alan Traven. When he was fired, that was taken from him—and his interpretation was that it happened because he was too good at what he did. Just like they had his entire life, those inferior to him conspired to rob him of what he deserved. To take back his power and to humiliate those who had stolen it from him, he kidnapped the Ziven girl, not for the ransom, but simply to demonstrate he was superior."

"But why is he trying to take it out on the FBI?" said Thorne.

"When he was involved in those entrapment cases, one of the suspects was black and had his attorney file a civil rights complaint. Since the FBI investigates all civil rights complaints, two Chicago agents interviewed Traven. He was never told, but the case was quietly closed because the facts really didn't meet the criteria of the law. Looking at the date of that interview, it took place just four days before he was fired. In his mind, filled with deep suspicions about everything, he probably decided that the FBI was ultimately responsible for ending his law enforcement career. It may well have been the reason he chose kidnapping as his crime of revenge; it would involve not only China Hills but the Bureau as well."

Thorne said, "So fast-forward to the present. Now there's a black FBI agent trying to put him in jail. He would think that blacks, on both sides of the law, are responsible for everything that has happened to him. From beatings as a child to losing his career as a cop."

"That's exactly right. And don't forget, he had three years of thinking that he was smarter than the FBI, then all of a sudden here's this black guy in his face, telling him it isn't so. Not only is he there to destroy this notion of superiority, but he's going to take his freedom as well."

"So his motivation is strictly revenge."

"Revenge which is meant to feed his ego, but for someone with a psyche as damaged as his, it's as futile as collecting water in a sieve," Trass said. "But don't underestimate him, he's extremely calculating."

"Then you don't think he'll demand a ransom."

"It wasn't about money with the Ziven girl, and it's definitely not now. Unless I miss my guess, he sees Alton as a ghetto-bred, handicapped, dope-smoking black who is allowed to be in the FBI simply because he is a minority, while Traven, a smart, strong white man, is reduced to working manual labor. I also suspect that at some time he had fantasized, like many cops, about becoming an agent, and this disappointment would also add fuel to his disdain for the Bureau. If that is true, he will see Alton as having taken the spot he could have filled. This type of personality looks for reasons to divide the world into those who are acceptable and those who aren't. Anyone like that will invariably judge those who are not white males as an enemy of his life. Based on his experiences as a youth, I'd be surprised if he doesn't also harbor an unbridled hatred for any minority, women included. I'm sure in his mind, he is being a patriot, not only for striking a blow for white males, but by ridding the landscape of another black woman with her menacing ability to reproduce future generations."

Thorne's secretary came into the room and whispered something in his ear. Thorne picked up the phone. "Hold on while I make a call. I think everyone's going to want to hear this."

When the agent at the house put Alton on the phone, he said, "Yes, sir."

"Ben, how's everyone doing out there?"

"We're hanging in."

"I just got word that the body from last night had an old fracture of the right forearm, so it couldn't have been Sarah." A relieved undertone went through the agents in the room.

"Thank God," Alton said.

"We're doing everything we can, Ben, so you've got to stay positive."

"That'll be a little easier now, sir, thank you."

"Just take care of your family; we'll take care of everything else." Thorne dialed another number, apparently a pager because he listened for a moment and then punched in a series of numbers. He then turned to Trass and asked, "Assuming that it was Traven who killed and burned this woman last night, why did he do that?"

"He's apparently graduated from humiliation to torture, and that's not a good sign. It's an indication that he is becoming completely contemptuous of society and the order that is its basis. He's willing to sacrifice everything to prove his point."

"What do you mean 'sacrifice everything'?"

"It means that in an indirect way he is becoming suicidal. Never by his own hand, but he is willing to die to prove he is the better man. And that makes him extremely dangerous because there is nothing too drastic that he won't do to further that end. Look at what he has just done—murdered an innocent woman just to scare Alton. But that said, he also does not want to get caught and convicted because that would mean the FBI was ultimately the winner. What this indicates in practical terms is that, although he has these suicidal tendencies, at the same time, he's not going to leave any evidence. So as paradoxical as it might seem, he is willing to die to prove his point, but he doesn't want to get caught doing it."

A muffled phone rang. Thorne said, "Excuse me for a minute." He walked back to his desk and slid open the large lower drawer. The phone rang again, louder. He picked it up.

It was Kincade, his voice graveled with sleep. "Did you page me?"

Speaking so he couldn't be heard at the other end of the room, Thorne said, "I've just been told that the body was not Sarah's."

"That's great. I told Ben it wasn't, but I wasn't really sure. Any new leads?"

"Nothing with any promise. After you called last night, I sent agents out to the west side to do a neighborhood around that apartment building. Of course, no one saw anything. But I'm going to send out a fresh crew this morning. You came pretty close to him last night."

"That was more accident than calculation."

"I'm not so sure about that. By leaving that woman's body where he left Sloane's, he has let us know that it's him without leaving one bit of evidence to prove it. Whatever you're doing, keep at it."

"Okay, I'll just keep stumbling around out there."

"Steve Trass got in last night from Quantico. He's briefing us right now." When Kincade didn't say anything, Thorne said, "He's a profiler, trying to help us develop leads."

"Did you tell him about the number 'three' being painted on the door?"

"Yes, but he hasn't discussed it yet."

"You'll let me know?"

"Next time we talk." Thorne hung up and went back to the table. "So what about that 'three' that was painted on the door?"

Trass said, "A mind as detached from reality as Traven's, it's almost impossible to say."

"I hate to ask this question . . . " Thorne didn't have to finish; everyone knew what it was going to be.

"Is he going to kill the girl?" Trass said.

"Yes."

"I'd like to say no, but I can't. I think the only question is when."

"So you think he's going to play with us for a while?"

"He did last night. I suppose it depends how big a jolt he got from it." Trass looked around the table. "Does anyone have any ideas what the number 'three' on the door might mean?" A couple of the agents answered no. "Well, he did it for a reason. I'm not sure of its significance, but there's a secondary benefit for him. In the future, he can leave another body with a number and we'll know it's him. That way he'll get credit without actually identifying himself, again leaving no evidence. Because of that number, I suspect what the SAC has said is true, that he's not through playing with us. Logically, the closer we come to him, the more likely he is to end Sarah's life, but it depends on how addicted he becomes to the close call. Not unlike sex in a public place, the crime's made worthwhile by the possibility of getting caught."

"If he's going to throw us another red herring, how soon do you think it will be?"

"He killed that girl the same day that he kidnapped Sarah. This kind of psychological degeneration, if anything, shortens, so I wouldn't be surprised if he hit within the next twenty-four hours."

"Any idea where?"

"Someplace where he feels he won't be caught, but afterward, we'll feel stupid."

# 23

"DID YOU GET UP AND CALL SOMEONE, OR WAS I dreaming?" Laura Welton asked Kincade as he came out of the bathroom tightening his tie. The Border collie vaulted to its feet and trotted toward the door.

"Sorry, I was trying not to wake you. It was the office."

"Were you going to leave without saying good-bye?"

Kincade smiled easily. "I figured one of us should get some sleep."

She sat up and pulled the sheet up over her chest. "You tossed and turned all night. What's going on, Jack?"

"What do you mean?"

"That's one."

"One what?"

"One strike," she said. "You've got extra clothes in the van, and it doesn't look like you're planning to go back to the motel for a while."

"Okay. There are some people who're going to be looking for me, and I'm trying to avoid them until this thing with Ben's daughter is over."

"You mean like bill collectors?"

"You might say that."

"I'm sorry but I need answers to be a little straighter than that. That's strike two."

Ever since he had first seen her, the thing he found most irresistible was her confidence. But at the moment, it was eliminating any possibility of compromise, leaving him with candor as his only option. "If I'm being vague, it's because you're better off not knowing."

"You mean you're better off not telling?"

He realized she was probably right; he was too embarrassed to tell her. "I suppose both. I'm sorry, Laura, you deserve better than this. I'll get my things and clear out."

"Do you know the one thing that men will always do better than women—*run*." Laura brought her knees up to her chest and leaned against them. "Do you think I jump into bed with every guy who has a good-looking dog?" She waited a moment for him to consider the question. "Whatever you've done, remember I've survived being Billy Sloane's stepsister. You know, kidnapping, murder—I know bad. But I also know good. You've got to tell me." She reached over and took his hand, pulling him onto the bed next to her.

As uncomfortable as exposing the shame of what he had done might be, there was an undeniably cathartic prospect to it. "Although I'm fairly certain this will qualify as strike three, I'll tell you. What do you know about bank burglaries?"

Kincade walked up the front stairs of the house and this time Alton opened the door himself. He looked just as somber, but there was something else in his expression, some new determination. "Did you get any sleep?" Kincade asked.

"I think so. How about you?"

"I got enough. How are Tess and your son doing?"

"You know, okay. Have you heard anything?"

"Just about the body. Thorne beeped me this morning."

"Jack, I can't sit here and wait anymore."

"Come on, Ben. You told me yourself last night that you weren't thinking straight. Out there it'll be worse."

"I've got to go with you. I swear I won't do anything. You call all the shots. I'll just ride along."

"No."

"What do you think it was like for me last night when I thought it was Sarah in that fire?"

"I can't imagine."

"I think you've got some idea," Alton said, his voice preparing to get angry. "Either I go with you, or I go off on my own, and I know you don't want to be thinking about that."

"Ben, it's not that simple . . . there's a problem."

"What?"

"I got the heads-up . . . OPR will be out here in a couple of days looking to put one behind my ear."

"The traps?" Kincade nodded. "I suppose that's my doing, sending the one in for latents. And the MO file."

"Hey, you did the right thing. It was just a matter of time. But right now I've got to keep myself scarce until we get Sarah back."

"That doesn't change anything, I'm still going with you. Just let me go tell Tess."

Kincade went out to the minivan to get his briefcase and B.C. When he came back Alton was already in his Bureau car. "What was Tess's reaction?"

"For the first time in twenty-seven years of marriage she looked at me like she may have made a mistake."

"Sure you shouldn't be staying home?"

"She just needs a little time. She'll figure out that it's best that I'm out there."

"It must be nice to have a wife you can have so much faith in," Kincade said.

"It is." Alton looked over at him and smiled. "There might even be someone out there for you."

Kincade could still see the disappointment in Laura's eyes when he had told her about the bank trappings. "You know, Jack, I thought getting involved with you was a pretty smart choice. An FBI agent wouldn't complicate my life with some of the things other men had." The statement was more a question, as if she wanted him to supply some defense or mitigation, but he knew there was none. He sat in silence and waited. Finally she said, "Well, is this an ending or a beginning?"

Kincade looked over at Alton. "Yeah, you never know."

As the car backed out into the street, Alton asked, "Where are we going?"

"I thought maybe we'd head out to his job site and interview everyone we can get our hands on."

He glanced over at Alton, who held on tightly to the wheel. Dull with fatigue and sadness, his eyes locked on the pavement that disappeared beneath the car.

As they exited the highway, Alton asked, "Who gave you the heads-up about OPR?"

Kincade looked over at him. "This can't go any further."

"Thorne?"

"Someone got a call from the Bureau. I got the impression it wasn't Thorne himself. That he would warn me is kind of surprising. I can't imagine myself on any SAC's endangered species list, let alone Roy K. Thorne's. Even if it is temporary."

"What do you mean 'temporary'?" Not wanting to further burden Alton with his problems, Kincade hesitated. "Come on, Jack, what?"

"I told him I'd give him a signed statement."

"I would have thought that self-preservation was a little higher on Jack Kincade's list of priorities."

"Hey, I stole. That makes me a thief. And I've never been much of a liar."

"I've got some bad news for you, Jack, you're not much of a thief, either." Both of them laughed. Alton said, "So you agreed to confess to keep working on this, didn't you?"

"Don't make it out to be a big deal."

"It is a big deal."

"Well, keep it to yourself, I don't want my life's work destroyed by a single thoughtless act."

The Bureau car pulled up to the construction site. "Jack, can I ask you something?"

"Why did I do it."

"It just doesn't make any sense to me."

"Believe me, I've been trying to figure it out. Somewhere I made a U-turn and didn't know it. When I was eighteen, I had it all figured out. I knew there was no way that I couldn't accomplish whatever I wanted. Everything was laid out in front of me: good family, good friends, good schools. It seemed almost too easy. Maybe it was. Maybe there has to be some fear of failure to keep you on track. I don't know. Whatever needed to be there, evidently wasn't. After my son was born, I guess I got scared—you know that circle of life stuff, you realize your own mortality—I don't know. Maybe I'm full of shit, maybe I just got bored. Whatever it was, you know something is wrong, but you don't know exactly what. Nothing has any feeling to it anymore. You become like one of those old black-and-white-movie zombies, that even if someone shot you, there wouldn't be any pain. You're desperate to latch on to any sensation, to be able to take just one deep, clear breath. To bring you back to life, then you'll turn over a new leaf. But then there's a second time, which you swear will definitely be the last. And of course it can't be." Kincade stared out the windshield. "I saw it in your eyes when we found Leah Ziven, that lust to beat the hell out of life. God, I was jealous. I'd give anything to feel that way again."

At that moment Alton wanted to tell him he would, but the darkness of Kincade's confession made him realize that redemption was not always a possibility. They got out of the car and started toward the construction office, their steps feeling ponderous, even futile, neither of them wanting to say what they both feared, that they would not find Traven. The next move would be his.

Shortly after midnight, the Chicago emergency services received a call that there was a car on fire on Lower Wacker Drive. The 911 operator dispatched the fire department and a single CPD patrol car. The officers arrived ten minutes after the firemen and were told that because the origin of the blaze was in the trunk, it would have to be pried open. Inside was a body.

Roy Thorne got the first call at a quarter to one in the morning. He was told that another female had been killed and her body burned on Lower Wacker, almost in the exact same space as the car under which Conrad Ziven had slid his stamp collection in order to get his daughter back.

Kincade and Alton had returned to Alton's home at about 10:30 the night before. When they walked in, Tess could see the exhaustion and disappointment on her husband's face. He had called her throughout the day and evening, more to be supportive than to update her. She had already fed the agents who were stationed there and insisted that her husband and Kincade also eat. She put a bowlful of stew on the floor for the Border collie, which it gratefully accepted with a brief, accelerated wagging of its tail.

By the time Thorne paged Kincade, he had dozed off on the couch. "Were the teeth pulled out?"

Thorne hesitated. "No."

"Goddammit!"

"I want you to get out to the scene. The body is already on the way to the medical examiner. We hand-carried Sarah's dental charts over to him yesterday. We should have some sort of verification within a couple of hours."

"I'm going to tell Ben. I know he'll want to go with me."

"Do you want me to tell him?"

"No, I'm at the house. I'll take care of it."

Kincade knocked softly on the bedroom door, waited a moment, and then stuck his head in. "Ben, could I see you for a minute?"

Tess reached over to the nightstand and turned on a small light. "What is it?"

Kincade looked at Alton. "She's got to know too, Jack."

Kincade walked halfway to the bed so he could speak in a lower tone. "Another body's been found. In a car on Lower Wacker . . . at the same location as the Ziven drop." He looked at Tess. Her face was distorted, twisting with fresh horror.

"Her teeth?" Alton asked, his breath shortened.

Kincade looked down. "They're intact." An involuntary gasp escaped from Tess's mouth. She tried not to cry, but large clear tears started working their way down her cheeks. Alton leaned over and put both his arms around her. "We should know something more definite in the next couple of hours. Thorne wants me to go out and take a look at the car."

"I'm going with you. Can you give us a couple of minutes?"

Kincade went out to the couch and picked up his jacket. B.C. was lying next to it. "Come on, boy. We're going for a ride."

A light rain had started. Kincade drove and headed east on the Eisenhower. There were few cars headed into the city, and Alton stared straight ahead through the pulsing windshield wipers, letting their patient rhythm steal his thoughts. They passed a lumbering semi and its heavy spray dissolved the world for a moment. Kincade cracked his window and breathed in the salted rain. Another misty curl blew in and chilled the left side of his face, making him wish the drive would never end.

On Lower Wacker, Kincade could see the scene of the fire ahead. He parked and Alton turned his head away from the charred, still smoldering vehicle. Kincade said, "Why don't you wait here?"

A single Chicago PD squad car guarded the area, which was roped off with the usual yellow tape with black marking. Kincade showed the officer his credentials and was allowed to cross the tape. The car, a full-size Buick, stood with its blackened trunk lid pried open and twisted. The interior was burned more extensively than the rest of the car. Evidently an accelerant had been used to ensure the thorough destruction of the body. He walked around to the front of the vehicle. Then he noticed it. Although the fire had blistered most of the paint of the once-blue hood, the faint outline of a large number "2" was barely visible. His eye traced the white paint that had been used to mark the hood. He walked around to the other side and examined it from a different angle. Borrowing the officer's flashlight, he looked at it again. As best he could tell, the number was the same width as the one on the apartment house door. And there was the slightest spattering around its outer edges indicating that it had been done with a spray can. Satisfied, he returned the light to the police officer and got back in the car.

When he didn't say anything, Alton looked over at him and was surprised to see him smiling. Alton straightened up. "What is it?"

"That wasn't Sarah's body."

"What?"

"Think about it. If he had pulled out this victim's teeth, we would assume, because of last time, that it wasn't Sarah. But by leaving the teeth in this time, we would assume it *was* her, at least until the medical examiner determined it wasn't."

"You're sure?"

"There's something else," Kincade said.

"What?"

"There's a number 'two' painted on the hood."

"So?"

"What was painted on the door of the apartment at the first fire?"

"The number 'three'?" Alton answered and then it hit him. "He's counting down." For a brief moment, Alton felt the reprieve of what Kincade had discovered. But then he realize what it ultimately meant. "That means she's next. Three, two, *one*."

Kincade had hoped Alton wouldn't figure out the implication of the countdown so quickly, but the important thing was that hope, and probably Sarah, were still alive. He began to pull out into the street when something else occurred to him. He stopped the car. "But next time I think I know where Traven's going to be."

# 24

BY 6 A.M., EVERYONE WITH THE EXCEPTION OF JACK Kincade was assembled in the SAC's conference room. The night before, after dropping Alton off, he had called Thorne and explained what he thought Traven's next move was going to be. Understanding the probability of what was being suggested, the SAC told him to get some sleep, and he would call out the troops first thing in the morning.

Thorne stood up at the head of the long table and the room immediately became quiet. "By now you all know that the medical examiner, through dental records, has determined that the body found on Lower Wacker last night was not Sarah Alton. Investigation at the scene revealed that the number 'two' had been painted on the hood of the car. I'll let Steve Trass explain the significance of that."

Trass stood up and, almost unnoticeably, moved off to one side of the room. "What I am about to say is something you may have already concluded yourself. This crime, like so many serial offenses, has come down to patterns. A criminal displays these patterns not out of desire but out of compulsion. And this compulsion is in response to whatever fantasy he is trying to achieve. In this case, Alan Traven has only one purpose—revenge. Revenge against an entity that he believes has stripped him of the only power he ever really had, that of a police officer and detective. All the villains in his little psychodrama are law enforcement agencies simply because they have rejected him. More specifically, he blames the FBI for its *role* in his dismissal, and most recently Ben Alton for his efforts to implicate him in the Ziven kidnapping and homicide. As demonstrated by his willingness to commit murder so casually, he is in a degenerating psychological state and if cornered, as I have already explained to the SAC, could become suicidal. In other words, there is nothing he is incapable of doing, no action is too extreme to prove his point. The woman found two nights ago has been tentatively identified through missing person reports as a prostitute, which makes sense because they are easy targets. It is their job to go with strange men in cars. I suspect the body last night will be another prostitute. Traven is killing these women primarily to terrorize Ben and his family as many times and as deeply as he can."

A female supervisor raised her hand. "What's the bottom line here: If he's killing women so indiscriminately, is there any chance that Sarah Alton is still alive?"

Trass smoothed his tie before he spoke. "That's the kind of question a profiler will never answer because there is simply no way to be sure, no matter how well we think we understand the criminal. She could already be dead, but you have to remember, this is a game to Traven. His victory will be all the more satisfying if he gives the opposition a chance to win, and they still fail to outsmart him. I think with Sarah that chance means keeping her alive until the last possible moment. The ME said that both burn victims were alive until the fires were started."

One of the supervisors interrupted, his voice incredulous. "That means that the first woman was alive when he pulled out all her teeth?"

"That should give some insight into how deranged he has become. By waiting until the last possible moment, he probably hopes that we will be haunted by the guilt of knowing that she would not have been killed if we had just been a little faster, a little smarter."

Thorne said, "The logical assumption is that he's leaving these numbers at the crime scenes as a taunt, counting down to Sarah. Do you think that's his intention?"

"That would be my guess. We have to assume that Sarah Alton is number 'one.' Now, what we need to figure out is where and when. I suspect *when* will be tonight at midnight. Number 'three' was two nights ago at midnight. 'Two,' last night at midnight. As I said in the beginning, patterns. That leaves *where*. Two nights ago it was at the same location where he dumped William Sloane's body, last night where the ransom drop was made in the Ziven kidnapping. Again, this is all part of the game he's playing. By using these same sites, he is saying, *You weren't smart enough to catch me three years ago, and you're not smart enough to catch me now, even though I'm going to the exact same places.* So where will he be tonight at midnight? I spent most of the night reading the Ziven case file. If he does not change his pattern, my guess would be that he will be in one of three places: the convenience store where Leah Ziven was abducted, the phone booth across from the bank where Mr. Ziven was called during the drop, or William Sloane's abandoned house where Leah Ziven's body was found."

The surveillance squad supervisor asked, "Any idea which is the most likely?"

"That's difficult to say. But if I had to guess, I'd go for the phone at the bank. I suspect it has a special significance for him. It was the location that led agents to the solution of the kidnapping, which eventually led to Traven's being identified as a suspect. But remember, that's just a guess."

Before Trass could continue, Thorne stood up and said, "Thanks, Steve. Okay, everybody, tonight we are going to cover all three of those locations. When we break up here I want them all scouted and everything in place—heads below the horizon— no later than six P.M. I know it's six hours ahead of time but hopefully he won't be looking for us to be that ambitious. I don't want anyone to underestimate this guy. He's surveillance-wise and has outthought us at every turn so far. If you can't get a good covered spot for a vehicle, do whatever is necessary to get inside a building. If you do wind up in a car, remember to keep far enough away so if he dry-cleans the area, he won't make you." Thorne turned to one of the supervisors. "Stan, I want you to get with Chicago Vice and see what you can do to cover areas of prostitution." He handed him a sheet of paper. "According to CPD those were some of the locations that the first victim worked out of. If the body from last night is identified before tonight, you'll have to scramble around and provide the same type of coverage for her areas. Any questions?" When there were none, he said, "Let's remember what's at stake."

After everyone left, Thorne beeped Kincade, who was again sleeping next to Laura Welton. He got up and went to the kitchen to call while she hurried into the shower. Finding his cigarettes on the counter, he took one out and started searching for a light. The second drawer he opened was overflowing with odds and ends, the ignored props of everyday life, the things a homeowner refuses to organize, a luxury of permanency—a couple of small jars of vitamins that had never been opened, a screwdriver, a broken radio headset, three or four tattered recipes cut from newspapers. Finally, he came across a book of matches with the name of the restaurant where Laura worked.

He lit his cigarette and dialed Thorne's private number. The SAC filled him in on Trass's briefing and the subsequent plan to cover the three locations. "Jack, I know Ben won't want to sit at home during all this. I understand how tough that would be, but I don't want him anywhere near these three sites tonight. I'm leaving it up to you to hold him prisoner and just drive around, keeping him occupied while we do what has to be done."

"I'll do my best, but you know how he is when he gets something in his head."

"Trass was pretty much in agreement with what you came up with last night."

"I hope we're right. Just keep your fingers crossed that Traven doesn't know we've figured it out."

They hung up and Kincade started the coffee maker, which Laura had filled up the night before. He took another drag on his cigarette and opened a cabinet above the sink looking for a cup.

He found a half dozen assorted mugs and chose the one most stained and cracked, its history comfortable, somehow necessary. The coffee started to drip and he deftly switched his mug for the pot. The thick peaceful aroma filled the kitchen.

"Since you can't seem to get the coffee out of that thing fast enough, I assume that you're taking it to go." She put her arms around him and rubbed his stomach. "Trying to sneak out on me again?"

He turned and put his arms around her. "That's what burglars do best."

"You slept very *audibly* last night. Snored like a chainsaw."

"Sorry, did it keep you awake?"

"For a while, but I kind of like the sound of a man being around."

"Confession must be good for the soul."

Kincade's cup was still under the coffee maker and it started to overflow. Laura quickly reached around him and carefully replaced his mug with the pot. She turned back to him and put her hands on his chest. "Jack, what's going to happen?"

Trying to lighten his voice, he said, "Well, technically it's the mood called Custody of the Attorney General."

When she didn't smile, he kissed her briefly, after which she buried her head against his chest. He closed his eyes tightly, squeezing into his memory the smells of burned coffee and damp red hair.

Finding a well-concealed vantage point for two of the three locations was surprisingly easy. The convenience store in Mundelein where Leah Ziven had been abducted was owned by a Peruvian man who lived in an apartment above it with his wife and three children. He had become a naturalized citizen of the United States four years earlier, and like most such immigrants was eager to demonstrate his patriotism. His cooperation at the time of the kidnapping, and during numerous subsequent interviews, was well documented. Once approached, he offered his apartment for the agents to use. In return, he and his family were put up at a downtown Chicago hotel for the night. Watching the parking lot was then simply a matter of installing some one-way shades in the apartment and keeping the surrounding Bureau vehicles apprised of any questionable movement.

The second location, Billy Sloane's house in Wheeling, presented the fewest problems of the three. One call to Detective Lansing secured access to the house, which had been padlocked as a crime scene ever since Leah Ziven's body had been discovered there. Surveillance would be very low-maintenance, since any car coming down its infrequently used, dead-end street would be immediately obvious.

The only site that took some creativity to cover was the phone booth in the area of the bank where Kincade and Alton had discovered Billy Sloane's identity. In hindsight, it had been chosen during the original kidnapping because of the difficulty of setting up surveillance around it. In the midst of a crowded commercial neighborhood, parking spaces were greatly limited. Any of the standard surveillance vehicles, such as vans or camper trucks, would have been obvious to someone like Traven. At first, Bob Newman from bank security was discreetly contacted to see if arrangements could be made similar to those at the convenience store. He offered complete access to the bank, but when the agents went inside to look for a vantage point, there were simply no windows, a limitation of security architecture, that overlooked the phone booth. Taking the time and causing the inevitable commotion of trying to recruit someone in the immediate area to assist the agents was considered too much of a risk because Traven had used the location three years ago and might know someone who could warn him. It was not likely, but even the smallest risk was now too great. The head technical agent finally solved the problem by designing a new surveillance vehicle out of an old dinged-up Triumph motorcycle he had spotted in the surveillance squad's garage. It had been seized in a drug case years earlier and then forgotten. On the back end were large fiberglass saddlebags, once used to transport cocaine. Cutting peepholes in the outside of each one, video cameras were rigged so that they could be controlled remotely from the bank across the street. Between the two cameras, a 270-degree periphery could be maintained. The motorcycle was placed next to a four-door sedan, which was parked in the last space all the way at the end of the lot, eliminating the need to see the other 90 degrees.

In the event Traven had obtained the FBI frequencies, every radio scrambler was reprogrammed with a new code that afternoon. All agents, with the exception of those covering the phone booth, were in place by 6 P.M. as ordered by the SAC. Because of the technical modifications, it was a little after 8:00 when the motorcycle was finally parked across from the bank.

Darkness came quickly, but then the time dragged. During the last hours before midnight, the agents, with their inherent disdain of waiting, found different ways to pass the time. Some dozed in shifts, while others retold timeworn stories that would not have been tolerated had there been an alternative. But as the final minutes of the day grew near, they became quieter, wondering how, if Traven had chosen their location, they would handle it. Conversations became compressed. Guns were checked and rechecked. Ammunition relocated for easier access. Radios tested. As the last few minutes evaporated, their handcuffs ratcheted softly, rhythmically as their thumbs pushed the single strand through the double.

In the last half hour, not a word was spoken on the air and very few anywhere else. Then suddenly it was midnight, and there wasn't a suspicious car or person in sight of any of the three locations. Everyone felt a small shudder of relief inside a much larger ache of disappointment.

At four minutes past, the crew inside the bank saw it on their monitor a split second before they heard the explosion. The cameras, apparently destroyed by the blast, went dead and the screen turned to snow. The weathered four-door sedan parked next to the motorcycle had contained a bomb. The trunk was the primary point of detonation, its lid thrown high into the air as the interior filled with a huge white, incendiary flame. All the assigned units scrambled to the parking lot, but the heat was too intense to do anything. They could see something in the trunk changing shape and shrinking as it burned; and they stepped back involuntarily in horror. One of them tripped over the trunk lid. And when he looked down, the agent saw a large number "1" painted on the inside.

# 25

ALTHOUGH THE RADIO TRANSMISSIONS WERE PAN-
icked and confused, Kincade immediately understood that the FBI
had been unable to prevent the murder that had been the focus of
everyone's efforts for the last twenty-four hours. Traven had intentionally established what the profiler called "signature patterns,"
fully aware that the FBI would recognize them and respond by
setting up surveillances at the likely sites. Once again he had anticipated them, setting the car, with its human cargo, in place before the agents could determine and interdict those patterns.

Ben Alton sat staring ahead, his face devoid of all emotion.
"Do you want to go over there?" Kincade asked.

He smiled a polite, tragic smile. "Could you take me home
please?"

Kincade wanted to tell him that there was always a chance
that it wasn't Sarah, but he had heard that too many times. His
hopes had been raised and then let free-fall twice before; that
was enough. Traven couldn't have ripped the life out of Alton
any more completely if he had hung him upside down and gut-
ted him. There was nothing left in him.

When Kincade pulled into his driveway, he got out and the
word "thanks" escaped from between his lips almost inaudibly.
At the door, he hesitated for a moment, drew in a breath, and
then pulled the door open as if it weighed more than he did.

Kincade sat there for a while wondering where his own anger was. For the first time in a long while, he was scared, not of anything physical, not even of Traven's inexhaustible capacity for death, but of his own inability to feel anything. Any other human being would have been filled with empathy and an accompanying blood lust, but he couldn't find a hint of either of those emotional counterweights within himself. It had been like that at the end of his marriage. After a night of drinking and gambling, his ex-wife would ambush him with a volcanic tirade, attempting to invoke his responsibilities as both a husband and father, and never once did he feel guilt or the normal accompanying panic to resolve the problems. He wasn't blocking out his emotions; they no longer seemed to exist. He backed out of the driveway and headed to the office.

Kincade found the SAC sitting alone at his desk, staring straight ahead. For a moment Thorne seemed surprised to see him, as if his presence was an act of surrender to the impending charges, which, by agreement, would be leveled only when the kidnapping was resolved. But then he remembered because of the hour that the office was deserted, something which Kincade had probably taken into consideration. With a short exhausted motion, the SAC waved him into a chair. He pulled open a drawer, took out a bottle of bourbon, and held it up questioningly to Kincade. When he nodded, Thorne went to the coffee table and retrieved two mugs, pouring a healthy dose into each of them. "The ME's got her."

Kincade swallowed half of his. "How long before we know?"

"I'm not sure." Taking a sip, Thorne answered mechanically, but then reexamined the question. "Do you think there's a chance it's not her?"

Now Kincade wondered why he had asked the question. His mind raced forward, and he realized it was unimpeded by the grief that had seized everyone else. Evidently there was an upside to just about everything, even self-destruction.

"To answer that, we've got to become Traven, if that's possible. If you were that smart, would you settle for three-two-one, the end? There is no *spectacular* finale. I know there was an explosion, and we were humiliated, but now that you've asked, it just doesn't have that big-finish feeling to me."

"I don't know, Jack. He's got me so confused. Pulling the victim's teeth out, leaving them in, three-two-one . . . I just don't know anymore."

"You have to remember his goal is to terrorize and embarrass us. If this is Sarah, did he accomplish that? I don't think so. When it is her, he's going to want us to know right then and there so the FBI will be disgraced for a long time."

The SAC picked up the phone and dialed. "Yes, this is Roy Thorne, is he there . . . Bob, how are you doing . . . I see . . . and how long will that take . . . You'll let me know . . . Thanks." He hung up. "This time there was some kind of incendiary chemical compound used. Something that burns at thousands of degrees. Not only was it throughout the trunk, there was an additional container of it placed near her head. The teeth and both jaw-bones were liquefied. Which I am sure was meant to confuse us, at least it has me."

"Is there any other way of determining if it was Sarah?"

"The ME says the body is a black female. He believes she was still alive when the fire was ignited. There's a procedure he's already completed, which I didn't fully understand. It has something to do with cartilage on the end of the ribs, which leads him to believe that her age is between sixteen and twenty-four years old. There were no old fractures. He says there are some chemical tests that will take a while, which might determine her age more precisely."

"What about the toxicology?"

"He didn't say. What about it?"

"If this is another prostitute, chances are pretty good that she would have traces of drugs in her system, which would indicate it isn't Sarah."

"Unless Traven made her take something, which doesn't seem likely."

Before Kincade could comment, Thorne had picked up the

phone again and hit the redial button. When he hung up, he said, "He's checking on it. He said you're right, it's extremely unusual not to find drugs in a deceased prostitute."

Kincade seemed to be listening to the quiet around him. "I didn't expect many people to be here, but there's nobody."

"I sent them all home to get some sleep. Why, is there something you think we should be doing?"

"Until we're told otherwise, we have to assume that the female in the trunk isn't Sarah. And if that's the case, then we've got to figure out where to be at midnight."

Thorne stood up and looked at his watch. "It's almost two. I'll put out the call at six. Hopefully by then I will have heard about the toxicology. Can you be back here at six?"

"I thought I was supposed to keep myself scarce for a while."

"This has become too critical; it's more important that you be here," the SAC said. "I could call headquarters and try to get some assurances that they'll leave you alone until this is over, but that can be chancy. I think I know a way to take care of any problems locally. Why don't you get some sleep."

"I'll go find a couch."

Kincade started to leave when Thorne said, "Jack, I am at a loss to understand how you can keep your objectivity through all this."

A soft, contradictory smile tilted Kincade's face. "There are certain advantages to being a sociopath."

Kincade slept very little. For four hours, every small, unidentifiable mechanical sound that had its origins somewhere in the hidden subbasements of the federal building seemed to reel him back and forth across the edge of unconsciousness. He checked his watch. It was after six and he knew the night staff would be busy calling in the troops. He wondered if the ME had called back with any answers, but then decided he didn't want to know, not right then anyway. He was in one of the supervisors' offices and started rummaging through drawers looking for toothpaste and a razor. In a filing cabinet, he found both and headed off to find the same shower Alton had used the first night they worked together.

At a few minutes past six, the SAC walked into Bartoli's office and sat down comfortably. "Good morning."

"Morning, I was just on my way to see if you needed anything."

With his chin resting on his hand, Thorne rubbed his index finger across his upper lip, searching for a starting point. "In twenty-seven years, I have never made a call to the Bureau to ask for a favor. What do you suppose would happen to your career if I called back there about you?"

"With your reputation? You could make or break anyone's career."

"Unfortunately I think you're right. So I want you to do something for me. I need to keep OPR away from Jack Kincade until this is over. I want you to do whatever is necessary to make certain of that."

Bartoli wasn't exactly sure where Thorne was heading but his instincts told him not to ask. "Of course I'll do what I can."

"Good." Thorne started to get up.

Still uncertain of the SAC's intentions, Bartoli decided to ask. "Excuse me for being forward, sir, but are you saying that if I can take care of this, you will make a call on my behalf?"

"Evidently you have misread my opinion of you. If you prevent them from coming out here, I promise *not* to call."

It was 6:30 by the time Kincade got to the SAC's office. The only other person there was Steve Trass. Thorne introduced them and then said, "We just got some good news. There was cocaine in the last victim's system." He handed Kincade the toxicology report that the ME had faxed over.

"So it wasn't Sarah," Kincade said, and then, quoting from the report, "'Also detected was trifluoperazine, an antipsychotic tranquilizer.' It makes sense that he would want her knocked out, otherwise, as long as she lay in that trunk, she might have made some noise to attract attention." Kincade went over to the side table and poured himself a cup of coffee.

Trass said, "Roy told me what you think Traven is trying to do. My guess is you're right. If that had been Sarah last night, he would have wanted everyone to know immediately, especially Ben. Either that or kill her and never let anyone know where she was so there would be no closure for the family. Which is still a possibility. But if Traven were going to let him know that she's dead, I think you're right about him devising a more dramatic ending."

Thorne said to Kincade, "I haven't called Ben yet. I think this is something he needs to hear in person. And since you seem to be closer to him than anyone, I'd like you to tell him."

"I know this is good news, but it does put him on that roller coaster again."

Trass said, "And that's exactly what Traven wants."

"I hate to darken this any more than it already is, but what are the chances of sexual assault?" Thorne asked.

Trass understood the SAC was uncomfortable with the question because he had not used Traven's or Sarah's name, implying that although he felt compelled to ask the question, he was trying to distance himself from any specifics. "In my estimation, extremely low. Through the psychiatric reports in his file, I've had an in-depth look inside Alan Traven's life. One of the things I noted was the absence of females after his mother. There is no mention of a woman anywhere. Given his relationship with his mother, I'd be willing to bet a paycheck he's impotent. The late Mrs. Traven's behavior with men probably snuffed out his sex drive. It's one of the reasons he's so tormented. And if you find that a little too theoretical, remember, the best prediction of what someone will do in the future is their behavior in the past. Leah Ziven was not sexually assaulted."

Apparently satisfied, Thorne said, "Good. Now the important question is what do we do next? Unless either one of you can think of something else, I say we cover the remaining two locations tonight. If in fact that wasn't Sarah last night, then it will be a great temptation for Traven to use one of them to continue to make fools of us." He looked at Trass for confirmation.

"That'd be my prediction," Trass said.

"It seems like the best bet to me," Kincade agreed. "Unless he decides to go outside his pattern."

"So far he hasn't."

Kincade took a sip of coffee. "And that's starting to bother me."

# 26

WHEN KINCADE WALKED INTO ALTON'S HOUSE, HE
saw only two agents. One was sitting sleepily in front of the tape
recorder, drinking coffee. The other was knotted into a ball on
the couch, his face turned inward, seeking sanctuary from the
early morning's pewtered light.

Alton came out of the bedroom, tying his robe. He was ashen
and obviously had not slept. "What are you doing here?"

Kincade motioned to the table in the kitchen and they both
sat down. "Ben, we're not sure, but we don't think that was Sarah
last night."

Suddenly, Tess came out of the bedroom, apparently having
overheard them. "Why do you say that?" she asked, her words
quick, demanding.

He told them about the toxicology report.

"That makes sense," Alton said. He looked over at his wife.

Tears rolled down her exhausted face. She hadn't slept, either, but instead had spent the night trying to maintain her san-
ity with memories of her daughter alive and well. Her first infant
cry in the middle of the night, its joy, its gift. Sarah's first day of
school, her backpack dwarfing her but not her enthusiasm. She
and Darian, warmly insubordinate, laughing at the dinner table.
The silly late-night calls from boys. But the strongest image was
of the first time a playmate struck her, her look of astonishment,
and Tess's inability to undo it, to make the world perfect again.

Alton squeezed her hand. "Are the other two locations being covered tonight?"

"They're already working on it."

The three of them sat there, afraid that any further discussion might prick the fragile balloon of optimism that floated around them. Finally, Kincade, a little surprised at the tone in his voice, said, "There's a reason Sarah is still alive. I don't know exactly what it is, but there's a reason. I told you we were going to get her back."

They all sat a while longer before Tess got up and put her hand on Kincade's cheek. "Thanks for being here, Jack." She went back into the bedroom and closed the door.

"Thorne has ordered the surveillances in place by noon. I'm going back to see if there's anything that I can do to help. I don't suppose there's any way to talk you into staying home tonight." Alton looked at him, his eyes filled with fresh resolve. "I'll be back around six."

At the office, Kincade was directed to the conference room. It was filled with people, each had an operations memo. Traven's photo was stapled to the front of each of them. Thorne was conducting the briefing, and Lt. Dan Elkins from the Chicago PD Bomb Squad was at his side. "In case our target has planted another car with a body in it, we are in the process of having municipal employees in both locations put up notices of parking bans under the guise of street cleaning so we can tow any suspicious vehicles out of the area. They will be taken to one of the two garages listed in the memo. There Lt. Elkins and his men will inspect them for explosives and incendiary devices. We do not want a repeat of last night. Team leaders, when your people are in place, contact the major-case room and let them know if you need anything." Thorne took a moment before he said, "One of the reasons Traven has kept ahead of us is that he understands our procedures, and how once we decide on a course of action, we lock into it. Tonight I want you to look for alternatives out there; you may have to make difficult decisions on the spot. Don't be afraid of that. We are not going to beat him by having tunnel vision or being inflexible. So stay loose and don't get too comfortable."

\*     \*     \*

As ordered, everyone was in place by noon. Thorne had come down to the major-case room and was sitting with Kincade as the surveillance team calls came in. Once again, because of its location on a dead-end street, no cars were parked in the vicinity of William Sloane's last residence. The only vehicle in the convenience store lot, other than the occasional customer, was the van belonging to the owner, who had again agreed to spend the night in a hotel. The immediate area around the store was posted with NO PARKING signs.

"How's Ben doing?" Thorne asked.

"He's pretty resilient, if you don't count him blaming himself for everything since the Garden of Eden."

"I assume he's insisting on being around tonight."

"Notice how that's not even a question."

"He is tough to box in. But, again, don't let him within a mile of the targets tonight. And, Jack"—Kincade looked over at him—"if we do get Traven, I don't care what you have to do, don't let Ben anywhere near him."

It was after seven when Kincade finally picked up Alton. He had B.C. with him, hoping the dog would help to keep him distracted. "How's Tess doing?" Kincade asked the question more to see how Alton was doing.

"She's okay. If she needs anything she can call me." He pulled a cell phone out of his briefcase and set it on the seat. "Anything more from the medical examiner?"

"Not yet. I thought we'd just scout around the outer periphery of both locations. But *real* loose. You know, where there's zero possibility of getting burned."

"You're the boss."

For the next four and a half hours there was no activity or traffic down the street that dead-ended in front of the Sloane residence, but at the convenience store, a steady flow of customers kept the surveillance crew busy on the radio. Each time someone pulled into the lot, their license plate was called downtown.

Just after 11:30, one of the agents at the Sloane location said,

"All units be advised we have a blue Chrysler inbound." Kincade glanced over at Alton who seemed to have stopped breathing.

"We're going to need that tag as soon as you can get it." It was Thorne, presumably still in the major-case room.

"Copy, CG One." Then after a few seconds, "There doesn't appear to be a front plate, and we don't have a visual on the back."

"Can you see how many occupants there are?"

"The best we can tell just the driver."

Alton had the mike in his hand. "How big is he?"

"He looks average size, but he's got long hair, down past his shoulders."

Alton looked at Kincade. "He's wearing a wig."

"They know that, Ben. Just let them work."

The agent from the Sloane location said, "He's pulled up to the curb directly in front of the house and is shutting it down. I can't be sure, but he has his hand up to his ear like he's making a phone call."

"Let us know if he gets out," Thorne said.

Alton felt his pager vibrate. "Not now, Tess," he said as he looked down at the readout. He didn't recognize the number but then saw a series of zeros after it. "Jesus Christ!"

"Who is it?" Kincade asked.

"I think it's him." He unclipped the pager and showed Kincade the readout. "Remember those zeros? When he paged me that night at the bar. Now everything makes sense—he wasn't counting down to one, he was counting down to zero."

"That means it definitely wasn't Sarah last night."

"That's right." Alton picked up his cell phone and started to get out of the car.

"Where are you going?"

"I don't want him to overhear the radio and know we're on him."

Alton dialed the number. The first ring wasn't complete when he heard Traven's amused voice. "Give me your number." When Alton didn't immediately respond, he said, "You do want a chance to see your daughter again, don't you?"

Alton gave him the number. With a cloying pleasantness meant to demonstrate the terrifying strength of his position, Traven said, "I'll call you right back." Alton got in the car.

"What'd he say?"

"He's going to call back."

Both men were trying to figure out what Traven was doing when the voice of one of the agents at the Sloane house thundered into the air. "There's been an explosion at the house!" It was followed by interminable silence. Then chaos. Finally Thorne's voice took over. "Everyone cease transmission. Who can see the house?"

"We're rolling up there now," an unidentified agent said. "The house is burning and so is the Chrysler. Two of our units are already there and making entry into the house. I'm going in." His transmission ended abruptly.

"All units proceed to the Sloane residence immediately," Thorne ordered.

Kincade started the engine. As he pulled away, Alton's phone rang. He turned down the Bureau radio. "Yeah!"

"Anything interesting going on?" It was Traven.

"You son-of-a-bitch!"

"I was going to let you talk to your daughter but now, because of your rudeness, I don't think I should."

Alton summoned every bit of control he had. "What do you want?"

"In case you haven't figured it out yet, that's not me over at Billy Sloane's; it's one of those disposable steroid freaks from the gym. Your daughter is safe and sound, for the moment. I assume a great American hero like yourself would like a chance to rescue her."

"I'll do whatever you want, but if anything happens—"

"I thought you would be a little more friendly seeing how I *didn't* invite you to the FBI barbecue."

"You know, someone is going to kill you."

"And I'm sure you think that lucky person is going to be you. Well, I'm going to give you the opportunity, probably not a very good one, but I am being more of a sport than I have to. I assume you're in the vicinity of the stakeouts. Start driving toward Libertyville. You have thirty minutes before the next barbecue begins. I assume you like dark meat? I know I do."

Alton glanced at his watch and put his hand over the phone and whispered to Kincade, "Libertyville." Kincade made a quick turn and headed in that direction.

"Is the agent from the gym with you?"

Alton knew that Traven was guessing, but he wanted him to think he was in control. "Yes. Is that a problem?"

"No, quite the contrary. I want both of you there. You'll find this little problem I have constructed for you will require a second set of hands to untangle. But if I see any more than your car in the area, I won't tell you exactly where she is, and then you can just follow the smoke to find out. And leave the radio on. I want to hear what is going on and be sure you're not calling on that scrambled frequency for help."

Alton reached down and turned up the volume until the nonstop traffic was loud inside the car. "Can you hear it?"

Traven didn't answer right away. An agent was yelling into his mike that they had gotten everyone out of the house; there were some serious burns, but nothing life-threatening. Thorne assured them that ambulances were on the way. Finally Traven said, "Sounds like my little distraction is keeping everybody busy."

"Come on, Traven, where do you want us?"

"All of a sudden that famous FBI camaraderie is not that important, huh?" When Alton didn't respond, Traven said, "There's a hardware store on One-seventy-six. I want you to tell me when you're there. And my watch says twenty-eight minutes left."

Alton took out a pad of paper from his briefcase and wrote "28 min left" and showed it to Kincade. He pushed the accelerator to the floor.

Seven minutes later, they could see the hardware store. "Okay, Traven, we're there."

"Three blocks up, take a right on Mill, and follow it to the river."

Alton repeated the directions and checked his watch. He wrote "20 min" on the pad. Kincade read it and slid through the turn onto Mill. "Okay, we're coming up on the river."

"Don't push it. You'll get directions as soon as I'm satisfied you're alone."

The road dead-ended at a small boat ramp. Directly behind them were large buildings on both sides of the street. Alton stared at the sweep hand on his watch while the traffic on the Bureau radio continued without a break. Thirty seconds later, he said into the phone, "Well, how long do we have to sit here?"

"You'd better calm yourself. You're going to need your wits about you," Traven said. "Now, behind you, the large brown frame building is a commercial garage. Inside you'll find three cars. She's in one of them. But which one? My watch says eighteen minutes. You'd better keep your phone with you." He hung up.

Alton said, "In the garage!" and they both jumped out of the car. The Border collie was at their heels. Alton tried the handle. The garage was unlocked.

He started in when Kincade grabbed his shoulder. "Hold it, Ben. He could have this place rigged. And unfortunately, since I'm the one who went to bomb school, I'd better go first."

"Okay, fine," Alton said, almost pushing Kincade through the door. "Just make it quick."

The structure had apparently been something else before it was a garage. It had thirty-foot ceilings, which were crisscrossed with steel structural beams and catwalks. At the far end was a wooden stairway which led up to a second-floor office. Next to it, a single flood lamp provided the only source of light inside the building. It was aimed at the back end of three cars, which were neatly lined up next to one another, their trunks each with a large "0" spray-painted on the lid. As Kincade got closer, he could see that there were thin cables strung from the trunk of the middle car to those on either side. "They're wired."

As both men stood frozen by indecision, Alton's phone rang. He pressed the button and held it up so Kincade could also hear. "Don't tell me the FBI is having trouble making up their mind."

"What do you want us to do?" Alton asked.

"Well, my choice is that you die, but if you guess right, all three of you may live. The trick is to figure out which one she is in and then open the other two at exactly the same time. You've got one chance in three. And it looks like you have less than twelve minutes left. Gooood luuuuck." Traven hung up again.

Kincade stepped closer and inspected the trunks. Each of the three locks had been punched and there was a single strip of gray duct tape holding the lids closed. He checked the wires that ran between the trunks. "These are Claymore wires."

"What does that mean?"

"Give me a minute to think." Alton checked his watch. Then Kincade remembered the dog. "B.C., come here." The Border collie sidled up to him obediently, cautiously wagging its tail. Kincade led it to the car on the left. "Find her, boy." The dog, not exactly understanding the command, gave the car a cursory sniff. Kincade went to the middle car and again said, "Find her." The dog, after an identical sniff, started wagging its tail and whining.

Alton immediately started tapping on the side of the trunk. "Sarah, are you in there? It's Dad. Are you in there?" A barely audible murmur answered. He checked his watch again. "Hold on, honey. We're going to get you out."

Without any discussion, Kincade and Alton went to the cars on either end and prepared to open the trunks simultaneously. Alton got a grip on the edge of the duct tape that held the lid closed and said, "On three." He glanced at his watch and then over at Kincade to make sure he was ready. Nine minutes left.

"Wait a minute," Kincade said. "Something's wrong."

"Come on, Jack, we've only got nine minutes to get out of here."

"The girl who was killed at the bank parking lot. She was so heavily sedated that she was unconscious. Why didn't he do that with Sarah?" He looked at Alton and could see that his panic was ready to explode. Kincade went over and grabbed his arm roughly. "Listen to me. He wanted Sarah to be able to tell us where she was. He wants us to open the other two first. Which means each of those would detonate, killing us, and at the same time set off the one Sarah is in. Again leaving no witnesses." He stepped back and took a long appraising look at all three cars again. "I'm no expert, but if I'm right about the two on the outside detonating the one in the middle, then the one Sarah is in is not booby-trapped."

"And what if it is, why wouldn't he just rig them all?"

"No, he wants us to guess wrong. That way he's smarter than us. If he was going to rig all three, this whole building would have gone up as soon as we cleared the doorway. He has to have his game."

Alton looked at his watch. "Just do something!"

"You're sure you want to try this?"

"Yes! Let's just get her out of there."

As they turned to the middle car, Kincade froze. "What's the matter now?" Alton asked.

"He's here."

Neither of them had considered that possibility. "You don't know that."

"He has to see it happen—he's here."

"But he would go up with the building."

"No, that's the beauty of the Claymores, they're completely directional. If you're standing in front of them, they'll cut you in two. If you're off to the side, they're just loud."

"Okay, okay, but we still have to get her out of there."

Kincade glanced around him. "Stand right where you are, but turn around with your back to me so you can watch for him. If he's behind you, he won't be sure of what I'm doing. As soon as I get her out of the trunk, shoot out that light, then we can get out of here in the darkness." He gave Alton a moment to think about it. "Ready?"

Alton slowly turned 180 degrees. "Ready."

Kincade ripped the tape off the lid and opened the trunk. Inside lay Sarah, bound and gagged, a Claymore mine taped to her chest. A smaller set of wires led from the device to a wooden box. Inside, their ends were soldered to the face of a wristwatch.

It showed three minutes until midnight, at which time the hands would complete the electrical connection. Kincade checked his watch; the timer was set six minutes faster than his. A practical problem from Bomb Tech school flashed through his head. They had to disarm a booby-trapped mock bomb. It was a long and grueling process and in the end most of the students were blown up despite their caution. It was supposed to teach you to expect the worst. Two minutes left. He had no time to worry about booby traps. Kincade got a firm grip on the wires, which led to the timer, closed his eyes, and yanked. Nothing happened. He then unscrewed the blasting cap from the Claymore, rendering it inert.

Alton couldn't help but look over his shoulder to watch Kincade lift his daughter out of the trunk. "Don't watch us!" Kincade demanded.

Alton turned back around, but it was too late. A long burst from an assault rifle erupted from above. One of the rounds bounced on the floor in front of him, sparking on the concrete, and then ricocheted up into his good leg, ripping through the calf. He went down, and his cell phone skidded away into the darkness.

Kincade carried Sarah around the side of the car as Alton scrambled around the opposite end. "Ben, are you all right?"

"I'm hit in the leg. But I'm okay."

"Can you come around the front of the car to us?"

"Yeah." Alton crawled, skirting the car, until he reached Kincade and his daughter. He tore at the tape holding the Claymore to her chest, but she was wrapped in several layers from her ankles all the way to her nose. He tore at it but only managed to rip off short, thin strips.

"Okay, now look at the door and remember where it is," Kincade said. "I'm going to take out the light, then you can get her out of here."

"Why can't we all stay until someone comes?"

"He's got an automatic weapon. He's going to circle around and start picking us off."

From a different location, a longer burst of gunfire exploded, bouncing off the floor around them. "I don't think I can do it. She can't walk, and I'm not sure I can carry her."

"Then drag her, goddammit!"

"My legs . . . she'll have a better chance if you take her, I'll stay."

Kincade smiled. "Sorry, Ben, it's my turn."

Seeing that nothing was going to change Kincade's mind, Alton handed him an extra magazine. "As soon as I get her to safety, I'll radio for help. Just stay down. I've got a shotgun in the trunk. That sounds like an AK-47, so don't do anything stupid." He squeezed Kincade's shoulder. "Just hang on, I'll be right back." Alton glanced at the door again and grabbed his daughter as best he could. "I'm ready when you are."

A single shot came from the overhead darkness and slammed into the back of the car with a sickening thud. Without looking over the top of the car, Kincade raised his automatic above it and fired five shots in rapid succession. He didn't expect to hit anything; he was just trying to get Traven's head down. With a surprisingly quick move, he stood up, fully exposed, and carefully took aim at the lone light. He fired one round and dropped down. There was an immediate pop, followed by an electric fizzle. The garage went black.

# 27

THE ONLY SOUND KINCADE COULD HEAR IN THE darkness was the rhythmic stop-and-start as Alton and his daughter dragged themselves across the floor. He tried to listen in the direction of the last shots to determine if Traven was moving to another position, but he couldn't hear anything. Kincade listened to Alton's progress, trying to figure out just how close he was to the door, but couldn't tell with any certainty.

Suddenly, a flashlight snapped on in the darkness and swept in an arc from the cars to the entrance, searching for Alton and his daughter. Unfortunately it found them ten feet from the entrance. Kincade stood up and fired a shot in the direction of the light. Even though it went out immediately, he knew he hadn't hit anything. Traven's footsteps, hard and sure, seemed to be moving toward Alton and Sarah. Kincade knew he was trying to get a better firing position, to block their exit, so he fired three rounds in the direction of the steps. They stopped. Kincade moved again. A short burst came toward him from the AK-47. He dove down and rolled away from the muzzle flashes. Then he heard Traven insert another magazine into his weapon and the bolt go home chambering the first round.

At the same time, the door that they had entered through swung open and a crooked rectangle of faded light marked the floor just inside of it. Kincade saw Alton, holding Sarah clumsily in his arms, half-crawl, half-dive through it just as a long burst from the assault rifle ripped the air, sparking the concrete in front of the door.

Kincade opened fire. Then, not fully understanding why, he ran toward Traven's position. The AK opened up again. Kincade tried to fire, but in the darkness he couldn't see that the slide on his automatic had locked to the rear. It was empty. He dropped the magazine out and slammed in another. Not knowing how many magazines Traven had, he silently reminded himself, *Fire discipline, Jack. Fire discipline.*

Kincade knew that Traven had no choice now but to get outside and kill Ben and his daughter. "Hey, Traven," he yelled into the darkness to momentarily distract the ex-cop, "is it my imagination, or is this not going well?" He then ran toward the door firing slowly, leaving a flashing trail of his route, letting Traven know that if he wanted to get outside, he was going to have to kill him first. A single shot came from a position surprisingly close to the door. Kincade returned fire and moved toward the muzzle flash. After a few steps, Traven fired a three-round burst, this time leading his target. The bullets struck the floor ahead of Kincade and concrete chips sprayed up into his face. He took two more steps and dove. Everything went quiet. Clamping his mouth shut, he forced his breath through his nostrils and listened for any movement. His forehead felt wet and he wiped it. He was bleeding; one of the concrete chips had caught him just above the eyebrow. He pushed his last magazine into his nine-millimeter and stood up.

Outside, Alton opened the trunk of his Bureau car and took a knife from his equipment bag. Quickly he cut through the tape binding his daughter's legs and arms. She immediately reached up and ripped the tape off her mouth. Alton was already loading a shotgun. "Daddy, don't go back in there!"

He handed her the keys. "Just get out of here. Get on the radio and tell them what's happening and that we're in Libertyville down by the river. Then go to where you see a bunch of people and call the police. Go on!"

Half using the shotgun as a crutch, Alton started limping back toward the garage. A long series of gunshots erupted inside. First the AK-47's distinctive *pop, pop, pop* and then Kincade's throaty nine-millimeter. The volleys became briefer and at shorter intervals, as if the combatants were closing in on each other.

When Alton finally made it to the door, he flattened himself against the wall and listened. He couldn't hear anything. There was only one thing he could do now. He dove through the doorway and rolled away from the light coming through it. Immediately taking up a prone firing position, he waited. There was nothing but silence. In the dark, the fear rose up inside him. He wanted to call out to Kincade, but that would expose his location. There was nothing to do but wait. As his breathing slowed, he could hear a low whimpering. It was B.C. He wondered if the dog had been hit.

The next minutes seemed like hours. Occasionally, he thought he heard something brief, indistinguishable, some slight scraping, its direction unclear. He would swing the shotgun at it, then the dog would sound its lament again. Alton could smell his own sweat. He wiped his upper lip and sniffed the air carefully. The only thing detected was burned cordite.

The dog had changed the pitch and rhythm of its crying. At least that was what Alton first thought, then the sound started growing in clarity. It was a siren, getting louder, closer. And while Alton found that reassuring, he was worried that Traven was using the sound to mask his movements within the garage. Alton took the opportunity to carefully move himself farther away from the door.

Suddenly a car stopped outside and the siren was cut off mid-yelp. He could hear at least two sets of feet running and then he heard, "Police officers!"

Alton flattened himself on the floor before answering. "I'm an FBI agent, Ben Alton, it was probably my daughter who called you. Sarah."

"Who else is in there?"

"Another agent, Jack Kincade, and the man who kidnapped my daughter."

"Is he armed?"

"Yes, with an AK-47."

"Do you know where he is?"

"No idea."

"Okay, stand by."

Alton watched the door out of the corner of his eye. He saw one of the officers lean in and quickly rake the interior of the garage with his flashlight. Ten feet away, Alton could see a body. Next to it lay the AK-47—it was Traven. Alton stood up, again using the shotgun to lean on. "It's okay," he called to the officers, "my partner got him." A closer inspection revealed that Traven had been wearing a bulletproof vest. Alton could see where he had been hit twice in the chest. Then he noticed his mouth. There was a small, curved tear in both his upper and lower lips. Alton rolled his head to one side. A large gaping hole in the back was still oozing blood. Kincade's shot had entered Traven's mouth and exited the rear of his skull.

"Jack!" Alton yelled. "Jack!" But there was no response. Both cops were now inside, one with his beam on Traven's body, the other swinging his randomly around the garage's interior. Twenty feet beyond Traven, the second light caught a pair of glowing eyes. It was B.C. The dog lay next to Kincade, its chin resting on his master's back. Everyone hurried over, and one of the officers rolled him faceup. He had been hit three times that they could see, twice in the stomach, once in the middle of the chest. The dog emitted a lonely howl, confirming what Alton had feared most.

# 28

AFTER THE MEMORIAL SERVICE BEN ALTON INTRO-
duced himself and his family to Jack Kincade's ex-wife, Saundra,
and their son, Cole. She was a nervously thin woman and wore a
dusty black business suit with lapels from another decade. The
boy was handsome and stood erect, his only weapon to combat
the situation a look of stoic confusion. Then, with some discomfort, Alton introduced Laura Welton as "a friend of Jack's." Laura
nodded formally to the former Mrs. Kincade. Remembering
good-looking redheads as being toward the top of Jack's long list
of weaknesses, Saundra said with cool suspicion, "Yes . . . how do
you do." Then, recognizing in the boy Jack's eyes and clever
mouth, Laura smiled at him warmly.

Tess reiterated to the boy and his mother that Jack—as was
the treatise of the eulogy—had saved their daughter's life and
was an extremely brave and unselfish man. The former Mrs. Kincade thanked her with a polite, but suspicious smile. Alton could
see that she was not sure if her ex-husband's role in the rescue
was being exaggerated due to his death—something not unheard
of after a line-of-duty death—or whether there had actually
been tectonic plates of goodness hidden beneath his disobedient
personality that had shifted into place in her absence. There
seemed to be a small sadness in the woman that the possibility
existed.

"I'm sorry to ask you this," she said to Alton, "but the owner of the motel where Jack was living called me. He asked if it would be possible for me to come and collect the rest of his things. I'm afraid I just can't bring myself to do that. I—"

"We'll take care of it," Alton said gently.

"You can use your own judgment what you think might be sent to me or Cole, if there's anything at all. You can do whatever you want with the rest of it."

"If it's all right with you, we're going to keep his dog. He helped save my daughter."

"I didn't even know Jack had a dog," she said, a little more of that sadness creeping into her voice. She looked tired, not from the drain of the ceremony but from being forced back into Jack Kincade's life, something she had evidently worked very hard to rid herself of. "I'm sure he would want you and your daughter to have it." She gave all four of the Altons a brief, stiff handshake and led her son to the waiting limousine.

After the internment, Alton walked Laura to her car. "Ben, I don't know if you knew, but Jack told me about the . . . banks." She could see in Alton's eyes that he hadn't been told. "I was just hoping that his son would never find out."

"I've had those four cases reassigned to me. I'd be surprised if we ever find out who committed them."

She kissed him on the cheek and got in her car.

Alton dropped his wife and son off at their house. He and Sarah loaded the dog into the car and headed to the Roman Inn. The owner, Jimmy Ray Hillard, still in his suit from the funeral, immediately recognized them from the church as well as the news reports. He shook their hands solemnly as his eyes filled. "Ol' Jack, he sure was one of a kind."

Alton held back a laugh. Yes, he was, he thought. As unhesitatingly and as unselfishly as Kincade had died, his most enviable trait wasn't that he didn't have a fear of dying, but that he didn't have a fear of living. He wrung every drop out of every moment. All at once Alton felt the additional loss that they had not become better friends. Like so many things in his life, it was something he had done his best to avoid—yet another distraction from the great Alton expedition. And now there was so much more he would like to have known about Jack Kincade.

The manager looked down at the dog nuzzled next to Sarah. "You keeping the pooch?"

"Yes, we are," she said.

"That's good. He could use a good home. Jack used to call him his 'fellow castaway.' Although he'd never admit it, I think B.C. was really important to him." Hillard went to a board behind him and took a key. "Whatever you don't want to save, just leave in the room. I'll get it cleared out."

When Alton pushed open the door, he could see his daughter's disillusionment. To a sixteen-year-old, men of unexplainable courage lived in the penthouses of the imagination. But the dusty room felt tarnished with squalor. The faded yellow walls were unadorned except for an occasional crack or catsup spatter. The piles of clothes and newspaper seemed far less charming without Jack to redefine their existence.

The dog nosed past her and took up a spot on the floor next to the broken recliner, as if it'd forgotten what had happened three nights before at the garage. Alton sat down at the warped desk. "Sarah, why don't you see if there is anything in the closet that Mrs. Kincade or her son might want?"

She pushed back the accordion-type door and saw a half dozen suits and sport coats hanging on a drooping wooden rod. On the floor was a single pair of dusty brown wingtips so old that their toes had curled up at nearly 45-degree angles. Alton watched his daughter as she made her way from one end of the closet to the other. He hadn't realized how graceful she had become, each small movement liquid, sure, like that of a trained dancer. Her perfect face glowing, she had become very much like her mother. She started to hum, a sweet, intimate soprano that was evidence of a burgeoning euphoria that she now seemed to find in even the simplest of tasks.

On the desktop, Alton could see the faint outline of the trap in the mist of black spray paint. Running his hand across it slowly, he smiled. Inside the top drawer was an envelope addressed simply to "Cole." It was unsealed and inside there was what appeared to be a letter.

"Dad, these clothes are pretty old. I don't think they're really worth saving."

"Okay, I'll take a look at them in a minute. Why don't you take the dog and see if he needs to go. There's a field out in the back."

She walked over and petted the Border collie on the head. "Come on . . . Dad, we've got to give him a real name sometime."

Alton had resisted pleas from Sarah for two days to name the dog, which would have been an admission that Jack was really gone. "How about Aias?"

"*A-yas*," she struggled with the pronunciation. "What kind of name is that?"

"It's from Greek mythology." He smiled. "Jack told me about him. He was a great warrior who never realized how important he really was."

"Let's see if he likes it. Come on, Aias." The dog stood up quickly and then followed her out the door.

Alton wasn't sure he should read the letter; it was between Jack and his son. He got up and went to the shelf above the refrigerator where Kincade's single glass sat next to a half-full bottle of Pistol Pete's Vodka. He poured an ounce into the glass and sniffed it. It had an industrial stiffness to it. Now he knew how Kincade had gotten into the habit of adding Tabasco. He tapped in a couple of drops and swished it around. Allowing himself the smallest sip possible, he couldn't believe the awful taste that flooded his mouth. He grinned.

He set it down and went over to the closet. Sarah's estimation of the clothing had been accurate. He doubted if even charities helping the less fortunate would want the shabby collection. It reminded him that Kincade's threadbare minivan was still parked at his house, and he would have to find somewhere to put it to rest. Alton started to close the accordion door, but then the thought that the suit coats should be checked stopped him.

If Jack had anything of value in the room, he would have put it either in the desk or, like a lot of men did, in his pockets. He patted down each suit jacket.

In what looked like the oldest sport coat, Alton felt something bulky. When he took it out, he was surprised to see a stack of fifty- and hundred-dollar bills rubber-banded together. A quick count totaled over $5,000. He couldn't imagine Jack Kincade with that much money, or, actually, with any money. Then he remembered the last depository trapping. The loss hadn't been that much but many gamblers kept an ever-available cash stake. Then he smiled, thinking about how mad Jack would have been leaving this life with money unspent. He decided to read the letter to his son. It was dated the day he had been killed.

*Cole,*

*Many times the biggest disappointments in our lives are brought on by the people we trust the most. I know your mother's and my divorce has been one of those disappointments, and you have accepted it with great understanding and courage. I, on the other hand, have not. I convinced myself that the best thing for you was not to see me. I now realize that I made that decision out of selfishness. But make no mistake about it, I love you more than my own life.*

*You will soon hear things about me, things that you will think are not true, but I'm ashamed to say they are. I am more sorry than you will ever know. Life's weaknesses will destroy you if you do not guard against them.*

*I am truly sorry for not being someone you could have been proud of. Never think that my betrayals are in any way your fault or your responsibility to set right.*

*Love,*
*Dad*

Alton tore the letter into small pieces, took it into the bathroom, and flushed it down the toilet, destroying the last evidence of his friend's misdeeds. Putting the money in the envelope, he sealed it and placed it in his inside coat pocket. He decided that when he gave it to the boy, he would also tell him how his father had confided in him the thoughts from the first paragraph of the letter. Holding the glass up, he said, "So long, Jack." He drank the entire drink in one burning gulp.

Outside Sarah was throwing a stick to the dog. He watched for a while as the black-and-white Border collie, without complaint or fatigue, brought it back time and again. Beyond the field was a tree line thick with hardwoods. Gone was the blaze of the mid-fall foliage: the callow greens, the blushed reds, the aureate golds. Only the spiny, rough-cut tweeds of winter remained, a season, which, although it had threatened to come early, Benjamin Alton no longer feared.

# About the Author

A Chicago native, Paul Lindsay is the author of four previous novels, including *Witness to the Truth* and *The Führer's Reserve*. After serving as a Marine Corps infantry officer in Vietnam, he joined the FBI and spent twenty years as a street agent in Detroit. He lives in Rye, New Hampshire, with his wife, Patricia.